"**What the hell are you talking about**" Jocelyn asked, her brow furrowing. "**I have not and would never tell Luther where Rosie Mendez is.**"

Landon snorted. "Yeah, right."

She bristled with self-righteous indignation.

But Landon didn't think she had any right to it. Any right to anything but a long prison sentence along with her real boss: Luther Mills.

"What are you accusing me of?" she asked.

"We all suspected it for a while," he said. "Nobody could be as bad a lawyer as you seemed to be."

She gasped. "How dare you—"

"How dare you destroy that evidence and let a guilty man go free to threaten and kill innocent people."

"What are you talking about? I never destroyed any evidence."

"Then how the hell did you fail to get indictments?" he asked.

"I didn't get enough for indictments because of sloppy police work."

He snorted again.

"What the hell do you think I've done?"

"I think you are the leak," he admitted. "I think you're the one working for Luther, that you've been working for him for years."

* * *

Be sure to check out the previous books in the exciting Bachelor Bodyguards miniseries.

* * *

If you're on Twitter, tell us what you think of Harlequin Romantic Suspense! #harlequinromsuspense

Dear Reader,

Welcome back to River City, Michigan—the fictional town I created that bears a striking resemblance to my hometown of Grand Rapids, Michigan, with the river winding through it and Lake Michigan less than a half-hour drive away. While River City and Grand Rapids might look alike, my hometown is not full of the rampant crime and corruption that has plagued River City. But all that crime and corruption has kept the Payne Protection Agency very busy over the years, especially during the reign of terror of one of the city's most dangerous and powerful villains.

This villain is so determined to avoid justice again that he is trying to kill or intimidate everyone involved with his upcoming trial—that includes the Payne Protection Agency, which has been assigned to protect the witness, the evidence tech, the judge's daughter, the prosecuting attorney and the arresting officer. This story is about the prosecuting attorney, Jocelyn Gerber, who is totally focused on putting the villain away for life—or she was totally focused until there are attempts on her life and she's assigned to close quarters with a sexy bodyguard, former vice cop Landon Myers.

I hope you enjoy the latest installment in the Bachelor Bodyguards series. I love writing this series because every book is like a family reunion with the Payne family. I hope the Paynes and the bodyguards who work for their agency are beginning to feel like your family, too.

Happy reading!

Lisa Childs

CLOSE QUARTERS WITH THE BODYGUARD

Lisa Childs

HARLEQUIN
ROMANTIC SUSPENSE

HARLEQUIN®
ROMANTIC SUSPENSE™

Recycling programs for this product may not exist in your area.

ISBN-13: 978-1-335-62899-2

Close Quarters with the Bodyguard

Copyright © 2021 by Lisa Childs

This edition published by arrangement with Harlequin Books S.A.

For questions and comments about the quality of this book, please contact us at CustomerService@Harlequin.com.

Harlequin Enterprises ULC
22 Adelaide St. West, 40th Floor
Toronto, Ontario M5H 4E3, Canada
www.Harlequin.com

Printed in U.S.A.

Ever since **Lisa Childs** read her first romance novel (a Harlequin story, of course) at age eleven, all she wanted was to be a romance writer. With over seventy novels published with Harlequin, Lisa is living her dream. She is an award-winning, bestselling romance author. She loves to hear from readers, who can contact her on Facebook or through her website, lisachilds.com.

For cat lovers, including me and my daughters, whose furry babies have stolen our hearts like heroine Jocelyn Gerber's cat has stolen hers!

Chapter 1

Landon Myers shook his head. The bodyguard could not have heard his boss correctly—because what Parker Payne had said made no sense at all. Landon leaned closer to Parker's desk and asked, "*Who* do you want me to protect?"

"Jocelyn Gerber," Parker replied.

When he'd resigned from the River City Police Department, Landon had hoped he'd never have to see that particular assistant district attorney again. "Why?"

"She's being threatened, along with everyone else associated with Luther Mills's upcoming trial." The notorious drug dealer had been charged with first-degree murder of a police informant. Mills thought himself so above the law that he'd shot the kid right in front of an eyewitness—the informant's sister.

Anyone else would have accepted a plea deal, knowing they'd be convicted. But Luther had gotten away with murder before, along with countless other crimes.

Landon snorted derisively. "What? Is Gerber's boss threatening to kill her if she loses this one like she has every other case she's tried to bring against him?"

None of those cases had ever made it past the grand jury, though, for an indictment—despite all the evidence she'd been given. Landon knew because he'd brought her some of that evidence only to have it mysteriously disappear.

"Luther's threatening her," Parker said. "The police chief learned about a plot Mills has in place to take out everyone associated with his trial. And Chief Lynch thinks Luther has help from within the police department and within the district attorney's office."

Landon snorted again. "Yeah, and I can tell you who. Her. Jocelyn Gerber is his help within the district attorney's office." That was the only thing that made sense for why Luther had never been tried before.

"If that's true, why would he be threatening her?" Parker asked him.

Landon leaned back in his chair, his knees bumping into the front of Parker's desk again. He would have pushed it back to accommodate his long legs, but the wooden chair was already against the paneled wall behind him. "So she'll do what he wants—like she has every other time River City PD got close to taking him down for his crimes—and the evidence against him will miraculously disappear." Along with the eyewitness. He probably should have been glad he hadn't been assigned to protect her; whoever was guarding Rosie Mendez had been given a death sentence.

Parker shook his head. "The district attorney wouldn't

have assigned the case to Ms. Gerber if she had any doubts about her."

"The district attorney should be trying the damn case herself," Landon said.

"Her doctor has ordered her to bed rest because of her high-risk pregnancy, and once she delivers, she'll be out for a while for maternity leave," Parker said.

Landon furrowed his brow, surprised his boss knew so much about the district attorney.

As if he'd read Landon's mind, Parker replied, "Amber Talsma-Kozminski is married to my brother Logan's brother-in-law Milek."

The Paynes were related to just about everyone in River City. The former chief of police was Parker's half brother, and the current one, former FBI bureau chief Woodrow Lynch, was now his stepfather.

An only child of only children who'd passed away a few years ago, Landon didn't have any family but for his fellow team members, who were also former vice cops like he was. But while he was the only Myers left in River City, Jocelyn Gerber wasn't the only assistant district attorney. Not in a city the size of theirs. River City, Michigan, was even bigger than Detroit but on the west side of the state near Lake Michigan. "The DA should have picked someone else for Luther's trial, after all the times Jocelyn has failed to bring charges against him despite the evidence we brought her."

"I'm sure that she didn't purposely drop those charges," Parker defended her.

"You left River City PD before I did," Landon reminded him. Parker had left the vice unit when his twin brother, Logan, started the Payne Protection Agency. He'd worked for Logan for a few years before starting his own franchise of the agency, which consisted of all former vice cops, like Landon. "You don't know Jocelyn Gerber."

"And you do?"

Landon felt heat rush to his face. If he didn't distrust her so much, he would have liked to know her better. With her long, silky black hair and long, lithe body, she was gorgeous. But she was just as treacherous as she was sexy—probably more so because she was so damn sexy. He shook his head.

"Well, you're going to get to know her since you'll be protecting her 24/7 from the threat to her life," Parker told him.

Landon groaned. "C'mon. She's not being threatened." She was the threat—to the case and maybe to him, as well, since he would have to spend so much time around her. She was definitely too damn sexy.

The sound of her heels striking the concrete echoed throughout the dimly lit parking structure. But instead of slowing down, Jocelyn Gerber sped up as she hurried toward her vehicle. She hadn't needed the chief of police phoning to warn her that she was in danger. She'd known the minute she'd taken the case against Luther Mills that she was putting her life at risk.

But neither the chief nor Luther Mills was going to scare her into giving up the trial. This time the charges would stick, and she would win.

She had to…

That win mattered most. No, putting Luther Mills out of commission mattered most.

A chill chased down her spine, and it wasn't just from the crisp autumn wind whipping through the parking structure. Someone was watching her. She was used to that. Since she'd been assigned this case, she knew everyone was watching her—waiting for her to fail again. But someone was following her now, too. She heard an echo from more than her heels. She heard the echo of louder footsteps—from someone bigger and heavier than she was.

She shivered.

Of course, it didn't mean that someone was following her. Maybe he was just heading to his vehicle like she was hers. But, since all the downtown offices had closed hours ago, there were very few vehicles parked yet in the structure. Most of the spaces were empty. The couple of cars she had passed, it sounded as though those footsteps had gone by them, as well. No lights blinked on, no horn tooted.

She pressed her key fob, but she wasn't close enough to her vehicle for her lights to blink or horn to toot. Where the hell had she parked?

She needed to get to her SUV. But just in case she didn't make it to her vehicle before the man caught up with her, she reached inside her purse, which hung over her shoulder next to her bulky briefcase. As she fumbled inside her leather bag, she turned her head to glance over her shoulder. She could see only a shadow behind her, but that shadow was enormous.

Her heart began to pound even faster and more furiously. The chief had warned that Mills would probably go after the eyewitness first. But what about Jocelyn?

She should have been safe—at least until the trial started. But it was weeks away and that enormous shadow was only feet away from her now. Her fingers finally closed around her weapon. She pulled it from her purse and whirled around to face her stalker, yelling, "Stay away from me!"

"That's going to be damn hard to do when I've been assigned to protect you," a deep voice drawled.

"Who are you?" she demanded to know as the man remained in the shadows. A hood was pulled over his head, and it shadowed his face like the dim light shadowed his entire body—his long, broad-shouldered body.

"Your bodyguard," that deep voice rumbled.

She shivered again and clutched her weapon tighter.

That was the other thing the chief had told her, that he was hiring the Payne Protection Agency to protect everyone involved in Luther Mills's trial. And like she had told him, that was a mistake. One that could prove fatal.

Was it going to prove fatal now—to her?

"Who are you?" she asked again, and she raised her weapon to point directly at his chest.

He chuckled. "You're going to tase me?"

She moved her finger toward the trigger of the weapon. She knew how to fire it to plunge those probes into his chest because, unfortunately, she'd had to use it before. Luther Mills wasn't the only criminal who had tried to hurt her.

"Yes." But before she could fire it, the weapon was snapped out of her grasp and she was spun around so that her back was pressed against his chest, his strong arms wrapped around her.

She screamed.

But he just chuckled again. He knew there was nobody around to hear her. To help her...

She struggled in his grasp, but his arms just tightened around her, stilling her movements. She tried to kick back, with her stilettos, but when her heel struck his leg, the shoe slipped off her foot. And she hadn't even fazed him; he was that strong, that muscular.

If this man really was her bodyguard, it was just as she'd feared. He was as big a threat to her as Luther Mills was—because, if she was right, someone within the Payne Protection Agency could be working for Luther. She had a horrible feeling that she'd just found out who—the man who had already overpowered her.

"Where are they?" Chief Woodrow Lynch wondered aloud as he looked around the nearly empty conference room.

Parker Payne shrugged. "They should all be arriving soon." Right now he was the only other person in the room, sitting at the other end of the long conference table from Woodrow. He seemed confident in his team, though, which should have eased Woodrow's concerns.

Woodrow had called the meeting at the Payne Protection Agency, so he could explain why he'd hired a private security company to protect everyone involved in the trial of a local drug dealer.

Luther Mills was not just any drug dealer. He was the biggest drug dealer in Michigan. Hell, probably in the entire Midwest, and he was so rich and powerful that he could hire or threaten anyone into doing what he wanted. And Woodrow had recently learned that some of those people Luther had either bought or manipulated were within the police department and the district attorney's office.

That was why he had hired the Payne Protection Agency. He was going to make sure that Luther Mills didn't hurt anyone else and that he finally went to trial for his crimes.

But not everyone was going to be happy with having a bodyguard. The assistant district attorney, Jocelyn Gerber, was certainly not happy. She thought he was stupid for trusting the Payne Protection Agency—at least Parker Payne's franchise of the agency—because every member of his team was a former vice cop. She suspected at least one of them could be working for Luther.

Of all his stepsons' franchises, Woodrow had chosen Parker's because of their connection to Luther Mills. He knew Parker and his team had tried for years to bring down Luther Mills, so he knew they would have a vested interest in making sure he was finally brought to justice.

But as Jocelyn had pointed out, they had tried for years with no success. She believed one of those former vice cops hadn't just been working for the River City Police Department but for Luther Mills, as well.

Could she be right?

If she was, instead of protecting everyone associated with the trial, Woodrow had just put one of them in even more danger. Which one?

Her?

Chapter 2

Landon had figured his protecting Jocelyn Gerber was a bad idea. But now he knew for certain he'd been right. She writhed in his arms, jerking around as she kicked at his shins. As her one remaining heel connected, he flinched, and a grunt of pain slipped out of his lips, stirring her black hair. "Stop struggling!"

"Let me go!" she yelled back at him.

But he kept his arms locked around her, holding hers down at her sides as her back pressed against his chest. He didn't trust that she didn't have another weapon on her. "What else you got in that bag of yours?" he asked.

In addition to not wanting to be tased, he didn't want to be pepper sprayed or shot either. And he suspected she might have a concealed-weapons permit to carry a gun as well as that Taser.

"None of your damn business," she told him.

"I'm your bodyguard," he reminded her. "Everything about you is my damn business now."

"You're not protecting me," she said. "You're the one hurting me."

He'd been careful not to hold her too tightly. But he was big and sometimes stronger than he realized. He immediately loosened his grasp, and she broke free and whirled around to face him.

As he'd suspected she would, she pointed another weapon at him, the small pepper-spray canister that was attached to her key ring.

He snorted. "I don't know why the chief and Parker think *you* need a bodyguard." Just as he'd worried, he was the one who needed protecting from her.

But while she had her finger on the trigger of the canister, she didn't press down on it. Yet. "I don't need a bodyguard," she said.

He suspected he knew why: She was working for Luther. She was the leak within the district attorney's office. Maybe he could use this opportunity to prove that to Parker and to the chief.

"But you got one," he said. "So you're going to have to accept that."

Her eyes were such a brilliant shade of blue that they gleamed even in the dim lighting of the parking structure. Then she narrowed them in a glare. "I don't have to accept *you* as my bodyguard," she said.

"Do you even know who I am?" he asked. What could she have against him personally? He'd brought her evidence to indict Luther Mills, and he wasn't the one who'd made that evidence mysteriously disappear.

She narrowed her eyes into slits of suspicion. "You obviously don't want me to know," she said. "Or you wouldn't have your hood up. You wouldn't have been slinking in the shadows."

"Slinking in the shadows…" He chuckled. "That's kind of what bodyguards do." Unobtrusively protecting their clients. But she wasn't his client; Chief Lynch was. She was just his principal, the person he'd been assigned to protect.

"Why?" she asked. "Wouldn't you be more effective if everyone knew you were protecting me?"

He shrugged. "I'm not making that call. That's up to Parker Payne and the chief. They might want Luther to actually make a try for you, to flush out whoever's working with him."

She tightened her grasp on her canister of pepper spray, and he instinctively took a step back. "Is that what you were really trying to do here? Make a try for me?"

He chuckled again. She was crazy. "You actually think I'm going to try to take you out?"

She glanced around the dark garage and shivered. "This would be a good place to try."

"I'm your bodyguard," he repeated, and this time his teeth were gritted when he said it. How damn dense was she? Maybe that was why she'd never gotten a grand jury to indict Luther—because she wasn't very bright.

"I only have your word that's who you are," she said.

He reached up and pushed back his hood. Not that seeing his face clearly would probably make her recognize him. So he added his name, "I'm Landon Myers. I work for the Payne Protection Agency. I have been assigned to protect you."

"You worked vice," she murmured.

She must have recognized him.

"Yes, I did."

His admission just had her tensing more. What was she worried about? Why didn't she trust him?

Did she realize that he was onto her? That he suspected she was Luther's leak in the DA's office?

If the meeting at the Payne Protection Agency had been meant to reassure her, it had done exactly the opposite. Jocelyn was even more on edge than she'd been before it—when Landon Myers had accosted her in the parking garage.

Now he was using her keys to let himself into her house. She wouldn't have turned them over, but he'd insisted on going inside first, on checking to make sure that nobody had broken in while she'd been gone. The minute he turned them and pushed open the door, the alarm began to blare.

"What's the code?" he shouted over it.

She wasn't about to give that to him. But she joined him in the foyer and surreptitiously punched in the numbers. When the alarm stopped blaring, she told him, "That's why I know nobody has broken in here. They can't get past my security system. That's why you don't need to be here."

"You heard the chief," he said. "He wants you and everyone else involved in this trial to have around-the-clock protection until the trial is over."

She'd heard him. And she hadn't had the chance to argue with him since everybody else had been arguing against the need for protection. She hadn't wanted anyone who needed protecting to lose it—like the eyewitness.

She could not lose the eyewitness. And she actually trusted Clint Quarters to protect Rosie Mendez. He was the one who'd turned her late brother into an informant. He blamed himself for Javier Mendez's murder. Unfortunately, so did Rosie. But because Clint felt guilty, he would do everything in his power to keep her safe. He'd already saved her from an attempt on her life tonight.

She shivered.

Landon must have thought she was cold because he closed the door, shutting them inside the dark foyer. She shivered again.

While she trusted Clint to protect Rosie, she didn't trust Landon. He had no stake in this trial. Clint had walked away from the River City PD because of his guilt over Javier's death. Why had Landon walked away?

Needing to see him clearly, she flipped on a light. The golden hue of the chandelier's bulbs made his thick light brown hair glow like gold, as well. His eyes were brown, too, but a richer milk-chocolate brown. He stared down at her, which was an uncomfortable and unfamiliar sensation for Jocelyn. She was tall and wore heels to make herself even taller, which was usually taller than most of the men she encountered.

Except Landon Myers.

He was tall. But he wasn't just tall. He was big all over—broad shoulders, huge chest and arms, long, thick legs. If he was working for Luther, like she worried he was, then he could have easily taken her out back in the parking garage. He could have snapped her neck with very little effort.

She shivered again—at the thought, and at the way he was staring at her. So intensely…

But he wasn't looking at her with the admiration most men looked at her with. He didn't seem to find her attractive at all.

"That's some fancy security system," he mused.

She nodded.

"Expensive."

She shrugged. She had no idea. Her parents had insisted on installing it. They were paranoid about protection. They would probably approve of her having a bodyguard following her around, but Jocelyn didn't.

"And not just the security system," Landon remarked as he glanced up at the chandelier and at the artwork on the walls.

Her house had probably been expensive. But like the security system, it was something else her parents had bought for her. She'd been happy with her small apartment downtown, close to the office. Her parents had wanted her to live in a more secure neighborhood.

But she wasn't about to share her private life with Landon Myers. "As you can see, I'm perfectly safe inside my house," she told him. "You don't need to stay."

He was already walking beyond the foyer into the dark living room. And as he walked, his hand moved toward his holster. He couldn't have heard anything, though. There wasn't anyone inside.

Then she heard it, too, the clatter of something falling onto the hardwood floor. Landon pulled his weapon and swung the barrel around, but before he could pull the trigger, she grabbed his arm. Muscles rippled beneath her fingers. "Don't shoot!" she yelled. "It's just my cat."

"Cat?"

As if to confirm it, Lady let out a pitiful meow. Jocelyn flipped the living room switch, but the light was dim from the lamp lying on the floor.

"That little thing knocked over the lamp?" Landon asked skeptically as Lady trotted up to them. The Singapura cat was naturally small-boned and light. But she was also active and athletic, too.

Sometimes a little too active and athletic. "She's naughty," Jocelyn said, but she smiled as she leaned over and petted the cat's smooth beige coat. "You're a naughty girl."

As if insulted, Lady walked away from Jocelyn and wound between Landon's legs.

His brow furrowed as he stared down at the animal. "I didn't figure you for a cat lady."

Her parents had not bought her the cat. They wanted real grandchildren, not furry ones.

"She came with the house." She must have belonged to the previous owner because Jocelyn had found her inside when she'd moved in. The cat had been alone and hungry for food and affection.

Landon turned his attention to her, asking, "And you kept her?"

Jocelyn could have turned her in to a shelter or even sold her once she'd learned how rare the breed was, but removing Lady from the house hadn't seemed right. And Jocelyn appreciated her company. Like she'd told her parents, Lady was as close as they were getting to a grandchild. Jocelyn was not about to wind up like her boss—missing out on a major case because she was having babies.

"Are you allergic to cats?" Jocelyn asked hopefully. And Landon must have heard that hope because he chuckled. He reholstered his weapon and leaned down to pick up the cat. "Not at all," he said.

The small cat looked even smaller in his huge hands. But instead of being frightened, she purred and rubbed against him.

"She likes me," he said.

"She's hungry," Jocelyn corrected him, and she headed toward the kitchen.

He was right with her every step—as if he still suspected an intruder could have gotten inside the house. If anyone had made it past the security system, Lady would have been hiding, not out knocking stuff over. Usually she shied away from strangers. But she kept purring and fawning all over Landon.

"Traitor," Jocelyn murmured.

"What?" Landon asked. But his mouth had curved into a grin, so he'd probably heard her.

The minute Jocelyn rattled the cat's box of food, the fickle feline squirmed from Landon's arms and jumped down to trot over to her bowl that her mistress dutifully filled.

"She is a traitor," Landon agreed.

Was he?

Was he a traitor to the police department and the city he'd once sworn to serve and protect? Jocelyn stared at him, wondering.

Could she trust him?

Not like the chief and Parker Payne did. She tried again. "You don't have to stay. I'm safe here."

"I have my orders," Landon said. "You were there— you heard."

She sighed. She'd heard too much—about that attempt on the witness, about the plan for all the body-guards to act like boyfriends, or in Detective Dubridge's case, Keeli Abbott was to act like his girlfriend. Jocelyn shuddered in revulsion. She didn't want a boyfriend at all, let alone someone like Landon Myers.

Someone she couldn't trust.

"Don't worry," Landon said as he walked out of the kitchen and headed back to the living room. "You won't even know I'm here."

Jocelyn doubted that. She followed him into the living room, where he shrugged off his jacket and undid his holster. After putting the weapon and his coat onto the ottoman next to the couch, he reached for his shirt, tugging it up and over his head, so that he stood before her with that enormous, muscular chest bare but for the golden-brown hair on it.

Jocelyn choked on her own saliva. How the hell long had it been since she'd had a boyfriend?

She couldn't remember the last time she'd seen a man shirtless. It had been too long ago, and it had never been a man with a chest like this guy's.

"You okay?" Landon asked her. And there was a wicked gleam in his brown eyes.

She nodded.

And he teased, "Cat got your tongue?"

Heat rushed to her face. But she refused to let him know he was affecting her, any more than he must have already guessed. She glared at him. "I'm fine," she said.

"Really?" he asked. "You look a little frustrated."

"I am," she agreed. But not how he was implying—

if that was what he was implying. She wasn't sexually frustrated. Not at all…

"I'm frustrated that you insist on staying here when I don't need protection," she said.

He shrugged, and muscles rippled in his arms and chest, as well.

She nearly choked again.

"I'm just doing my job," he told her.

Was that all he was doing, though? Or was he working for Luther Mills as well as the Payne Protection Agency?

Fortunately, he'd returned her Taser, so she would have that if he tried anything. It wouldn't kill him, but at least it would give her time to get away from him.

And she needed to get away from him now—before she did something stupid, like continuing to stare at his chest. But before she turned away, she felt socially obligated to tell him, "There is a guest room upstairs."

Actually, there were three of them. The house was entirely too big for just her, but her parents had not yet given up their hope for her to get married and have children.

He shook his head. "I need to stay down here, make sure nobody tries to get in." He narrowed his eyes with suspicion. "Or out…"

Had he guessed that she was thinking about ditching him? Probably. She'd made it a little too clear that she didn't think she needed protection.

She certainly didn't need him to protect her. But maybe she did need protection—from him.

The Payne Protection Agency.

Luther had heard of it. A person couldn't live in

River City and not know about it. But he didn't just know the agency. He knew Parker Payne.

He leaned back on his bunk and laughed. Parker Payne had tried for years to take him down. Instead, the former vice cop had nearly been taken down.

Too bad Parker hadn't died when that hit had been put out on him years ago. So many assassins had tried…and failed. Regrettably.

Maybe Luther should put out another hit on Parker Payne and on every damn bodyguard working for him.

Luther knew all of them. Clint. Hart Fisher. Tyce Jackson. Landon Myers and that little hottie, Keeli Abbott. They were all former vice cops who, like Parker and Clint Quarters, had tried for many years to take down Luther and his organization. But eventually, they'd all given up and quit the River City PD.

Luther ran his fingers over the cell phone that was still warm from his last, lengthy conversation. He'd been apprised of the situation.

The chief knew that Luther had gotten to someone in the police department. Obviously, he didn't know who yet, or Luther wouldn't have gotten all the information he just had—that the chief had hired the Payne Protection Agency to guard the witness and everyone else associated with the case against him.

Someday soon, when he was free, he would have to thank Chief Lynch for making it all so easy for him. Now he wouldn't just take out the witness and the other people going after him; he would take out all those former vice cops, as well.

He would take down everyone who had tried to destroy him for so many years. But it wouldn't take him years to accomplish his objective.

Just days…
Or hours…
And all of them would be dead.

Chapter 3

Landon listened to the echo of her heels striking the wooden steps as she went upstairs to her bedroom. He was tempted to follow her, and not so he could use that guest room she'd mentioned. He'd rather share her bed. And for a moment, the way she'd looked at him, he'd thought she might not mind sharing with him.

Sure, she didn't like him. That was obvious. But she hadn't been able to stop staring when he'd taken off his shirt. He grinned again, like he had then. Teasing her had been fun but futile.

She hadn't taken the bait. She'd just ignored his innuendos. Looking the way she did, she had to be used to dealing with unwanted advances.

But he wondered if his advances would have been unwanted. She had been staring at him.

His body tensed and hardened. But he dragged in

a deep breath and exhaled it. While he couldn't help being physically attracted to a woman as beautiful as Jocelyn Gerber, he couldn't act on that attraction—because he couldn't trust her.

In the glow of the lamp he'd lifted back onto an end table, he stared up at the coffered ceiling over his head. The house was a mansion, the security system highly rated and expensive. And he'd recognized some of that artwork on the walls. It had been original, not prints.

He didn't think the salary of an assistant district attorney was enough to cover all her purchases and expenses. So where the hell was she getting her money?

Luther Mills?

It would make sense that he'd been paying her off to lose that evidence. But Landon needed evidence to prove that she was on the take. Luther threatening her, too, had proved her innocence to some, but not to him.

He didn't think she was really in danger.

He suspected he was the one in danger. Maybe he shouldn't have given her back that Taser. But her using that on him was the least of his concerns at the moment.

Clint was protecting the witness. He let a ragged sigh slip through his lips. While he was close to everyone he'd worked with in the vice unit, he was closest to Clint. They even rented a house together, a small one that was nothing like Jocelyn Gerber's.

Clint had nearly died tonight. And in order to protect Rosie Mendez, he still could die. Luther would probably be happy to take out Clint along with the eyewitness. Hell, Luther would be happy to take out any of them or all of them.

They'd all tried really hard to bring him down. Landon wanted to make certain that this time justice was finally served. It wouldn't be, though, if Jocelyn was working for the drug dealer.

He needed to know.

As his thoughts stopped racing, he noticed that the house had fallen silent. There was no creak of floor-boards overhead. Jocelyn wasn't moving around any-more. Neither was her damn cat.

So it was time for Landon to move around, to see what he could find in her house. Hopefully, she had some kind of home office or den someplace where she might keep financial records.

With the security system she had to keep everyone out, she might not even lock up her records. He hoped that was the case. And he hoped that home office was downstairs, so he wouldn't have to risk getting tased.

Before leaving the living room, he grabbed his Glock out of the holster. Despite the security system, he didn't want his weapon far from his reach. He knew he might need it, either for protection from Luther's crew or from Jocelyn Gerber.

Along with his shirt, he'd taken off his boots, too, so he moved softly across the hardwood floors, which creaked only slightly with his weight. The house was some kind of Tudor design with dark trim and plaster walls. It was rich and almost untouchable looking— like Jocelyn.

He'd touched her earlier, though, when he'd strug-gled with her in the parking garage. And he'd wanted to touch her again. He would get the chance if he pre-tended to be her boyfriend. The chief and Parker had suggested the ruse to fool Luther's leaks. They didn't want the ones within the police department and DA's office to know that the chief was aware of them.

But Landon had a feeling the leak in the DA's office already knew. He just had to prove she was the leak.

Her den was easy to find. Its double doors opened off the opposite end of the living room from the kitchen. Through the glass panes, he could see her desk. A computer sat on it along with a pile of folders.

The doorknob turned easily. Just as he'd hoped, she hadn't locked up anything. He pushed open one of the double doors and slipped inside the room. Like the living room, it had a coffered ceiling, but in here the beams had been painted white and so had the paneling on the walls. When he flipped on the lamp on the desk, which was also white, the entire room glowed. Unlike what he'd seen of the rest of the house, this space was bright and feminine—like Jocelyn.

Had the rest of the house been decorated by someone else? Had she lived here with someone else? A former husband? Maybe she'd gotten the house in a divorce settlement. He turned his attention to the files and the computer sitting atop the desk. He flipped on the computer to a log-in screen and cursed. He was no hacker, and he didn't know Jocelyn Gerber well enough to guess her log-in or password.

So he pressed the power button, turning it off, and reached for the folders instead. They appeared to be case files. Was it legal for her to remove them from the DA's office? Were they copies of information?

Some of the cases appeared to involve Luther, or at least some of his crew. Landon's former and current coworker Tyce Jackson had taken down quite a few members of that crew when he'd gone undercover within Luther's organization. None of them had turned on Luther, though, but they'd still gone free despite the vice unit's efforts to put them away.

Was that because of Jocelyn?

She hadn't worked every single case, but she'd been assigned quite a few of them. Too many of them…

But would Luther really have threatened her if she was working for him? Unless that threat was just a cover, so no one would suspect she was his mole.

But Landon wasn't the only one. Sure, he hadn't convinced Parker, and the chief obviously didn't suspect her. But his team members did. He'd seen the suspicion on all their faces tonight. They all had their hands full with their own assignments, though. So it fell on Landon to get the proof.

And, despite her top-notch security system, Jocelyn was unlikely to leave that lying out on her desk where a visitor or cleaning lady might see it. So he reached for one of the desk drawers. While he tugged on the handle, the drawer didn't budge. Then he noticed the lock.

So this was where she kept the things she didn't want anyone to see. Too bad the lock was flimsy. He grabbed her letter opener and easily jimmied open the drawer. A gasp slipped through his lips at what he found.

This wasn't evidence of her collusion with Luther Mills. If anything, it might have been proof of her innocence—if he was the one who'd sent the threats.

The first thing he'd seen was a paper with letters pasted to it that spelled out: *You're dead, Bitch!*

There were papers beneath that one, some written in thick black marker, some neatly typed, but all contained similar death threats.

Why hadn't she mentioned them during the meeting?

When they'd arrived, they'd seen a threat the judge had received regarding his daughter. A slashed-up photograph of the beautiful heiress. While none of these had photos of Jocelyn included, it was clear that the threat was meant for her—to end her life.

Jocelyn jerked awake just as she'd finally closed her eyes. She could not sleep with someone else in her house, especially when that someone was Landon Myers.

He was shirtless…

And ridiculously muscular and sexy and…

Suspicious. She could not trust him. While he was probably in his early thirties, like she was, he had worked vice long enough that he should have been able to bring down Luther Mills. But that hadn't happened until after he'd left the department.

There had to be a reason for that—like he had been working for Luther the years he'd been in the vice unit. Was he working for him now?

Instead of protecting her, did he intend to get rid of her? She reached beneath the pillow next to hers, where she'd stashed her Taser gun. Would the shock be enough to stop him? Or would she even have time to fire it at him?

He had a real gun with bullets. He didn't have to get close to her to kill her. But he was close.

Just below her.

She scooted up against the headboard to listen for any noise. Was he asleep? It wasn't as if she would be able to hear him snoring unless he snored really loudly. She did hear something, though—the metallic creak of hinges. Somebody was opening a door.

She waited for the blare of the alarm but then remembered that she'd shut it off. She hadn't turned it back on before going to bed like she usually did because her damn bodyguard had distracted her.

And if that wasn't her bodyguard moving around downstairs, it could have been someone who'd taken advantage of the security system being off. Someone could have broken inside her house.

She pulled the Taser from beneath her pillow and stepped lightly onto the floor. She moved quietly toward the door. But she had to unlock and open it. And the hinges on her door creaked like the ones she'd heard.

Damn.

Now whomever she had heard might have heard her, as well. It didn't matter if it was the bodyguard or an intruder. She was in danger no matter who was out there. With her Taser in both hands, she moved to the back stairwell, which descended into the kitchen. She drew in a deep breath as she stepped onto the tile floor. The ceramic was cold beneath her bare feet. She shivered, but being cold wasn't the reason.

She heard another creak—from behind her. But she had no time to whirl around, and point her weapon, before strong arms closed around her. A scream tore from her throat as she struggled in the grasp of her attacker.

Through the thin cotton of her nightgown, she could feel the heat of his body and even the bareness of his chest. The bodyguard was the one who'd grabbed her.

Now what did he intend to do with her?

Kill her?

Or…

Her pulse quickened in anticipation as he turned her

in his arms, and her breasts pushed against his chest as she panted for breath. "What—what are you doing?" she asked. But she didn't sound as angry and haughty as she wanted to sound.

"What the hell are you doing?" he asked.

"I—I heard someone moving around and remembered that I hadn't turned the alarm system back on," she said.

He cursed. "How the hell did we forget...?"

Because he'd taken off his shirt and she'd lost all her common sense. Maybe she'd been too focused on work lately. Maybe she needed more of a personal life than she'd been allowing herself.

Of course, she didn't want a husband or children like her parents wanted for her. But maybe a date every once in a while wouldn't interfere too much with her work.

What was Landon's excuse for forgetting, though? Had she distracted him, as well? She nearly snorted. She doubted that. He didn't seem at all attracted to her. But now...

The light from the microwave clock and various other appliances illuminated the kitchen enough that she could see him and the way he was looking at her, his dark eyes gleaming. He stared down at her nightgown. She wore no bra beneath the thin cotton, so her nipples pushed against the fabric, the tips taut as if begging for attention.

A strange tension began to wind inside her, from her breasts to her core. How could she be attracted to this man? She didn't even trust him.

It was purely physical—because he was so damn good-looking. His gaze met hers now, and his eyes looked more black than brown, as if his pupils had dilated. He leaned down until his mouth nearly touched hers.

Maybe it would have…had something not crashed somewhere else inside the house.

"That damn cat…" Landon murmured.

But she shook her head. "You don't know that. Not with the alarm being off."

He released a ragged breath before stepping back and finally letting her go. "You're right. I'll check it out. You go back upstairs."

She shook her head again. If someone had broken into her house, she sure as hell wasn't going to hide. She wanted to see who the intruder was. "I have my Taser," she reminded him as she raised the weapon.

"And that's not going to be effective if Luther sent a crew here like the one he sent to Rosie Mendez's apartment."

She shivered again because she knew he was right. If that many people had broken into her home, they both needed to run. But Landon wasn't running away from danger.

He raised his weapon and turned toward the kitchen doorway. He'd taken only a few steps before he turned his head and looked over his broad shoulder at her. "Stay behind me," he advised her.

As if his body alone could protect her from a barrage of bullets. But it was so big and muscular that maybe it could. She stayed close to his bare back as he headed out of the kitchen and across the living room.

No gunfire rang out—only his curse again.

"That damn cat," he said as he pushed open the door to her office. It creaked; she suspected it was what she'd heard earlier. It must have creaked when he'd closed the door to her office and locked the cat inside.

"What the hell were you doing in my office?" she asked him.

"I— What?" he asked as Lady streaked out between them. She'd knocked the files on Jocelyn's desk onto the floor along with a glass paperweight that had shattered against the wood.

"I didn't let her in there," she said. She was always careful to keep the cat out of her office since the feline was so active. "So you must have. What were you doing?"

Then she saw the drawer that had been forced open. He hadn't even bothered to put the letters back inside it. They lay across the keyboard to her computer.

"What the hell were you doing?" she demanded to know.

He gestured at those letters. "What the hell were you doing?" he asked. "How come you haven't told anyone about those threats?"

"That's none of your damn business," she said. "Nothing in this office is. You had no right to come in here."

"I'm your bodyguard," he said. "Those threats are damn well my business and so is whatever else you're hiding."

She shivered once more—but it was at the coldness of the look on his face. "Just what the hell are you implying?"

"I'm not implying anything," he said. "I'm flat out accusing you of not being truthful." He pointed toward those threats. "And those letters are proof."

She snorted. "Those letters are proof that I'm good at my job."

He snorted now. And her face heated with indignation. He was one of those—one of the officers who blamed her for not being able to get an indictment off sloppy police work. Figured.

"That's what those threats are about," she said.

"You're saying none of them have anything to do with this case—with Luther Mills?"

Because he'd already accused her of not being truthful, she couldn't shake her head—because she honestly didn't know. Did Luther Mills want her dead?

Anytime the phone rang in the middle of the night, it wasn't with good news, like Luther Mills had been shanked in jail and nobody was in danger any longer.

Parker reached for the cell phone vibrating next to his bed with the expectation of only bad news, especially with as determined as Luther seemed to be to take out the eyewitness. Suspecting it was Clint calling, he didn't even look at the phone before answering, "Tell me you're alive."

The caller's gasp sounded soft and feminine. "Who do you think could be dead?"

He swallowed a groan as he recognized Jocelyn Gerber's voice. The assistant district attorney already seemed on edge. Woodrow had warned him that she also didn't trust his team. Parker had chosen not to share that information with his team, who he already knew didn't trust her either.

Especially the man protecting her.

"Tell me!" she demanded.

"Nobody's dead," he assured her, although he couldn't know for certain, not with all the attempts Luther had already made on the eyewitness.

"Then why did you say what you did?" she asked, as if she had him on the witness stand and was going to interrogate him.

"Because usually when the phone rings at this hour, it's not good news," he pointed out. "Why are you calling me now?" If there had been an attempt on her life, Landon would have called him—unless he'd been injured during that attempt. "Is Landon all right?"

"No," she said.

And Parker gasped now. "What's wrong?"

Sharon murmured in her sleep and turned toward him on the bed. So he slipped out of it and moved to the hall to finish the call.

"What happened?" he asked.

"He snooped through my office," she said.

And Parker's brow furrowed with confusion. "What? I thought you two were going to your house after the meeting."

"We did," she said. "He went through my home office, even broke into my desk."

Parker swallowed a curse. Damn it. What the hell had Landon been up to? But he could guess—trying to find evidence that Jocelyn Gerber was Luther's mole in the DA's office.

"I want a different bodyguard," she demanded. "I'd prefer not to have one at all, but the chief insists that everyone involved with the trial has one."

Parker swallowed a groan now. Had she called the chief? Hopefully, she was just going by what he'd said during the meeting when everyone had been arguing against having protection.

"That's not possible," Parker told her. "Everyone else has already been assigned to another principal."

"Principal?"

"Person to protect," he replied.

A frustrated-sounding sigh rattled his cell phone. "What about one of your brothers' agencies? I'd prefer to have someone who hasn't worked in vice anyway."

"And the chief prefers that you do," Parker reminded her. "You and Landon will need to work this out." Before the lawyer could argue with him any more, he clicked off his cell.

Why was she so angry with Landon? Because she felt like he'd invaded her privacy? Or because he'd come close to finding whatever she might be hiding?

Could Landon be right? Could she be working for Luther Mills?

Parker hoped like hell Landon was wrong—because Jocelyn Gerber was too close to everyone else involved in the trial. She could help Luther get to any of them at any time.

And Landon.

She would be able to get to him all the time. Instead of protecting her, he might wind up needing protection from her. Especially now with as furious as she sounded with her bodyguard.

Parker had been worried that the eyewitness might not survive the night. Now he was worried about Landon.

Chapter 4

His friend was in pain, and Landon hated seeing him like this. It wasn't the shoulder Clint had injured jumping out a window to save Rosie Mendez the night before that was hurting Clint—it was the guilt. That had been weighing heavily on him since Javier Mendez had died.

Clint blamed himself for the kid's death, and he was not the only one. Rosie Mendez blamed him, too. She thought Clint had forced the kid to become an informant for him. She thought he'd planted the drugs on her brother that he'd found when he'd busted the kid. But that wasn't the case. Landon knew the kid had wanted to bring down Luther as a way to make amends to his sister. Despite all her efforts to keep him away from the drugs that had ruined their mother's life, Javier had been selling for Luther.

But Landon doubted Clint had told Rosie that. He

wouldn't have wanted to add guilt to the pain of her loss. Watching Luther murder her brother had already traumatized her.

But it hadn't scared her like it should have. She was insisting on working her shift as an ER nurse, which was why Clint had called Parker with the request for Jocelyn to talk some sense into her.

So Landon had brought Jocelyn to the safe house where Clint was staying with Rosie. The condo was in a converted warehouse in the nearly abandoned industrial area of River City. With metal-and-brick walls and a security system even better than Jocelyn's, it was safe.

Or it had been, until Landon had brought Jocelyn there. "You sure about this?" he asked as he stepped closer to where Clint leaned against the kitchen counter. The condo was open concept, almost like a loft, except for the bedroom, which was closed off with the door shut. Rosie Mendez must have been in there because Landon hadn't seen her since Clint had let him and Jocelyn in a few moments ago.

Clint cocked his head. His blond hair was mussed as if he'd been running his hands through it, and his green eyes were rimmed with dark circles as if he hadn't slept at all. Landon knew the feeling. He hadn't slept at all the night before either, and nobody had been shooting at him.

"Are you sure?" Clint asked.

And it was clear he was asking about Jocelyn. He shared Landon's suspicions. But those threats Landon had found had gone a long way to assuage his doubts about her. At least some of those had to have been from

Luther's crew. And none of his crew did anything without his ordering it. He nodded.

But his finding those threats had made Jocelyn distrust him. She eyed him even more suspiciously than she already had. And he'd overheard her call to Parker.

His lips curved into a grin. Too bad for her that Parker hadn't replaced him. Then he remembered how close he'd come to nearly kissing her last night. And his grin slipped away. No. It was too bad for him that Parker hadn't replaced him.

It wasn't easy being so close to Jocelyn Gerber—not with as gorgeous as she was. She wore another of her suits with the tight skirt that molded to her curves. Her black hair hung like a silk curtain around her shoulders. She looked more like a model than a lawyer. Maybe she modeled on the side and that was how she afforded her house and furnishings.

A door creaked open and Rosie Mendez stepped out of the bedroom. The young woman wore scrubs with her hospital badge pinned to one of the pockets. That was why Clint had wanted Jocelyn to talk to her. But Rosie didn't know because she asked, "Why are you here?"

"You need to stay here," Jocelyn told her.

Rosie's brown eyes narrowed in a glare directed at Clint before she turned back to the ADA. "What about you? Are you staying in a safe house?"

Jocelyn shook her head. "It's not necessary for me," she replied. "You're the only witness. If *you* die, the case is over. If I die, someone else will just take over the case. So it makes no sense for Mills to kill me."

"Unless the DA on his payroll takes over the case," Landon said. Maybe that was why she'd been sent all those threats, so she would give up the case to whoever really was working for Luther. Jocelyn glared at him now. Despite the chief's meeting, she still refused to accept that anyone within her office could be working for Luther. Landon had thought that was because she was the leak and didn't want her department investigated.

But now he wondered if she was just naive.

"We're not talking about me," Jocelyn said. "We're talking about the key witness for the prosecution."

"We're talking about *me*," Rosie Mendez interjected. "I'm a person—with a life."

"A life you're going to lose if you don't stay safe," Jocelyn said. She looked around the condo. "And you're safe here. Far safer than you were staying in your own place, where Luther knew where to find you whenever he was ready to get rid of you."

Rosie snorted. "You better get to know Luther better if you intend to prosecute him. He can find me anywhere. He has people in the police department and in your office. You don't think that he already knows where I am? Where you are?"

Jocelyn shivered. She was probably thinking about all those death threats Landon had found locked in her desk drawer.

"She's right." Clint surprisingly came to Rosie's defense. "Luther probably has eyes on this place already." But then he added, "That's why you can't leave, Rosie."

"No, you can't," Jocelyn agreed.

Thinking about all those threats he'd found, Landon felt compelled to agree with Rosie. "So you should stay here, too, Ms. Gerber."

She glared at him again. "You said that the guards outside haven't seen anyone watching the place. You said no one followed us," Jocelyn fired back at Landon. Then her face flushed as she must have realized she'd just contradicted what Clint had said. She turned toward Rosie now. "That doesn't mean that Officer Quarters— that Clint—isn't right. You said so yourself that Luther probably already knows where you are."

Rosie nodded. "So there's no more reason for me to stay here than there is for you."

"You have to testify," Jocelyn said, and only now did she sound frightened. She wasn't worried about losing her life. She was worried about losing her case.

"I will testify," Rosie assured her.

"Not if you're dead," Jocelyn told her. "If you leave this place where you are safe, you're risking your life, but most of all, you're risking justice for your brother. Do you want his killer to go free?"

Seeing her in action like this, arguing her case, Landon was surprised that she'd ever lost, let alone as many times as she had. And those niggling doubts grew again.

But maybe she'd pushed too hard, because tears pooled in Rosie's eyes just before she ran back into the master bedroom.

"Damn it!" Clint cursed.

"I'm sorry," Jocelyn said, but she sounded unapologetic. "She needed to hear it, though."

"It's too much," Clint said.

"Parker told us that you wanted Jocelyn to come here and talk some sense into the witness." Landon reminded him of the reason for their visit. After those threats, he would have preferred to bring her to a safe house to stay, not just visit.

"I wanted ADA Gerber to talk some sense into

her," Clint said, "not manipulate her and make her feel guilty."

"It will be her fault if Luther Mills gets away with her brother's murder," Jocelyn said.

Thinking he might need to protect his principal from his best friend now, Landon stepped between them. But then he realized what she was doing—taking no responsibility, just as she had when she'd failed to get those other indictments against Luther or some of his crew. She'd blamed sloppy police work then.

He snorted his disgust. "You're already setting up someone else to blame if you lose this case, too."

She bristled with righteous indignation. "I don't do that," she protested. "I just want my witness to make it to the stand." She turned toward Clint now. "And if she doesn't, then that's your fault."

Landon opened his mouth on the curse word he was tempted to call her, but Clint cut him off. "She's right," he said. "It's my job to protect Rosie Mendez."

"Make sure you do your job," Jocelyn told him as she headed toward the door. "Because with her testimony, I won't lose."

"This time," Landon muttered as he trailed her toward the door. He reached around her and pressed the security code into the panel to open the big steel door. Jocelyn had turned back to glare at him, so he didn't think she saw the code he inputted. But as he walked out the door, he could see his friend was concerned that he'd made a mistake.

Clint had obviously wanted Jocelyn to convince the young woman to take no chances with her safety. But after having Jocelyn come to the safe house, Clint was clearly worried that he might have put Rosie in danger himself.

But Landon was the one who'd brought the ADA. If something happened to Rosie, Landon would take the blame for it. His friend already carried too much guilt.

Despite the cool breeze swirling around the sidewalk as they stepped outside the condo, Jocelyn's face stayed hot. She wasn't embarrassed, though. She was angry. How could Landon think she was to blame for failing to get indictments or losing cases?

It was clear that he'd thought it was her fault, and he wasn't the only one. Clint Quarters had seemed to share Landon's low opinion of her.

Did they think she was incompetent? Or worse?

Landon wouldn't even look at her as he held open the door of the black Payne Protection Agency SUV for her. His attention was on the bodyguards protecting the perimeter of the condo. "Be extra careful," he advised them before he closed her door and walked around to his side.

"You're worried," she said after he slid beneath the steering wheel. He was such a big man that despite the size of the vehicle, his shoulder nearly touched hers over the console between them. She was worried, too, but even more so after realizing he was, as well.

Despite what she'd told Rosie, she didn't think she would lose the trial if she lost Rosie's testimony. There was evidence, too, that would impact a jury even more than eyewitness testimony that the high-priced defense lawyer would tear apart on cross-examination. But she didn't want anything to happen to Rosie Mendez—

anything else. She'd already been through enough with losing her brother.

Jocelyn knew what it felt like to lose loved ones to violence. All these years later, her heart still ached with loss.

"We shouldn't have come here," Landon said.

Jocelyn shook her head. "No. Rosie needs to know how much danger she's in."

"You don't think she knows?" Landon asked. "She saw her brother gunned down in front of her. She knows better than anyone else what an animal Luther Mills is."

She shivered. While violence had affected her and still did because of the career she'd chosen, she hadn't personally witnessed it happen. She'd only seen the aftermath. "He is an animal," she agreed.

"And anyone who works with or for him is an animal, too," Landon said, and his deep voice rumbled with emotion.

Had she been wrong to suspect him? She had no doubt that someone in the police department had helped Luther over the years, though. According to the chief, someone was still helping him now. She could believe that. But to think someone within her department…

She knew everyone too well. Nobody worked in the district attorney's office for the money. Maybe some did for politics—to move up. But most, like her, did it because they wanted to take criminals off the street.

That was why people became police officers, too. "Why did you leave River City PD?" she asked.

He shrugged, and his broad shoulder bumped against hers. "Parker offered me the job. Clint was leaving, too. And Tyce and Hart and Keeli…"

She winced as she thought of all the bodyguards. Luther's mole in the vice unit could have been any of them. And now each of them was protecting one of the people he'd threatened. Which one was the mole?

She was beginning to believe it wasn't Landon. He seemed to want Luther off the street as badly as she did.

"You're that close to them?" she asked. "That you would leave a job you loved…just because they did?"

He snorted. "I wouldn't say that I loved it."

"You didn't enjoy working in the vice unit?"

He glanced across at her, and his brown eyes were hard. "I didn't enjoy watching perps I arrested walking away with no charges."

She narrowed her eyes. "Are you blaming me for that?"

He cursed, but it wasn't at her. His focus was on the rearview mirror.

"What?" she asked.

"We're being followed."

She whirled around in her seat, but there were so many vehicles behind them, as they headed downtown to her office, that she couldn't tell which one he was talking about. "Where? What one?"

But instead of answering her, he pulled out his cell phone and punched in a number. A deep voice emanated from the speaker. "This is Parker."

"Landon," her bodyguard identified himself.

"Everything all right?" his boss asked, and his voice sounded as tense as it had when she'd called him late last night. "What?" he asked anxiously. "What is it?"

"I—" Landon kept glancing into the rearview "—think we're being followed."

"You have backup," Parker reminded him. "I'll have them intervene."

"I can lose whoever this is tailing us," Landon said. But he hadn't sped up. He hadn't switched lanes. It was almost as if he wanted the vehicle to follow them.

She shivered again.

"Good," Parker said. "So what's the problem?"

"I'm not sure where I picked up the tail," Landon admitted, and a muscle twitched along his tightly clenched jaw. "They're good."

"So what are you saying?" Parker wondered. "That the people following you probably aren't some of Luther's flunky drug dealers?"

A ragged sigh slipped out of Landon's lips. "I hadn't thought of that, but it's true."

"They could be cops." Jocelyn uttered her first thought aloud.

Landon glared at her. Even though he didn't work for River City PD anymore, he apparently wasn't any more willing to consider that one of them could be Luther's mole than she was to suspect one of her coworkers.

"I don't know who the hell they are," Landon said.

"If you don't need backup to intervene, why did you call?"

Landon sighed again before slowly admitting, "I might not have noticed them earlier."

"Okay…"

"We just left the safe house," Landon said. "We just left Clint and the witness."

"You think you might have led them there?" Parker asked.

"I don't know if I led them there," Landon said, his voice gruff with guilt, "or if they were already there."

Even though she was still mad at him for his comments and over his snooping the night before, she automatically defended him. "Rosie and Quarters said that Luther Mills probably already knew where they were."

The thought made her sick with concern and fear for their safety. She wasn't the only one afraid.

Parker Payne said, "I'll send more bodyguards to the safe house—make sure none of Luther's crew tries anything."

"Good," Landon said, and now he uttered a shaky sigh of relief.

"You focus on protecting Ms. Gerber," Parker added.

He glanced across at her. "That would be easier to do if she took her own advice and stayed in a safe house instead of insisting on going into her office."

"Parker has more important things to do than listen to us argue." She reached over and pressed her finger on the disconnect button on his cell phone. Payne needed to get more protection on the witness.

"I don't need to go into a safe house," she said. "Luther is not going to have me killed because, like I told Rosie, it doesn't matter if anything happens to me. The trial will still go on."

"But will the new prosecutor get the conviction you seem pretty confident you'll be able to get?" he asked.

She had been confident—until she'd learned about Luther's plan to take out everyone associated with the trial. Sure, that included her, but he wasn't going to start with her. He would use all his resources to get rid of Rosie first.

"You are so sure someone in my office is a traitor," she said. "It seems like you'd be happy to go to work with me and try to figure out which one it is."

He glanced across at her, and his gaze was speculative. "That's exactly what I plan on doing."

Was that why he'd searched her office the night before? She intended to ask him, but he suddenly jerked the wheel, sending the SUV into another lane but barely missing the vehicles already in it. Horns blared, and she cursed.

"Hang on," he advised her. "I'm going to get rid of our tail."

The vehicle he thought he'd noticed following them? Or their backup?

She didn't entirely trust him yet. He could still be working for Luther and just very good at hiding it.

Luther clicked on his vibrating cell phone to a curse. "What the hell's going on?" he asked.

"I'm following the lady DA like you said," his caller replied. "But her bodyguard is trying to lose me."

Blaring horns emanated from the cell phone.

"Aren't you trained for this kind of driving?" Didn't the police academy have some kind of a class for it? Like how not to lose a suspect?

"Yeah, but he was trained for it, too."

He? Who was protecting Jocelyn Gerber? And how the hell would he be able to focus with her around? She was too damn good-looking to be a lawyer.

"Don't worry about the lady DA," Luther advised him. "Focus on Rosie Mendez. You already lost her once." Last night—when she was supposed to have died. Instead, Clint Quarters had literally leaped to her rescue. *Damn him.*

"What about Gerber, though?"

"I can have Jocelyn Gerber taken out anytime I

want," Luther said, and a self-satisfied smirk crossed his face. He didn't just have help in the police department; he had help within the district attorney's office, too.

And that person could easily get to Jocelyn. She, and whoever her bodyguard was, would never see the threat until it was too late.

Until they were both dead.

That was going to happen. Luther wanted them all gone: everyone associated with the trial and every damn bodyguard of Parker Payne's agency, including Parker Payne. Luther needed to send a message—a very loud message—that nobody better ever try to take him down again.

Or they would wind up dead…

Chapter 5

Landon lost the tail—almost too easily—as if the person had suddenly given up. Of course, they had probably already known where he and the ADA were headed. Anyone who knew Jocelyn Gerber knew where she spent most of her time: divided between her office and the courthouse. The two buildings were close, so close that the parking garage that stood between them serviced them both. After pulling into a space designated for the staff at the district attorney's office, Landon glanced around the garage.

It was early, so not all the spaces were full.

Jocelyn reached for her door handle, but Landon reached across and covered her hand with his. "Wait for me to make sure it's safe," he told her.

Her willowy body bristled, but she stayed inside until he walked around the SUV and opened her door. "You don't have to pretend to be my boyfriend," she said.

"I didn't open your door because I think we're on a date," he assured her. "I just want to keep you safe."

And to find out the truth about her.

"I'm safe," she told him as she headed toward the side of the parking structure where doors opened into the district attorney's office. She gestured at the guard who sat near the metal detectors at the entrance.

Landon opened his jacket to show his holster to the middle-aged guard. "I have a permit and the chief of police's permission to carry inside this building," he told him.

The man nodded. "I know, Myers."

And Landon grinned as he recognized the former police sergeant. "Good to see you."

"You, too," his former boss said with a grin. But when he turned toward Ms. Gerber, his grin slid away. "Ms. Gerber."

She nodded at the man as she proceeded through the metal detectors. She didn't wait for Landon, just kept going.

The guard shook his head as Landon rushed off to keep up with her. He was obviously not a fan of the assistant district attorney.

Landon suspected not many of her coworkers were. The ones they passed did the same thing the guard had; if they were smiling or talking with someone else, they tensed and stopped—talking and smiling. Jocelyn didn't seem to notice or care, but Landon took note.

Her keys jangled as she pulled them from her purse and unlocked her door. Like her desk at home, this one was piled high with folders. They also covered the credenza behind her and the top of a filing cabinet. He pointed at it. "Too busy to use that?" he asked.

She glanced at it. "It's too full to hold any more."

And there was no space in her small office for another filing cabinet. A chair barely fit behind her desk and another in front of it. "Why do you have so much work?"

She tensed again. "Because I want it."

A chuckle followed her pronouncement, and Landon glanced at the man standing in the doorway. "Jocelyn wants every case—every trial," the gray-haired man remarked. "And if she doesn't get it, she goes behind our backs to the DA and steals it."

Jocelyn chuckled, as well, but like her coworker, it held no amusement. "Still stings that she gave me Luther Mills's trial, huh?"

"Gave?" The man snorted. "You stole that, and you know it."

Why had she wanted it so badly? Because Luther was paying her to lose it?

"Amber thought I was the best attorney for the trial."

The guy shook his head. "Was that it—or was it because you're the only female ADA?"

Jocelyn chuckled again. "Are you claiming the DA is guilty of reverse sexism in the workplace?" she asked.

"I'm not saying anything I wouldn't want her to hear," he replied, "because we all know you're her eyes and ears in the office while she's off having her baby."

Jocelyn bristled again. But she didn't deny being the tattletale her coworker had basically accused her of being. If everyone else suspected the same thing he did, it explained why they'd all stopped talking when she'd arrived.

Landon held out his hand and introduced himself

since Jocelyn didn't seem so inclined. "Landon Myers."
He didn't bother explaining what he was.

"Mike Forbes," the man replied, as his gray brows
lowered over narrowed eyes. "Myers? You a cop still?"

Landon shook his head.

Before the guy could ask anything else, another man
joined him in the doorway. This one was younger and
thinner—his body and his blond hair. He had the lean
build of a runner. "Hey, Forbes, quit giving Jocelyn a
hard time. She just wants what we all want—Luther
Mills behind bars."

As she looked at this man, her smile lit up her already beautiful face and stole Landon's breath. She'd
never looked at him like that. "Thank you, Dale."

The blond guy smiled back at her. Maybe he was the
one person in the DA's office who didn't care what she
told the boss. Or he wanted to be more than a coworker.

Something about the way he looked at her had
Landon's stomach muscles tightening and his hands
squeezing into fists.

But then the guy reached out a hand to him. "Dale
Grohms," he introduced himself.

"This is Landon Myers," she said before he could.
Then she added, "He's my boyfriend."

And now the guy's smile slid away. He definitely
wanted to be more than her coworker.

Landon waited until both men left and she closed the
door behind them before saying, "I thought you didn't
want me pretending to be your boyfriend."

"I don't want you *acting* like my boyfriend," she
said.

And he frowned. "I don't understand."

"I can tell people that you are," she said. "But I don't want you…touching me…or…"

That feeling in his gut, that he'd had watching her smile at Dale Grohms, intensified now. He wasn't sure what the hell it was, but he didn't like it. He didn't like her much either, but that didn't stop him from being attracted to her. And he knew, after the night before, that it wasn't just one-sided. Not with the way she'd looked at him.

Before she could move behind her desk, he stepped closer to her—blocking her path. Her body came up against his, and she sucked in a breath and stared up at him. "What—what are you doing?"

"Calling you out," he told her. And he wanted to do that—about so many things—but this one was suddenly most important to him.

"Calling me out?" she repeated, her brow furrowing slightly.

Her skin was so creamy and flawless, her features so perfect. She was that kind of beauty that seemed as untouchable as she claimed she wanted to be. But he didn't believe her.

"You're a liar," he said.

"What?" She was also full of self-righteous indignation again as her blue eyes widened with shock.

"You wanted me to touch you last night," he said, "when I held you in the kitchen."

"You grabbed me," she said.

"You didn't fight me off," he said. Not like she had in the parking garage earlier that evening. "You didn't pull back when I started leaning down…" And he began to lean down again. "You didn't push me away…"

She didn't this time either, even as her body tensed. It was as if she waited for it—wanted it—just like he wanted to kiss her. Even if there'd been another crash, he wouldn't have denied them this time. He brushed his mouth across hers, lightly at first, but then her lips parted on a soft sigh and he deepened the kiss.

Her lips were as silky as her hair looked. Needing to know, he slid his hands into the long, smooth locks as he held her head to his. He slid his mouth over and over hers before tracing her fuller bottom lip with the tip of his tongue. Then he slid his tongue inside her mouth and tasted her.

And he was shocked by the hotness and the sweetness when she always acted so bitter and cold. Her fingers slipped into his hair, too, and she kissed him back. Passion burned through him, heating his body, making his pulse pound.

He couldn't remember ever being so damn attracted to anyone else. Why her?

Finally, as if remembering what he'd said, she moved her hands from his hair to his chest, and she pushed him back. But her lips stayed open as she panted for breath. Her skin was flushed. She was attracted to him, too.

She didn't try denying it now. She just moved around her desk and murmured, "I—I need to get to court soon."

Landon wasn't sure if she actually had a trial to go to, or if she just didn't want to stay alone with him in her office. With the door closed and the attraction between them heating up the place, the room felt even smaller than it was.

And Landon felt like he was suffocating. He was

tempted to open up the door for some air, but when he glanced at it, he noticed, through the window in the wood, that the two men who'd left her office hadn't gone far. They stood just out in the hall, looking toward her office. Neither could have missed that kiss.

Had they bought it? Did they believe he was her boyfriend? Or did they suspect he was really her bodyguard? He hadn't kissed her to convince them, though. He'd kissed her because he'd wanted to.

And, damn it, he wanted to do it again.

But he couldn't let her distract him from protecting her or from finding out if she or one of her coworkers was also working for Luther.

Despite all the hours that had passed since that kiss, Jocelyn's lips still tingled from it—from the heat of it, the passion.

She couldn't remember a kiss ever affecting her like that, a man ever affecting her like that. She'd had to force herself to push him away. She'd had to force herself to focus on the job that had previously always consumed her.

All she cared about was getting justice, just like Dale Grohms had said. Forbes didn't believe it. He thought she was lobbying for the same job he was—their boss's.

Jocelyn didn't have to be in charge. In fact, she didn't think she'd like it because she wouldn't be able to try as many cases as she did now. Forbes had been right when he'd said she wanted them all.

She did—to make sure they weren't lost. But despite how hard she worked, she didn't win every case. In fact, she'd had a string of losses that haunted her. A string that had seemed to end when some of the vice unit had quit River City PD to go to work for the Payne Protection Agency.

Could she really trust Landon?

He hadn't respected her order for him to not act like her boyfriend. But as he'd pointed out, she hadn't pushed him away when she'd had the chance. Sure, she could have used the excuse that she knew her coworkers were watching them, and she hadn't wanted to draw any more attention than his following her around already had. But she hadn't realized Mike and Dale were outside her office yet until she'd settled, with shaky knees, into the chair behind her desk.

Despite the cool night air blowing through the parking structure, her face was burning. And it wasn't just with embarrassment over her coworkers witnessing that kiss. She was hot because that kiss had been damn hot.

Landon Myers was damn hot. His body, his mouth… his hands slipping through her hair as he'd held her head to his. She stifled the moan that rose in her throat as desire rushed over her again. She had to remind herself that kiss had just been part of his cover; it hadn't been real. He didn't even seem to like her.

But he did seem determined to protect her. He walked so close to her that his body brushed against hers with every step they took. He wasn't trying to turn her on, though. He wasn't even looking at her. Instead, he peered around the dimly lit structure, as if looking for killers lurking in the shadows. And he was ready for those killers, with his gun drawn and held at his side.

Even though he wasn't trying to affect her, his closeness did. Jocelyn's pulse quickened, and her breath burned in her lungs, as if stuck there. It didn't matter how close he was to her, though. In the courtroom, he'd been forced to sit in the gallery a few seats behind the prosecutor's table. But she'd been aware of him the entire time, had known he was watching her, and her skin had tingled with that awareness—with that attraction.

Her body had flushed with heat and desire, like it was now. But then a sudden chill raced down her spine, and she shivered.

"Somebody's watching us," Landon murmured.

So he'd felt it, too.

She glanced around now, staring into the shadows at the few cars left in the parking lot. "Where?"

He shrugged even as he covered her hand with his. She'd thought he was reassuring her, and she leaned closer to him. But instead, he clicked the key fob she held in her hand. The beep of her horn and the flash of her lights startled her so much that she stumbled. She might have fallen had he not caught her and steadied her with his arm around her.

He held her for just a moment—as if waiting for her to regain her balance. But when he touched her, she lost her balance, lost her focus. She could see only him, feel only this damn attraction to him.

His gaze held hers and he leaned slightly toward her, as if he intended to kiss her again. But before his mouth touched hers, he jerked back. Then he quickly guided her toward the passenger's side of the black SUV and opened the door for her.

She didn't know if he was in a hurry to get some distance between them or if he was really worried about whoever was watching them. "Didn't Parker say that he had backup bodyguards following us?"

"Not anymore," Landon said. "They were needed to help guard Rosie Mendez."

Jocelyn nodded. "That's good. She's the one in danger."

Landon gently nudged her into the seat, and before closing the door, he reminded her, "She's not the only one."

He could have been talking about the evidence tech or the judge's daughter who'd been threatened, too, or the detective who'd investigated the murder and arrested Luther.

But she knew he was talking about her. She wished he hadn't seen all those threats. She watched as he rounded the front of the SUV to the driver's side, and a twinge of panic struck her heart.

If she was in danger, then so was he.

Because, with how determined Landon was to protect her, if anyone truly wanted to hurt her, they would have to hurt him first.

Had Jocelyn and that giant with her seen him? He held his breath with concern that they might have. But then he expelled that breath on a ragged sigh. It didn't matter if they had. This was the parking garage where he parked, too—since he worked at the same place Jocelyn worked.

But they must not have noticed him behind the tinted windows of his car since they walked past him to a black SUV that must have been *his*.

Who the hell was he?

Boyfriend?

He shook his head. He wasn't buying that story. Jocelyn Gerber was too damn ambitious to let anything get in the way of her aspirations. She wanted the district attorney's job. Hell, she probably wanted even more than that, and she had the resources to go after whatever she wanted.

And she didn't care who else wanted or deserved it more.

No. The only way to stop her was to get rid of her.

Luther Mills was supposed to do that. But for some reason he wanted to wait. He thought he needed to kill the others first.

But *he* wasn't going to wait. He had to get rid of Jocelyn—and whatever the big guy was to her—*now*.

Chapter 6

She went straight from working at the office to working at home. Landon stared through the leaded-glass doors of her home office, watching her as she studied the papers strewn across her desk.

Was she working on the case that she'd started today, with a preliminary hearing in court, or was she working on Luther's case? Or worse yet, had she received another threat she hadn't shared with him?

He just knew that someone had been watching them a short while ago in the parking garage. Even though he hadn't seen them, he'd felt their presence and the intensity of their stare. He reached for his cell and punched in the contact for Parker. While he was confident he could protect Jocelyn while they were in her house, he needed to make sure she was safe everywhere else—especially the parking garage.

He needed backup at least there.

Hell, he probably needed backup everywhere since she was so damn distracting to him. What the hell had he been thinking to kiss her?

Because all he wanted was to repeat it.

It was a good thing she'd locked herself away in her office. She was out of his reach. And out of the reach of whoever had been watching them.

He'd been especially vigilant on the drive back to her house, making sure nobody had followed them. He hadn't seen anyone, but that didn't mean they hadn't been there, still watching.

Waiting for the chance to make good on all those threats she'd received.

Parker's voice emanated from his phone, but it was his outgoing message. Landon's brow furrowed as he tried to remember if his boss had ever not answered a call. He couldn't remember.

He punched in the number again, murmuring, "What the hell's going on…?"

The call connected this time, but it wasn't Parker's voice he heard. The sound of sirens and a disjointed conversation emanated from his cell now. He only caught bits and pieces of it—only enough to scare the hell out of him.

"Parker!" he shouted. Had his boss been wounded? Why the hell wasn't he speaking into the phone?

Then he heard his voice in that disjointed conversation, just a word here and there as Parker conversed with a few other people.

And finally that conversation must have ended, for, at last, he spoke directly into his cell. "Have you heard from him?"

"Who?" Landon asked.

"Clint," Parker replied.

And Landon knew—all those sirens and the urgency of that conversation…

"He's been hurt," he said.

"Shot—we think," Parker replied. "There was an ambush at the safe house."

"Did—did they get the witness?" Landon asked.

"We don't know," Parker replied. "Clint got her away from the scene, but we don't know if she'd been hit, too."

Landon groaned. "It's my fault," he murmured. "I knew I shouldn't have brought her there."

"What?" Jocelyn asked. She stood in front of him in the open doorway of her home office. "What's going on?"

He ignored her, as anger gripped him. It had to have been her. She had to be working with Luther.

"Let me know when you hear from him," Landon told his boss.

"The same," Parker replied.

But Landon doubted Clint would call him for help. After the ambush, there was no way he would trust Landon again, not as long as he had Jocelyn with him.

He clicked off his cell and slid it back into his pocket with a slightly shaking hand.

Jocelyn stepped closer and gripped his arm. "What's wrong? What happened?"

He looked at her then, and anger coursed through him. But he was angrier with himself than he was with her. How had he kissed her? How had he been attracted to a woman like her?

"You tell me," he said as he pushed past her into the office. He glanced around even though he'd already searched in here for the answers he sought. "When did you tip Luther off to where Rosie Mendez was?"

She gasped. "Wh-what happened to her? Is she dead?"

Landon shrugged.

And she tugged on his arm, as if she was trying to shake him or maybe pull him out of her room. "Tell me!"

"I don't know," he said. "Clint got her away from the ambush. But he was shot—" His voice cracked with emotion. Where the hell was his friend? Was he okay?

"Call him," Jocelyn urged him.

Like Clint would answer his call.

After what had happened, Clint was probably struggling to trust anyone right now. Especially him.

"Why?" Landon asked. "You need to find out where he is now, so you can update Luther?"

"What the hell are you talking about?" she asked, her brow furrowing. "I have not and would never tell Luther where Rosie Mendez is."

Landon snorted. "Yeah, right."

She bristled, her willowy body tense with that self-righteous indignation.

But Landon didn't think she had any right to it. Any right to anything but a long prison sentence along with her real boss: Luther Mills.

"What are you accusing me of?" she asked.

"We all suspected it for a while," he said. "Nobody could be as bad a lawyer as you seemed to be."

She gasped again. "How dare you—"

"How dare you," he interrupted. "How dare you destroy that evidence and let a guilty man go free to threaten and kill innocent people."

"What are you talking about? I never destroyed any evidence."

"Then how the hell did you fail to get indictments?" he asked. "My unit worked damn hard to get Luther Mills off the streets. We built cases for you. Gave you what you needed—"

"Bullshit." She interrupted him now. "I didn't get enough for indictments because of sloppy police work. It had nothing to do with my abilities as a lawyer."

"Of course not," he said. "You would never take any responsibility for what you've done." She'd always been quick to blame the cops instead of herself.

Something like a growl emanated from her throat. "I haven't done anything but my job," she insisted.

He snorted again.

"What the hell do you think I've done?"

"I think you are the leak within the district attorney's office," he admitted. "I think you're the one working for Luther, that you've been working for him for years."

She pulled her arm back and began to swing her hand toward his face. He was ready for her—ready to catch her wrist and stop her from hitting him.

But she stopped herself. Then she stumbled back a step against her desk and began to laugh. Maybe it was a relief for her for the truth to finally come out.

Jocelyn felt tears streak from her eyes as her stomach ached from laughter. How the hell could *anyone* accuse her of working for Luther Mills?

At first she'd been insulted, so insulted that she'd been tempted to lash out. But then it had struck her how hilarious the ridiculous accusation was. So hilarious that she could barely stop laughing.

But she forced herself to draw in deep breaths and calm herself. "You're insane," she told him.

Landon arched his light brown brows. "*I'm* insane?"

His inference sobered her up, and she drew in one more deep breath before replying, "Yes, you are, if you actually believe I could be working for Luther Mills."

"I'm not the only one who thinks you are," Landon told her.

And now her stomach ached with nausea. Was it possible? Could other people believe she'd work for a killer? That she would help an animal like Luther Mills evade justice?

She shook her head. "Anyone who thinks that is insane," she said. Or complicit.

Was casting doubt on her a way to remove it from himself?

"Explain to me how you failed to get all those indictments?" he asked.

"I've told you before," she said. "Sloppy police work. I never received the evidence that the arresting officer claimed we had."

Landon narrowed his dark eyes and stared at her with suspicion. "That's a lie. You lost it."

"That's not true," she said. "I'm very careful to never lose the chain of custody with evidence. I double- and triple-check."

"So it just disappeared?"

"Or it was never collected in the first place," she said. She'd always thought that was the case, but now she was beginning to wonder...about a lot of things.

"You're blaming the police," he said. "Why the hell would we claim we had evidence that we didn't? We wanted to take Luther off the streets even more than you do."

She snorted now. "I doubt that."

"What? You have a personal beef with him?" he asked. But again he sounded doubtful, like he thought her path would have only crossed with Luther because she was working for him.

"I have a personal beef with all criminals," she said. "I want to take them all off the streets."

"That's why you try to take all the cases at work?" he asked. "For justice?" He sounded skeptical again.

She nodded. "That's right."

"Not for your career?" he asked.

Mike Forbes had gotten to him. "Despite what my coworkers think, I am not after my boss's job."

"Just justice," he murmured again. Then he opened his arms, gesturing at the room. "How the hell do you afford this place?" He pointed toward the office walls. "The artwork? Your vehicle? Hell, that alarm system even."

"I didn't buy it," she admitted.

"No," he said. "Luther did."

She lifted her arm again, but before she could even begin to swing her hand at his infuriatingly handsome face, he caught her wrist and jerked her up against his body. "Let me go!" she said through gritted teeth, and she tried to pull free of his grasp.

But his arms tightened around her. "So you can hit me? Or go get your Taser?" He shook his head. "Not going to happen. I'm not letting you go until you tell me the truth."

"I'll tell you the truth," she agreed. She would tell him everything—things she hadn't talked about in years. But only on one condition. "If you tell me the truth."

He didn't release her, but he drew back slightly and stared down at her, his brow furrowed. "About what?"

"About who within the vice unit was working with Luther," she replied.

He laughed now—not uproariously like she had, just a gruff chuckle. "You really are insane."

"Think about it," she urged him. "That evidence you and your coworkers supposedly collected never made it to the DA's office. It was gone before it got to us. Where did it go?"

He tensed now, and his brow furrowed. Then he shook his head. "No...no way in hell was anyone I worked with working with Luther. We all wanted to nail him. We all still want to nail him."

Even Parker. That was why he'd accepted the assignment from his stepfather, the chief. He wanted to make sure Luther was finally brought to justice.

She arched a brow now with skepticism. "Really?"

"Of course."

"Then why did you quit?" she asked. "Why did you give up?"

He flinched as if she had struck him. "I tried," he said. "For years...but with no results, with no accountability for what he'd done. He kept getting away with it—no matter what evidence we found against him."

She pursed her lips now. "Evidence you claim you found."

"We did," he said. "I had it. A gun. A recording..." He shuddered as if abhorred by whatever had been on that tape. "But they disappeared."

She felt a twinge now. So they had been working toward the same goal all those years. And someone else had been undermining them.

"You know I'm not the one who told Luther about the safe house," she said.

"I do?"

"You were with me all day," she said. "How would I have talked to anyone without you knowing about it?"

He stared down at her, but he didn't look quite as suspicious anymore.

"You can check my phone," she told him. "You can see every contact I've had. None were with Luther or any of his crew."

He released a shaky sigh. "So Luther just knew, the way he knows stuff…"

"Through his sources," she said.

"Within the police department and your office," he said.

She snorted. "I still don't believe anyone within my department would work with him."

"You have a lot higher of an opinion of your coworkers than they seem to have of you," he said.

She flinched now. She told herself repeatedly that it didn't matter. She wasn't looking to make friends at work; she was looking for justice. And to ensure that justice was served, she sometimes had to step on some toes.

"You think highly of the people you work with," she pointed out.

"I'm not claiming Luther doesn't have a leak within the police department," he said. "I fully believe that he does. In fact, it makes a lot of sense."

About how that evidence had disappeared. Anyone could have gained access to the evidence locker and destroyed it. So maybe it wasn't someone who he'd personally worked with in the vice unit. But it made more sense that it was.

"I'm talking about the people you work with now," she said, "at the Payne Protection Agency."

He tensed again. "What?"

"They all know where that safe house is," she pointed out. "One of them must have told Luther where the witness was."

He gasped—like she had. While his mouth was open, he didn't spew any denials. He didn't argue with her. He just looked, once again, like she'd slapped him. Then, finally, he shook his head again. "No."

"You'd rather believe I did it?" she asked. Maybe he thought she'd sneaked in a call while she'd used the ladies' room. It was the only time she'd been out of his sight that day.

He nodded. "Yes, I would. It makes more sense." He glanced around her office.

And her face heated with embarrassment. She'd promised him the truth. "I didn't buy this house, and neither did Luther Mills," she said before he could hurl that accusation again. "My parents bought it and the artwork and the security system. They're paranoid about my not being safe enough."

"Having seen those threats, I understand why," Landon interjected.

"They have not seen those threats," she said. She couldn't imagine how scared they'd be if they had. "They're paranoid about safety because my grandparents were murdered."

He sucked in a breath. "I'm sorry."

"It happened years ago," she told him.

"I'm still sorry," he said. "That kind of pain doesn't lessen."

"Sounds like you speak from experience," she mused.

He nodded. "My parents are gone. My grandparents, too. None of them were murdered, though. Just health issues. Cancer. Heart attacks. I must not have good genes."

He looked healthy to her. He looked strong and vital. He felt that way, too, as he continued to hold her. His hand around her wrist, his other arm around her back.

"How were your grandparents murdered?" he asked.

She closed her eyes as she remembered what she'd seen—all the blood. "They were killed during the course of a home invasion robbery. Tortured…" She shuddered, and now his arms tightened around her. He pulled her close to his chest. "The thieves must not have believed they didn't have much money or jewelry in the house. As rich as they were, they were smart, too. They kept their valuables in safety-deposit boxes in banks."

"Were you there?" he asked.

She shook her head. "No. But I found them."

"Oh, my God. How old were you?"

"Sixteen," she said. "I just got my license and drove my new car over to show them. They'd bought it for me." She shuddered again. "The door was open. I shouldn't have gone in."

Because she'd never gotten those images out of her head. He hugged her closer, and his hand stroked her hair. "I'm so sorry…"

Her breath escaped in a shaky sigh. But she pulled back. "It was a long time ago," she reminded him.

"But you don't ever forget something like that," he

said. "I still remember my first crime scene." He shuddered. "And I didn't even know the victims. I couldn't sleep until we arrested their killers. Were your grandparents' killers ever arrested?" He wasn't a cop anymore, but he still thought like one.

She nodded. "It took a few years for them to be found. And a few more years for the trial. But they were convicted and sentenced. They killed four more people before they were put away, though."

More families had been devastated like hers had been. Like Rosie Mendez was by her brother's murder.

"That's why I do what I do," she said. "I have no need for money or for a job title. My only need is for justice."

"I'm sorry," Landon said again. And she knew he wasn't offering condolences now, especially when he cupped her face in his palms and tipped it up to his. "I'm sorry," he said again, "for ever doubting you."

"I doubted you, too," she said.

His lips curved slightly into a weak grin. "You don't anymore?"

"No."

"Why not?" he asked. "I don't have a story like yours. I didn't go through the kind of tragic loss because of violence like you did."

But he'd endured loss all the same. It didn't matter how his family was gone—just that they were gone. All of them. At least she had her parents still, no matter how crazy their overprotectiveness sometimes drove her.

"Do you have any siblings?" she asked him, hating the thought of him being all alone.

He shook his head. "Nope. I'm the only child of only children."

She winced, feeling for him. "So you have no family. You're on your own now."

He chuckled. "Not at all. I have family."

She gasped as a horrible thought occurred to her. "Are you married?"

He didn't wear a wedding band, but then, plenty of married men did not, especially when one of the requirements of their job was to occasionally pose as someone else's boyfriend.

Laughter rumbled in his chest, pushing it against her breasts. "Hell, no!"

Maybe he shared her views on marriage, as an unnecessary distraction.

"My family is my coworkers," he said. "They're my friends."

She felt a pang now. She had family—her parents, who loved her so much. But she had no real friends. She admired and tried to emulate her boss, but Amber Talsma-Kozminski was not a friend. She wasn't like the girls who'd worried about Jocelyn after her grandparents had been murdered. They'd been concerned about how much she'd changed. Then they'd begun to complain about how she wasn't fun anymore and eventually they'd stopped trying to talk to her.

When she'd lost her grandparents, she'd lost her innocence—that part of herself that had believed that all people were inherently good. She knew better now.

She knew there were monsters like Luther Mills in the world who had no conscience, who felt no empathy when they took the lives of others. And sometimes those monsters were not that easy to spot.

Like the people who'd murdered her grandparents. One of them had been a teenager who'd mowed their lawn. Her grandmother had fed him cookies, and Jocelyn had had a crush on him. But then, she'd just been a kid herself, so she couldn't feel too bad about missing his true nature. She'd learned to be more careful now about whom she trusted. Maybe that was why she had no friends and rarely dated.

"Are you sure you can trust your friends?" she asked him.

"Yes, I'm sure," he said, "with my life."

"What about the witness's life?" she asked.

"Clint would gladly give up his life for Rosie Mendez's," Landon said with pride in the man who was obviously the closest of his friends.

"What about the others?" she asked. "Would they die to protect the person they've been assigned to?"

His mouth curved into a slight grin, and he chuckled. "I'm not sure about Keeli and Detective Dubridge. She might kill him herself."

During the meeting, Jocelyn had heard how the detective had talked to her—how he'd called the petite blonde Bodyguard Barbie. She wasn't entirely sure she would blame Keeli if she did kill him. But Jocelyn needed his testimony to corroborate what Rosie had told him at the scene of her brother's murder.

"Keeli aside, everyone else feels the same way I do about our assignments. We would willingly risk our lives to protect our principal."

She tilted her head and studied his handsome face. "You would?"

He nodded. Then his gaze slipped down to her

mouth and he murmured, "I hope that's all I give up for you, though."

"What else is there?" she asked.

But she knew. His heart. She felt a twinge in hers now, too. That had to be fear, though—just fear. Then her heart began to pound—fast and furiously—as he lowered his head to hers.

His mouth had just brushed across hers once when gunfire rang out, so loud that the windows rattled. Then the glass shattered as bullets broke through the windows.

Landon pushed her to the office floor and covered her body with his. And she had her answer. Yes, he would give up his life for hers.

As the gunfire continued to ring out, she only hoped that he wasn't about to die now. But with so many bullets striking the house, sending shards of glass raining onto them and the floor, she doubted he could avoid getting hit.

Chief Woodrow Lynch was not happy. He had still not found the leak within his department or within the district attorney's office. Hell, he couldn't even get a handle on the guards at the jail. Some of them had to be helping Luther. The drug lord had to be communicating with his crew somehow because they kept coming after the people associated with the trial.

The witness had barely survived all the attempts on her life. There'd been some issues with the evidence technician, as well. More threatening photos sent to the judge and even a break-in at his daughter's apartment.

And now the prosecutor.

But Woodrow wanted to keep that quiet. He hadn't

even told his wife. Yet. Of course, he hadn't seen her yet. The minute he got out of his vehicle and stepped into the house, she would know that something else had happened.

Hell, she probably already knew. Penny Payne-Lynch had an eerie sixth sense in which she just knew things were going to happen before they actually did. Well, she knew when bad things were going to happen.

So she probably knew.

He drew in a deep breath, bracing himself to push open the door and step onto the driveway. But his cell vibrated before he could reach for the door handle. "Chief Lynch," he said as he accepted the call.

It could have been his wife calling him from inside the house, wondering what was taking him so long to get inside, but it wasn't her number on his screen. He knew he'd seen it before, but he hadn't added a contact in his phone for the person. "Hello?"

"Chief," a female voice said. "This is Amber Kozminski." She sounded breathless. Maybe she'd gone into labor. Even though she was the district attorney, she wasn't trying Luther's case because she'd been ordered to bed rest weeks ago.

"Is everything all right?" he anxiously asked her.

"You tell me," she implored him.

"About…?" he asked. His wife had warned him not to upset the heavily pregnant woman. Penny had emotionally adopted the woman's husband and brother and sister-in-law even though their father had been accused of killing her first husband years ago. She pretty much adopted everybody she met but was especially protective of the Kozminskis. Amber wasn't supposed to know about the threats to everyone involved with the trial. She wasn't supposed to worry at all.

But she sounded very worried. "Chief! I need to know if Jocelyn is all right."

So she had heard. How?

He'd been trying to keep it so quiet. And even if Penny had, with her uncanny ability, figured it out, she wouldn't have told Amber.

"How did you hear about what happened?" he asked, because it was clear that she'd heard.

"What does that matter?" she asked.

"It matters," he insisted. "A lot…"

Because he was trying to contain that damn leak. The dispatcher had passed the report of shots fired at the ADA's home on to him directly—because he'd had Jocelyn Gerber's address flagged. And he'd sent out his most trusted detective to investigate those claims.

So who had called Amber? Which one of them?

"Somebody in my office called me," she said. "They told me there was a shooting at Jocelyn's house. I need to know if she's okay."

She wasn't the only one who needed to know that. He hadn't heard back from his detective yet. Or from Landon Myers…

Had he and the assistant district attorney survived that shooting?

Chapter 7

What the hell had happened? Landon still didn't know. One minute he'd been kissing Jocelyn and the next...

That had been his first mistake. Kissing her. That wasn't part of his assignment—at least, not when there was no one to witness his acting like her boyfriend. The only person he'd been fooling with that kiss was himself.

He was her bodyguard—nothing else. And he wasn't doing a very damn good job. Sure, he'd knocked her to the floor. But he should have noticed the person outside before they had even started shooting. Hell, he should have heard the vehicle drive up.

But he'd only heard it drive off, and after that he'd helped her up from the floor, anxiously asking, *Are you all right?*

She'd silently nodded at him, her blue eyes wide and bright with fear. *Are you?* she'd asked.

He'd nodded back at her. *But we need to get out of here.*

I—I have to find Lady, she'd said as she looked around her home office, her eyes wide with terror.

She's not in here. She didn't get hit, he'd assured her. *She's hiding. And we don't have time to look for her. We need to leave. Now.*

No. We have to stay for the police.

The sirens had already wailed in the distance. *That's why we have to leave,* he'd pointed out. *We don't know who—if anyone—we can trust in the police department.*

She'd gasped. But she'd stopping arguing with him. She'd just shoved some things in her briefcase and closed the office door before hurrying out with him.

"Where are we?" she asked as she looked around the house he'd brought her to, which was nothing like hers. The entire place could probably fit inside her living room. It was just two bedrooms, one off the living room and one off the kitchen, with a bathroom in between them.

"This is where I live," he said.

She pointed toward the gun in his hand. "Then why do you need that?"

"Because other people might know that I live here," he said.

"Nobody's trying to kill you," she said.

It hadn't felt like that earlier when all those bullets had been flying into her house. It had probably just been one clip, though—from one gun—not like the onslaught Clint and Rosie had faced down at the safe house.

"I'm not the only one who lives here," Landon said.

She glanced around again. "I thought when you laughed at the thought of being married…"

"That I didn't have a serious relationship?" he asked. "My roommate is Clint. He's probably the most serious relationship I've had—friendship."

The women he'd dated hadn't understood the long hours of being a vice cop. They hadn't appreciated his being late or missing dates altogether, so those relationships had never gone beyond dating. Not much had changed since he'd become a bodyguard, though. Protecting someone around the clock left even less time for dating.

Maybe that was why he'd kissed Jocelyn.

No. He'd kissed Jocelyn because he'd wondered for years what it would be like. If his lips would stick to hers like the kid's tongue did to the flagpole in that Christmas movie he and Clint watched every year.

"Clint!" he called out as he moved through the few rooms, checking to see if his friend had come home.

"You thought he might have brought Rosie here?" she asked, and she peered around now, too—looking inside the bedrooms and bathroom.

"He's too smart to have done that," Landon said. Smarter than he was. He should not have brought Jocelyn here. He needed to get her somewhere safe. But what she'd said…about the people who knew about the safe house…

No. She had to be wrong. Nobody he'd worked with could be colluding with Luther. They'd all wanted to bring him down just as much or even more than he had. Landon pushed a slightly shaking hand through his hair. A shard of glass nicked his skin before falling onto the floor with a few other pieces.

"You're bleeding," Jocelyn said, and she grabbed his hand to inspect the wound.

Her skin was so silky. And as he knew, she wasn't at all as cold as he'd thought she was. She was warm. Hell, she was hot. So damn hot...

He wanted to kiss her again. Last time he'd done that, though, they could have been killed. The shots fired into the house had gone wild, hitting everything in her office but them. He couldn't believe the shooter had been one of Luther's crew. Even the young ones were more familiar with firearms than their shooter had seemed to be.

So it could have been someone else—someone who'd sent one of those other threats she'd received.

"I need to call Parker and the chief," Landon remarked.

"You need to get a bandage on this," she said as she continued to hold his hand. "It won't stop bleeding."

The blood was just oozing, though—not flowing. "It's nothing."

His friend was out there somewhere, according to Parker, bleeding, as well. Landon should have immediately gone out to look for him. But then Jocelyn would have been alone and unprotected in her home when the shooting happened...in her office with all the windows.

He'd thought her house was safe with its high-tech security system. But now he wondered if anyplace was safe. "We need to get out of here," he said.

But he wasn't sure where they should go. Dare he trust the others? He knew for certain it hadn't been any of them outside her place shooting at them. Any one of them would have hit them. They were that good of shots.

And even better people.

No way. He wasn't going to let her distrust of his team affect him. They were his family. The only family he had.

"I need to call Parker," he said, "and find out where I should bring you."

"Home," she said. Then she glanced around. "My home."

"This place not nice enough for you?" he teased. He knew it wasn't much. But he and Clint worked so much that they didn't need much.

She tensed again, as if she thought he was insulting her. "I wouldn't have the house I do if my parents hadn't bought it for me," she said. "I was happier in my apartment downtown, and that was much smaller than this."

He believed her. She would have gone for the convenience of having a place close to work over the grandness of her big house. But she'd moved to make her parents happy.

He had seriously misjudged her. And he felt so bad about it that he couldn't argue with her. But he wasn't going to bring her back to her house either. "Your place isn't as safe as your parents thought it would be," he pointed out. "We need to put you in a safe house."

"Because that worked out so well for Rosie Mendez?"

He flinched.

"C'mon," she said, and she tugged him—not toward the outside door, though, but toward the bathroom. "We'll put a Band-Aid on this and then you can call Parker."

And he remembered why her coworkers found her threatening and annoying. She was bossy and controlling. Now he knew the reason why she was...because of how she'd lost her beloved grandparents.

So he let her tug him along with her, and something tugged at his heart, making it ache in his chest. It had to just be sympathy.

Nothing else.

He would never fall for anyone like her—whatever her reasons for being bossy and controlling.

Jocelyn stared down at her hand, which was smeared red with his blood. An image flashed through her mind of the last time she'd had blood on her hands. And her knees weakened and wobbled. She swayed slightly and might have fallen into the sink if strong hands hadn't closed over her shoulders and steadied her.

"Are you okay?" Landon asked.

She looked up at him. He was so big. So strong...

So heavy. She could remember the weight of his body lying atop hers, pressing her down to the floor, protecting her. He could have been killed.

His blood was on her hands because it was her fault he'd been hurt. "Thank you," she murmured.

She couldn't remember if she'd done that yet.

His brow furrowed. "For what?"

"For saving me," she said. "You reacted so quickly."

He grimaced. "I shouldn't have had to react," he admonished himself. "I should have noticed him getting close to the house before the shooting ever started."

But he'd been kissing her.

And she hadn't wanted him to stop—even when the shooting started. She was losing her mind. Maybe she had been working too hard—like everyone always told her she was.

But with so many criminals on the streets, she felt as if she still wasn't working hard enough. That she wasn't doing enough. That wobbly feeling in her knees began to spread, making her tremble. Landon's arms wound around her, pulling her against his chest.

"You're not okay," he said.

She couldn't stop shaking. "I don't know what's wrong," she murmured. She hated this weak and helpless feeling.

"You're in shock," he said. "I should take you to the hospital."

"I'm fine," she insisted, even though she didn't feel that way. She felt so strange—so unlike herself. So out of control...

"You're not fine," he said. He drew back and stared down at her, into her eyes.

And she shivered at the intensity of his stare. It was as if he was peering right inside her, as if he could see something no one else could.

"You're scared," he said.

She tensed as she realized that she was.

"That's good," he said. "You should be. You should have been after receiving those threats. And knowing that Luther's determined to take out everyone involved in his trial, you should be very afraid. I was worried when you weren't."

"Is that why you thought I was working for him?" she asked. "Because I didn't seem scared?"

"That and all those times you failed to get indictments," he said.

Frustration gripped her. But she wouldn't defend herself again. That only made him think she was unwilling to accept the responsibility for her losses. She shrugged it off. "I don't know... Maybe I could have done more."

"Not without the evidence," he said.

"We need to look into that," she said. "Find out where it went. But first we need to find Rosie." She could not lose her eyewitness to the murder Luther had committed. He often didn't carry out his dirty work himself.

Even when he wasn't in jail, he usually sent out his crew instead...as if he didn't want any blood on his hands. But it was still there, no matter what he did.

Landon released her. But the bathroom was so small that his body still touched hers as he reached around her and turned on the water in the sink. First he put his hand, that was still bleeding, under the faucet, and then he put hers under it, washing away his blood.

A little sigh of relief slipped through her lips. That was always the hardest for her—to see the blood in the crime-scene photos.

Landon looked at her again, like he was looking through her. "It's good to be scared," he told her.

She snorted. "Yeah, right..."

"I was worried when you weren't because it's hard to protect someone who doesn't realize they're in danger," he said. "Or they know, and they don't care."

She flinched. She'd fallen into that second category. "It doesn't make sense," she said.

"That Luther would try to kill you? I know it's difficult for you to accept, but someone in your office is working for him," he said.

She released a ragged sigh. She couldn't deny that it might be true. With Luther, really anything was possible. "But why try for me now?" she asked. "Why not wait until closer to the start of the trial?"

He shrugged. "I don't know. Maybe he doesn't want to risk a postponement that would leave him in jail longer."

That was true. If she was killed now, there was time for another assistant DA to get up to speed on their case.

"I don't know…"

"I don't know if it was Luther behind the shooting either," Landon admitted.

And she was relieved that he shared her doubts.

"You have all those other threats," he said. "It could have been any of them."

She'd thought those threats were empty. That was why she hadn't reported them to the chief. But now she realized that had been stupid. She'd been stupid. Like Landon had pointed out, it was smarter to be afraid. Then she would be careful.

She wasn't just afraid for her life anymore, though. She was afraid for her heart, too.

That was fear Landon must have seen when he'd looked so deeply into her eyes. She was afraid she was starting to fall for him.

But then he tensed and drew out his weapon. "Shhh…" he said, even though she hadn't been about to say a word.

She listened, though, to the sound of their breathing and the creak of a door opening. Someone was here.

She doubted it was Clint Quarters. He wouldn't have risked bringing Rosie here, where other people would know to look for them. No. This was someone either looking for Rosie and Clint or for her and Landon, to finish what they'd started—to finish them off.

Where the hell had everyone gone?

Were Rosie and Clint dead? A dead man couldn't drive, and Luther had learned that Clint had driven away from the ambush. But that hadn't been the only ambush that evening…

Someone had shot up the assistant district attorney's house. He punched in the number for the person he figured had done that.

"Hello?" the caller greeted him curiously. He wouldn't have recognized the number. Luther kept having to change cell phones—kept having to destroy the ones that might have been traced back to him.

"What the hell did you do?" he asked.

"Do?" the person innocently asked. Too innocently.

"I heard about the ADA getting shot at," Luther told him. "I did not give the order for that."

What the hell was happening? Why was no one listening to him? At least his source at the police department was keeping him informed—had let him know about the call of shots fired at the ADA's house and about the break-in at the judge's daughter's apartment.

He just wanted eyes on Jocelyn Gerber and the judge's daughter, Bella Holmes. He didn't want either of them dead. Yet.

"I didn't—"

"Don't lie to me!" he shouted, drawing the attention of a guard passing his cell. But the guard only glanced back at him once before turning around and acting as if he hadn't seen a thing.

Nobody saw what he was doing. So how had the damn chief of police gotten wind of his plan to take out everyone associated with his trial?

"I didn't hit her," the man finished. "She and the guy she calls her boyfriend are fine."

"Boyfriend?" Luther snorted. That bitch was too uptight to have a lover.

"Big guy—light brown hair, brown eyes."

"Landon Myers." Had to be Landon.

"Yeah, I think that's his name," the guy replied.

Luther chuckled. The former vice cop could be pretty damn uptight, too. "He's her bodyguard."

"He's going to fail," the guy replied.

Luther opened his mouth to reiterate his order to keep Jocelyn alive for now. But then he thought about it.

He needed the judge's daughter alive. He couldn't use threats against her to influence the judge to rule in his favor if she was dead.

But it didn't really matter to him when Jocelyn Gerber died.

He uttered a ragged sigh. "When you get the chance, do it," he agreed.

The guy chortled. "I'll get the chance soon. Very soon."

As Luther clicked off the cell, he felt a moment's regret. Jocelyn Gerber was so gorgeous, it really was a shame that he wouldn't be able to look at her much longer.

But then he shrugged off that regret. It would be good to have at least one person dead that he wanted gone.

Chapter 8

Landon pushed Jocelyn behind him. "Get in the bathtub," he whispered. "Stay down." She would be safe in the old steel claw-foot tub if the shooting started—as long as the shooter didn't take him out. Then Jocelyn would have no protection at all.

There wasn't even a window in the bathroom through which she could escape. But she did as he'd ordered.

And again, he was glad that she was finally afraid. It would make protecting her a hell of a lot easier. As long as he wasn't outnumbered too much. How many people had come after them this time?

The door creaked as it opened all the way before softly snapping shut again. And then the floorboards creaked with the weight of the intruders. There had to be at least two, as he heard two distinctly different sounds of footsteps. He'd partially closed the bathroom door, so he could only peer out through the crack between it and the jamb. He heard the front bedroom door open. He didn't have much time. They would open this one next. So he slipped out—with his gun drawn and his finger twitching against the trigger.

"Don't shoot," a female voice yelled. And a blonde stepped between him and another man holding a gun.

"Keeli!" Landon exclaimed. He jerked his barrel up to point at the ceiling.

Spencer Dubridge did the same and expelled a shaky breath. "Stop doing that!" he growled, but the comment was directed at Keeli.

"It's my job to protect you," she reminded him as she stepped back.

"It's okay," Landon called out to Jocelyn. "It's Detective Dubridge and Keeli."

The ADA must have already discerned that because she stood in the open doorway to the bathroom. But she arched a black brow and asked, "Are you sure it's safe?" as the two continued to bicker.

He grinned. Who knew Jocelyn Gerber could be funny?

He was actually beginning to like her as well as understand her. The grin slid away from his mouth. That wasn't good, though. She was already too much of a distraction. He forced himself to turn away from her and focus again on the detective and his diminutive but fierce bodyguard.

"Clint's not here," he told them.

"I'm not looking for Quarters," Dubridge said. "I found who I'm looking for."

Landon furrowed his brow with confusion. "Me?"

"Both of you," Dubridge replied as he turned toward Jocelyn. "The chief sent me out to investigate the shooting at Ms. Gerber's house. But by the time I—"

"We," Keeli interrupted him.

Dubridge sighed. "Whatever. You guys were gone. What the hell happened?" he asked. "Who shot up the place?"

"I don't know," Landon admitted.

"You didn't see anyone?" Keeli asked the question and narrowed her eyes to study him.

Heat rushed to his face. It was as if she knew what he'd been doing—that he'd been distracted. "It all happened so quickly."

"There were no spent shells inside the house," Dubridge remarked.

"The shooter didn't get inside," Landon replied.

"Were you inside or outside?" Dubridge asked.

"Inside."

"You didn't return fire?" he asked, and now he exchanged a glance with Keeli.

Landon's face burned now with embarrassment. He knew he'd been a piss-poor bodyguard, but now they knew it, too.

"There was no time," Jocelyn said.

He was surprised she would defend him.

"He saved my life," she added.

And Keeli and Dubridge exchanged another look. They knew he could have done more, that he could have caught the person who shot at her if he'd been more alert.

Less distracted…

Or maybe that was less attracted—to the person he was supposed to be protecting.

He'd saved her life this time. But there would be

more attempts. Landon just wasn't sure who was coming after her—some of Luther's crew or one of the people who'd sent her those other threats.

Jocelyn looked around her house and shuddered. She hadn't wanted to move here. She hadn't wanted the house her parents had insisted on buying for her. But she hated seeing it as it looked now, with the windows of her home office shot out, pictures knocked to the floor and holes torn through the paneling she'd painted white.

At least Lady had finally come out of wherever she'd been hiding. She'd run right to Landon the minute they'd opened Jocelyn's front door. He'd carried her into the kitchen to feed her.

"I already called the company we recommend for crime-scene cleanup," Spencer Dubridge assured her. "They'll secure the place tonight and then can start on repairs once you or your insurance agency okay their estimate."

She nodded. She wouldn't have thought of all of that—of what her parents must have had to do to clean up and repair her grandparents' home. Of course, once those repairs had been made, they'd sold the house right afterward. Nobody had ever wanted to go back there again—least of all her.

She wasn't sure she wanted to be back here now, but Spencer had insisted. And she knew she and Landon shouldn't have left the scene until police had arrived. But he hadn't trusted the police.

Or so he'd claimed.

She studied the dark-haired detective. Should she trust Detective Dubridge? He was ambitious. But then, everyone thought she was, too, because she worked so hard. Maybe he worked hard for the same reason she did, though—to get criminals off the streets.

"What about the crime-scene lab?" she asked him. "Has anyone been here yet?" The techs usually took a long time to process a scene, but she'd caught no sight of the van. She hadn't even seen any police tape cordoning off the area.

Spencer shook his head. "No. The chief sent me out because he wants to keep this quiet. I'm supposed to be the only one to investigate." He glanced at Keeli Abbott, who moved around the home office, inspecting the damage. "I took pictures and bagged the spent shells I found on the street outside. Whoever shot at the house shot from the open window of their vehicle."

"A drive-by, then…" That should have scared her, but she actually breathed a sigh of relief. "That has to be Luther's people."

Spencer shook his head. "Luther doesn't send just one shooter to a scene. I don't think he had anything to do with this."

"Then who?" she asked.

Spencer held up a plastic evidence bag. It didn't contain the spent shells he'd picked up. It contained the letters from her desk. "Any one of these people…"

She shivered.

"Why didn't you report these?" he asked.

She shrugged. "I didn't consider them any more credible threats than when people tell me in court that they're going to get back at me." That happened so often, a perp swearing vengeance as bailiffs dragged them out of court. It was only every once in a while that she was accosted outside court; that was why she carried the Taser—to protect herself during those rare occasions.

Dubridge pointed toward the shattered front windows of the office. "Looks pretty credible to me. You should have reported the threats."

"I really didn't think I was in any danger," she said. "At least, not here. My address is not a matter of public record."

"Anyone can do a deed search," the investigative detective said.

"But my name isn't on the deed," she said. "It's in the name of my maternal grandparents' trust, with no way to trace it back to me." Her parents had wanted to be doubly careful to protect her.

"Then someone must have followed him," Dubridge murmured.

Landon had just stepped out of the kitchen, where he must have left Lady. But he was deep in conversation with Keeli on the other side of the large living room. While they both glanced over at the people they were supposed to be protecting, they did not appear to be eavesdropping on them.

Keeli wasn't just petite and protective. She was appealing. Was Landon attracted to her? Had they ever been involved? Something cold chased over Jocelyn, like she'd been doused with ice water.

"Don't you trust him?" she asked.

"Myers?" Dubridge asked, and his dark eyes widened with the question.

"All of them," she said. "The Payne Protection bodyguards who used to work vice. Do you trust them?"

He glanced over at Landon and Keeli now himself,

and his voice deep with conviction, he replied, "With my life."

"You do?"

"I used to work with all of them," he reminded her. "They're good people, hardworking, honest people. I trust them. It's our current coworkers you and I need to worry about."

She shivered again. "You believe the chief, then— that there are leaks in our departments?"

He nodded. "In fact, I would sooner believe that a coworker of yours knows where you live than that someone followed Landon Myers here. He would have noticed the tail right away."

He'd noticed the one that had followed them from the safe house after her meeting with the eyewitness. And as soon as he'd noticed him, he'd lost him.

She drew in a shaky breath, bracing herself to accept the truth. Someone she worked with might have tried to kill her. Someone she worked with was also informing for the enemy.

Dubridge, who was usually all business, slid his arm around her shoulders and squeezed her reassuringly. "We'll find out who," he promised. "We'll keep you safe."

"I'm not worried about myself," she said. At least, not just herself...

She was worried about Luther Mills getting away with not just one murder but quite a few more.

Like the witness and the evidence tech and the judge's daughter and...

Hers.

He felt like he was on the damn witness stand right now, and he didn't like it one bit. At least his boss wasn't interrogating him in person—just over the cell phone pressed to his ear.

"How did you know about the shooting at Jocelyn's house?" Amber Talsma-Kozminski asked him.

He shouldn't have called her. But he'd wanted to know himself if any of those bullets had struck Jocelyn. He'd also wanted to be the first one to talk to his boss about the shooting that would be attributed to Mills, so that he would get the case before she assigned it to anyone else.

He still couldn't believe she'd assigned it to Jocelyn. Not when he had more experience than the young female lawyer. He was the better man for the job.

He was also the better man for Amber Talsma-Kozminski's job as the district attorney. And he would have that job, too. Someday...

As long as he didn't get caught.

He figured that Kozminski wasn't just being curious about how he'd heard about the shooting. She sounded suspicious. Had someone realized that there was a leak in the district attorney's office? That he was the leak?

He had to be careful—so damn careful—right now. He couldn't claim that Jocelyn had called him; unless she was dead, she'd call him a liar. He could cast doubt on someone else in the office. He considered it, but no name but Jocelyn's came to his mind at the moment.

"Are you there?" Amber prodded him, and the suspicion in her voice was even more evident, along with the impatience. "I asked you—"

"I heard about the shooting from a friend at the police department," he said.

Someone in the police department had called him—

Luther's someone in the police department. So he wasn't lying.

And because he wasn't lying, Amber must have heard the truthfulness. "I need to know who," she said.

He uttered a rueful sigh. "I'm sorry, boss. I promised this person I wouldn't say anything. They know the chief was trying to keep the shooting quiet, and they're worried they'll get in trouble."

That was all true, as well.

"This is important," Amber persisted. "Jocelyn could have been killed."

Could have been.

So she hadn't been.

That damn bitch had survived despite his emptying his entire clip of bullets into that house. How the hell had she done that?

Then he remembered the size of the guy who'd been hanging around her. Like Luther had said, he had to be a bodyguard. And he'd guarded her successfully.

This time.

Next time he would make certain that he took them both out. And he needed to do it soon—before anyone discovered that he was Luther's leak.

Chapter 9

Where the hell had they gone? Nobody had heard from Clint and Rosie since the shooting. Parker had gathered several people in the conference room because he wasn't the only one worried about what had happened to the missing eyewitness and her bodyguard. At least he knew where Jocelyn and Landon were now, and that they were okay since they sat around that table, too.

"You're sure he was hurt?" Parker asked his sister Nikki about Clint.

"There was blood on the sidewalk where he'd pulled the SUV," Nikki said. "And I swear I saw him get hit at least once."

A twinge of pain struck Parker's heart. But he wasn't the only one bothered by the news. Landon Myers looked sick. He and Clint were close—so close that they shared a house in the city.

Clint hadn't gone there. Landon had already checked. Jocelyn Gerber sat next to Landon. She looked sick, too.

But she wasn't worried about Clint. She was worried about the witness. "What about Ms. Mendez?" she asked Nikki. "Had she been injured?"

Nikki shrugged. "Like I just told my brother, the SUV came under heavy fire. She could have been."

Jocelyn gasped. "That is unacceptable. The Payne Protection Agency's main responsibility was to make sure that nothing happened to the witness—"

Usually Landon was pretty patient, but now he lost his temper. "Do your damn job," he told Jocelyn, "and you won't need Rosie's testimony."

"What do you mean?" she asked, and her blue eyes looked bright, almost as if she was about to cry. Despite how tough she always acted, Landon had hurt her feelings. "Of course I've done my job."

"Offer those shooters a plea deal to turn on Luther. There are plenty of them in custody, thanks to the Payne Protection Agency," Landon said with pride. "Even you should be able to get through to one of them."

Jocelyn glared at him. "Then I need to go down to the jail," she said as she rose from her chair around the conference table. "We're obviously wasting our time here."

Landon grimaced, and Parker mouthed *I'm sorry* at him. He'd had no idea that Jocelyn Gerber would be so difficult for his friend to handle. Landon got up to follow her out, but he paused at the door and turned back. "Let me know when you find Clint."

"Do you have any ideas?" Parker asked. "He's not answering his phone."

"And I can't even pick up a signal for it," Nikki added.

Landon shook his head and turned back toward the door. But then he stopped and swiveled around. "What about his cabin? Did you check there?"

"What cabin?" Parker had never figured Clint for the outdoors type. All he ever remembered him doing was working—first as a vice cop and now as a body-guard.

"He just bought the place a little while ago," Landon said.

"He didn't mention it."

Landon grimaced again. "Yeah, he probably wouldn't have said anything about it to you…"

Parker felt a pang. And now he knew what his brother Cooper had gone through when he'd become the boss to his friends. It wasn't always as easy to maintain that friend relationship when you were suddenly the one in charge. "Why not to me?"

"It's the cabin Cooper owned."

"My brother?" As far as Parker knew, Cooper had never owned a cabin, unless he'd been keeping things from him, too.

"Officer Cooper," Landon said.

The man who'd killed Parker's father. He shuddered. He'd never intended to go back there. Ever.

"He bought it really cheap from the guy's estate, which just recently got settled," Landon said. "It had been in probate for years…"

"Does anyone else know about it?" Parker asked.

Landon shrugged. "I think everybody in vice knew he'd bought it. He'd been trying to buy it off the estate before it even got settled."

So everybody but Parker knew about it. Of course, Parker had left vice long before these guys had.

"Do you remember where it is?" Landon asked.

Parker nodded. He would never forget. Now he had to go back. He only hoped that when he did, it wouldn't end as it had the last time—in another death.

Since the shooting at Jocelyn's house, a heavy pressure had settled on Landon's chest. It was a mixture of guilt and anxiety—over her shooting and over the shooting at the safe house. That guilt and anxiety had caused him to lash out at her during the meeting moments ago.

And that had only intensified his guilt. He shouldn't have snapped at her to do her job, but her concern seemed to be just for her case and not for the people who could be out there—hurt, dying even. Then she'd disparaged the Payne Protection Agency's ability to keep the witness and everyone else safe, infuriating him even more.

She seemed furious, as well, bristling with anger. "Let's get to the jail, then," she said as she stomped on her stiletto heels down the hall ahead of him.

He groaned and uttered an apology. "I'm sorry."

And she whirled around on the tip of one heel to face him. A black brow arched over one of her bright blue eyes. "What?"

"I'm sorry," he repeated.

"For what?" she asked.

"For making that crack about you not doing your job," he clarified. "I know that you work your ass off." Actually, her ass was perfect and perfectly displayed in all those tight little pencil skirts she wore with her suits.

She definitely needed to change before they headed over to the jail, or she might cause a riot.

Hell, she was causing a riot in his chest right now, as his heart began to pound even harder than it had been since the shooting hours ago.

She sighed. "I'm sorry, too," she said. "I know you're worried about your friend."

Tension gripped him, tightening his jaw as he gritted his teeth. He could only nod.

"If you want to go look for him while I go to the jail…"

He shook his head now. "You're sure as hell not going to the jail without protection."

She snorted. "Like what could happen at jail? There are guards."

"Guards who must be smuggling phones in to Luther," Landon reminded her. "Or helping him get messages to his crew other ways. You can't trust them."

She tilted her head and narrowed her eyes, as if wondering if she could trust him. Hadn't he proved himself yet? Hadn't he shown her that he wasn't working for Luther any more than she was?

"I know you would rather be going with Parker to that cabin to look for Clint," she said, "than going to the jail with me."

He couldn't deny that he was worried about his friend. But Clint wasn't the only one he was concerned about. After the shooting at her house, he was stressed about her, too, and worried about how he had nearly failed to protect her.

That weight on his chest pressed down even more, stealing away his breath. And he shook his head. "My job is to protect you."

But she was more than just an assignment to him. He wanted to keep her safe because he was beginning to care about her.

Before, he'd thought they'd had nothing in common—because he'd suspected she worked for Luther—but now he realized they had too much in common. All either of them cared about was work, protecting people from criminals. Since he hadn't been nearly as effective as he'd wanted as a vice cop, he'd switched to being a bodyguard. But he was worried that he might not be any more effective as a bodyguard—if he let her distract him again.

It was better that they keep infuriating each other than caring about each other.

Sympathy tugged at Jocelyn's heart. She knew how it felt to lose someone you loved, and Landon clearly loved his roommate. They were more than just coworkers; they were obviously very good friends.

She was already anxious for Parker to find Clint and Rosie alive and well. But now she didn't just worry about that because of the case. She worried about him because of Landon, because she didn't want him to lose someone else he loved.

He'd already suffered enough loss and no longer had any family left in his life. Still standing in the corridor outside the conference room, they had to step aside as the others walked past them.

"I'll find them," Parker told Landon. "I'm also bringing in Logan's team to help with backup, so everybody will have extra protection."

"We're fine," Landon said. "Even Dubridge didn't

think the shooting at her house had anything to do with Luther or his crew."

Parker narrowed his eyes as he looked speculatively at Jocelyn. "You have someone else after you?"

"Yes," she replied, and she felt her defenses rising again. They really thought so little of her. "Despite what Landon thinks, I win more than I lose, so I've sent a lot of people to prison. They're usually not very happy about that."

But she knew none of those people would have been able to find her very easily or at all since she and her parents had been so careful to hide her home address. No. It probably had been someone from her office— the real someone who was working for Luther Mills. But her pride was already stinging too much for her to admit that they were all probably right about there being a leak in her office.

Parker nodded. "Doesn't matter who's after you. You need extra protection."

Landon sighed. "You're right."

"I thought you'd already left for the jail," Parker said. "So Logan's guards were going to catch up with you on the way there."

"We're heading there now," Jocelyn assured him as she walked with him down the hall. "I will talk to those shooters and get one of them to turn on Luther."

Following behind them, Landon snorted. And her sympathy for him ebbed.

"You really don't think that I can do my job," she murmured as she stopped at the outside door and turned back toward him.

"I think it's going to be hard to turn anyone against

Luther," he said. "Especially after he killed Javier Mendez for becoming an informant."

"It was your idea for us to go there," she reminded him.

Parker uttered a ragged sigh and shook his head. "Why the hell can't any of you get along?" he wondered aloud.

They could. It was just safer—for both of them— if they didn't. But she doubted Landon was about to admit that any more readily than she was.

"I can't stay to mediate this squabble," he said. "You two are going to need to work this out on your own."

"Go," Landon urged him. "Find Clint and Rosie."

Parker nodded and headed out the back door to the parking lot. Landon caught the door and looked around outside before letting her exit with him. All of the black Payne Protection Agency SUVs looked alike, and there were several of them since some of the other bodyguards had stayed behind in the conference room.

Landon must have noticed it, too, because he murmured, "Parker shouldn't be heading there alone," as one of those black SUVs drove out of the parking lot.

"Maybe some of his brother Logan's team is meeting him at the cabin," she suggested. Since Parker seemed adamant about everyone else having backup, she doubted he would go anywhere without some of his own.

Landon released a shaky breath and nodded. "You're right. I'm sure they are."

"And I'm sure Clint is okay," Jocelyn said. "He probably just doesn't know who to trust."

She knew the feeling. Could someone in her office

really have fired those shots into her house? Have tried to kill her?

She shivered, and not just because of the cool night air blowing around them, tangling her hair across her face.

"He knows he can trust me," Landon said. Then he reached up and pushed her hair back from her face. "And you can trust me, too."

She drew in a shaky breath. She wanted to be able to trust him—to believe, like Detective Dubridge did, that no one working at the Payne Protection Agency was also working for Luther. But she was scared to trust the wrong person.

Maybe it was safer just to trust no one at all. That was probably what Clint Quarters had decided, why no one had heard from him. Or the alternative was that he was dead—and Rosie didn't dare to trust anyone.

Jocelyn could understand that, but she didn't want Landon to have lost his friend. Even though she struggled to bring herself to trust him completely, she did care about him. Maybe too much…

He must have cared, too, because he began to lower his head to hers. But he was moving too slowly, so she rose up on tiptoe and pressed her mouth to his. Then she moved her fingers to his nape to hold his head down to hers as she kissed him deeply.

He groaned, and his hands moved to her back, clutching her close—but then within seconds, he was pushing her away and shoving her down. And just as her body hit the asphalt, she heard the shots ringing out.

Someone was shooting at them. But Landon hadn't hit the asphalt with her. Instead, he'd drawn his weapon and was returning fire.

"Get down!" she screamed at him, afraid that he would be hit. She had just uttered the words when he dropped to the ground. And she knew that she'd probably warned him too late.

He must have already been hit.

Chapter 10

Landon grimaced at the sight of the jail. "We should be going to the hospital," he said. "Not here."

"You said you weren't hurt!" she exclaimed as she turned in the passenger's seat of the SUV and studied him over the console.

"I'm not," he said. "But you are." He stared at the torn sleeve of her suit jacket. The skin visible through the tear was scratched and swollen and oozing blood. "You're bleeding," he said. "You might need stitches."

She shook her head. "I'm fine. Thanks to you."

He was the one who'd hurt her. The shots had missed them both wildly. The vehicle from which they'd been fired had moved fast—too fast for the driver to take any real aim at them. That was why Landon hadn't been hit.

She probably would have been less injured had he not pushed her down. But when he'd heard the vehicle pulling into the lot Parker had left, he'd instinctively known there was going to be trouble. Fortunately, he'd heard the motor and opened his eyes.

Or he might have just gone on kissing her...until they were both dead. Because if he hadn't reacted, the shooter might have just stopped the car and shot at them. Then he wouldn't have missed. But he'd been driving fast, so fast that Landon hadn't gotten a good look at the driver or the vehicle.

He shook his head. "You could have been killed."

"We don't know that he was shooting at us," she said. "He could have been expecting someone else to be coming out of the Payne Protection Agency."

"He could have been." But Landon suspected he had been shooting at them. At her.

So had the other bodyguards when they'd rushed out to the lot at the first sound of gunfire. Nikki Payne-Ecklund hadn't wanted them to leave the agency, but Jocelyn had insisted on being brought here, to the jail.

She really thought she might turn some of Luther's crew against him. She'd never been successful at that before Luther had murdered Javier Mendez. He doubted she would succeed now. But because he had suggested it during the meeting, he had to support her.

So he'd driven her here. He hated the thought of her being inside the jail, though. And he hated it even more when he wasn't allowed into the small visiting room reserved for meetings with lawyers.

"We're right here," one of the guards said.

That was the problem. The guard was probably working for Luther just like his young crew member had been when he'd ambushed Clint and Rosie at the safe house.

"Nothing will happen to her," the older man assured Landon.

He was not reassured.

"What the hell's going on here?" he asked.

The guard shrugged. "I don't know what you're talking about."

"You don't think the chief of police and the district attorney's office have figured out that someone on the inside is helping Luther?"

"On the inside?" the guard asked, as if he didn't understand.

Landon figured he didn't just understand but that he probably knew exactly who was helping Luther Mills. Like probably himself.

Landon was not going to budge from outside the door. But that door was steel and the walls solid concrete. If Jocelyn was screaming inside the room, he wouldn't be able to hear her. He would never know—until it was too late—that she had needed his help.

Jocelyn glanced around the hotel suite where Landon had brought her after the jail. She'd wanted to go home, to her own house, to her cat.

He'd assured her that he'd shut the feline into the laundry room, where her litter box was, and that he'd given her plenty of food and water.

Besides her cat, what Jocelyn wanted most was her bathroom. She needed a shower, and not just because Landon had knocked her down in the parking lot. She needed a shower to wash away all the comments the perps had made when she'd tried to talk to them.

The things they'd called her…

The suggestions they'd made to her.

She shuddered.

"That bad?" Landon asked.

She tensed with defensiveness. Her parents were always trying to get her to quit her job. They didn't understand that she just didn't want to be a prosecutor; she *needed* to be a prosecutor. "Don't," she said.

"Don't what?" he asked.

"Don't tell me that I shouldn't be doing this job," she said. "That I'm not equipped for it."

He stared down at her, his brow furrowed with confusion. "Why the hell would I say that?"

"My parents do all the time," she said.

"Then I guess they don't know you very well," he replied.

A tightness she hadn't even realized she had in her chest eased now.

"You're tough," he said. "You can handle anything."

That tightness turned to a warmth that spread throughout her chest. "I'm glad you realize that."

"You're tough," he said. "But you're not invincible. That's why we came here instead of back to your house."

He'd rented a hotel suite, not just a room. So there were two bedrooms—with two separate beds—and a big bathroom between them. She wondered if he could afford it, or if the Payne Protection Agency had picked up the tab. Ultimately the police department would—since the chief had hired them because he didn't trust his own officers to protect those associated with the case.

The sky was already getting lighter outside, dawn making the blinds glow at the windows. She glanced at the window and shivered.

"We're safe here," Landon said. "The backup Parker promised is outside, guarding the perimeter."

And he was inside with her.

"I wish I'd been allowed in that room at the jail," he said. "I hated thinking of you alone in there through all those hours of interviews."

"Unfortunately, I wasn't alone," she remarked.

"Do you think you got through to any of them?"

She shrugged and flinched as the torn jacket rubbed against her scraped shoulder. "I think you were right. That they're all too afraid of Luther to risk testifying against them."

After the attempts on her life, was Rosie too afraid now? Jocelyn wouldn't blame her if she was. She had not enjoyed getting shot at either.

"I don't know," Landon said as he continued to stare down at her. "You're pretty damn scary yourself. I'm sure you threatened the hell out of them and got them thinking."

People commented on her appearance all the time, but those compliments never affected her. His comment— about her being scary—might not have even been a compliment, but given her profession, she took it as such and smiled.

He chuckled. "You're happy about being scary."

She nodded. "Yes." But then she looked up at his handsome face grinning down at her, and she was the one afraid—very afraid—of how he made her feel.

Of how much she wanted him.

His mouth curved down as the grin slid away, and his brown eyes darkened. "You are so damn scary," he murmured with a shaky breath.

"You're afraid of me?" she asked. If he would have

admitted that earlier, she might have thought he had something to hide—like his association with Luther Mills. But she didn't believe that anymore.

If he was working for Luther, he wouldn't have risked his life for hers. He would have just let her get shot, killed. But instead, he'd saved her life.

"I'm terrified," he said.

The thought that he could be afraid of her had a laugh bubbling up from her throat. "Yeah, right."

He touched her with just his fingertips sliding along her jaw. "You do," he insisted. "You scare me because of how damn much I want you."

Then his mouth lowered to hers, covering it, as he kissed her. There was such heat, such passion, in the kiss.

Her heart pounded, her skin heated…and that fear she'd felt intensified. But now she was afraid that he would stop, that something would make him stop like it had the other times he'd kissed her.

He was tense, too, as if he was braced for the same thing. But no gunfire rang out. There was no sound but their pants for breath as the kiss went on and on.

Not wanting him to pull away, she slid her hands around his nape, holding his head down to hers. His thick hair was soft against her skin. She wanted to feel it against more than her fingers.

But he pulled back and broke the kiss. Maybe he just needed air because he panted for breath—like she did.

She wanted him. So she reached for him again, tugged at his shirt. She dragged it from his jeans and over his abdomen. His stomach rippled with sculpted muscles. The man was so damn perfect.

But the shirt caught on his holster and went no farther up. A protest slipped through her lips.

And he grinned. But he didn't pull off his holster. Instead, he undid the buttons on her suit jacket. He was careful of the scrape on her shoulder when he eased it down her arms. It dropped to the floor. Then he lowered his lips to her shoulder and gently kissed the wound. "I'm sorry," he said.

"You saved me," she said as she reached for the button of his jeans.

"Is that what this is about?" he asked. "Gratitude?"

She snorted. "This is about greed. I want to feel something besides fear and frustration. I want to feel passion." And with him, she felt that more intensely than she ever had before.

He grinned again. "What about pleasure?"

"Can you give me that?" she asked, knowing she'd issued a challenge.

One he obviously accepted as he swung her up in his arms. He carried her into the bedroom where he'd brought her overnight bag. They weren't spending the night, though, since it was already almost morning. Light filtered through the blinds on the window.

He laid her on the bed. But before following her down, he removed his gun and holster, setting them on the table next to the bed. Then he pulled his shirt up and over his head. Next he reached for the button of his jeans. He undid it and lowered the zipper.

And Jocelyn's breath rasped out along with the sound of the zipper lowering. He was so damn sexy...

Just looking at him brought her pleasure, had heat coursing through her body. Had certain spots tingling and throbbing with desire.

He kicked off his jeans but left on his knit boxers. His erection strained against them, though, begging to be released. She reached for him, but he didn't join her on the bed. Instead, he knelt beside it, and he started undressing her now. He moved his hands down the front of the sleeveless blouse she'd worn beneath her jacket. He carefully and slowly released every button.

Why were there so many buttons?

Her breath caught each time his fingertips brushed across the skin he exposed. Her heart pounded fast and furiously. She wanted his hands on her, wanted him touching her.

A moan of frustration slipped through her lips.

And he chuckled.

Then her blouse parted. She arched up and jerked it off her shoulders, uncaring of the scrape on her skin. That pain was nothing compared to the tension winding so tightly inside her. She felt as if she might snap.

Before he could torture her any more, she unclasped her skirt and lowered the zipper. Then she wriggled out of it until she lay on the bed clad only in her blue silk underwear.

A groan emanated from him now, and it sounded as if he was being tortured. He stared down at her, his face flushed and his nostrils flaring. "You are beautiful…"

When he said it, the praise affected her because she suspected he wasn't one to throw around empty compliments. From the look on his face, he was obviously sincere.

Her skin heated even more just from his look. Then he touched…running his fingertips along her every curve, from her neck to the arch of her foot. Despite the heat, she shivered as sensations raced through her.

Then he unclasped the front closure of her bra and pushed it away from her breasts. And he touched them…cupping them in his hands as he stroked his thumbs across the peaks of them.

She arched up from the bed as that tension wound painfully tight. "Landon…"

She needed him like she couldn't remember ever needing anyone else. She needed him to ease the tension, to give her the pleasure he'd promised.

Then he moved his hands from her breasts to her waist. He pushed her panties down, his hands skimming over her ass and along her thighs as he discarded the scrap of silk. He continued to stroke her legs and hips as he leaned across her. And as his hands moved over her, his mouth closed around a nipple. He nipped lightly at it, and she cried out.

He pulled back. "Did I hurt you?"

She shook her head in denial. But she was hurting—so bad. She'd never felt as out of control, a feeling she usually hated. But for some reason with Landon it felt liberating.

She reached for him, running her hands over all his hard muscles. But he didn't let her pull him down onto the bed with her. Instead, he stayed beside it, just leaning over her body. His mouth moved from her breast, over her abdomen to her core.

She arched up again and cried out at just the heat of his breath touching her there. Then his fingers slid inside her, as his tongue flicked over her most sensitive part. And she cried out as the tension eased a little.

"Wow," he murmured. "You're responsive."

She was desperate and needy. And what he'd just

done wasn't enough. She clutched at his shoulders, trying to pull him onto the bed with her—onto her.

But he held back. She heard something tear. Then she glanced down and saw him rolling a condom on the length of his erection. He was big everywhere. So damn big...

Finally he joined her on the bed, but he held his weight off her. Lowering only his mouth to hers, he kissed her deeply—over and over again. His lips nipped at hers; his tongue teased hers.

"Landon." She murmured his name again—in an unspoken plea.

And finally he lowered his body to hers.

She lifted her legs and locked them around his waist, as he eased his erection inside her. He was so big that she had to shift and arch and move to take him deeper. And still she could not take all of him.

He moved his hips with gentle thrusts. But instead of easing the tension, he just built it more.

She was going out of her mind. She raked her nails down his back to his butt, clasping him against her. Then she nipped her teeth into his shoulder and rubbed her breasts against his chest.

He shuddered. "You're driving me crazy."

"Good!" She didn't want to be the only one slipping into madness. She arched her hips more, trying to take him deeper, trying to move him faster.

He chuckled, but the sound was gruff, like his pants for breath. His chest moved with his harsh breathing, the soft hair brushing over her nipples.

She bit her lip. And he brushed his tongue across it. Then he arched back and moved his head lower until his tongue brushed across a nipple. Pleasure moved from that point to where she throbbed in her core. She needed more, though.

And then his thumb was there, brushing over her as he slid deeper inside her. He moved her legs higher and thrust deeper yet.

And finally that tension broke as an orgasm moved through her. The intensity of it had her crying out as her body shuddered. He kept thrusting, pushing her to another one before the first had even finished.

The second was even more intense, and she shouted his name now. Then he tensed, and a low groan tore from his throat as his big body shuddered against hers for a long while.

He flopped onto his back next to her as he panted even louder for breath. "You are so damn scary, Jocelyn Gerber."

But she was the one who was scared now—to her core. She'd never experienced anything as intense or as pleasurable as what they'd just done, as what he'd just given her. She was afraid that it—and he—might begin to matter to her—too much. She'd vowed long ago to focus only on her job. She'd wanted no distractions.

But she'd never met anyone who distracted her as much as Landon Myers did. He was the far bigger threat to her than Luther Mills ever was.

Luther lay back on his uncomfortable bunk and closed his eyes. But he couldn't close his ears to all the chatter around him. He knew Jocelyn Gerber had survived another shooting attempt. He knew because she'd been in his house. The jail had become his house because of her—because she'd managed to outwit his high-priced lawyer and make sure bail had been denied him.

He owed the bitch for that. Hell, he owed her for a lot. She'd spent last night trying to turn members of his crew against him, trying to get them to finger him for giving the order to kill Rosie Mendez and Clint Quarters, and then she'd promised them lighter sentences.

He blew out a breath and even managed a chuckle. That was her problem. She couldn't entirely forgo justice. If she'd offered to drop the charges in exchange for their testimony, she might have found someone willing to talk. But his men knew that if they were in here— in his house with him—they wouldn't survive betraying him. He would kill every last one of them, just like he intended to kill every last person associated with his trial.

Maybe he'd made a mistake in starting with the witness, though. Maybe he should have started with Jocelyn Gerber.

But it didn't matter when she died. His men wouldn't talk to her. Nobody dared to turn on him—not since his killing Javier Mendez. He just had to make sure the only thing that came of his killing Javi was a lesson to everybody not to betray him. He could not get a murder conviction and life sentence out of this.

That was Jocelyn Gerber's intention—to send him to prison for the rest of his life. So, yeah, hers had to end soon before she could make good on her intention.

Chapter 11

What the hell had he done?

Landon hadn't just crossed the line with Jocelyn Gerber; he'd trampled all over it. He couldn't believe how stupid he'd been. His assignment was to protect, not to fall for her. Not that he was falling.

He had no time for love. No time for a relationship. And he couldn't afford any distractions right now, not with Luther Mills trying to get away with murder.

Landon had spent too many years trying to bring Luther to justice to help him escape it now. If something happened to Jocelyn, there was a damn good chance that Luther would not be convicted.

Like Spencer Dubridge, Landon believed the person who'd shot up her house was someone she worked with, someone who knew where she lived.

They were at her office at the district attorney's now. While she sat behind her desk, speaking on the phone,

Landon stared out the window in her door, watching people watch them. He recognized the two guys he'd met, but they weren't the only ones taking an unnatural interest in him and Jocelyn.

"I'm going to get some coffee," Landon told Jocelyn, but he said it more for those standing outside her office than for her benefit. When he jerked open the door, he startled a young man who jumped and lost a folder he was carrying.

Landon bent down to help him pick it up and noticed the guy was shaking. "I'm sorry," he told him, then narrowed his eyes and asked, "Are you okay?"

The young man nodded. "Yes. I just—I just had to bring them to Ms. Gerber. I'm a paralegal."

Landon took the folder from his hand and promised, "I'll make sure she gets it."

A sigh slipped through the young man's lips and he murmured a grateful "Thanks" before rushing away.

Just as he'd told her, Jocelyn was scary as hell. Even scarier to Landon now that he'd had sex with her. He'd never felt anything as intense as what they'd shared. Hell, he wasn't even sure what it had been, and before he'd been able to figure it out, her cell had blared out an alarm.

It must have been her wake-up call for work—since she'd scrambled to get ready to come into the office. But it had been Landon's wake-up call to remind him that keeping her safe was his job—not seducing her.

But he wasn't exactly sure who had seduced whom. She'd seemed to want him as badly as he'd wanted her. As he still wanted her...

His hand shook, and the folder nearly slipped from his grasp. He glanced down at it and noticed it was a dossier on her coworkers. Despite her arguing that nobody in her office could be Luther's mole, she must have had her doubts, or she wouldn't have asked the young paralegal to compile the information for her.

No wonder the kid had been so nervous. He hadn't wanted any of his coworkers to know that he'd helped her investigate them. He shouldn't have been the one doing it. Landon was the one who needed to help her, not just to keep her safe but because he personally wanted to deal with whoever the hell kept shooting at them.

So, after making sure his backup bodyguards were within sight of Jocelyn, Landon continued down the hall toward the employee break room. He wasn't much of a coffee drinker, but he approached the pot a few other people loitered around. Mike Forbes and Dale Grohms glanced up at him with feigned surprise. They'd been close enough to her office to overhear him telling Jocelyn where he was going.

He smiled as he reached for a cup and the pot. "Good morning, gentlemen."

"Morning?" Dale asked. "It's a little later than that now."

"That's because Jocelyn was late this morning," Mike Forbes said. "What's up with that lately? Your fault?"

Landon chuckled. "What makes you think I have anything to do with it?"

"You've become her shadow lately," Forbes said. "And I'm not buying the boyfriend act. Who are you really?"

"You don't know?" the young paralegal asked from

where he stood behind the men. "He's a bodyguard with the Payne Protection Agency."

Had Jocelyn had the kid investigate him as well as her coworkers? How did he know who Landon was? Landon studied the kid now, wondering if he'd been more nervous over running into him than he'd been over having that folder on him. Had he met the kid before, back when he'd been working vice?

Could he be one of Luther's crew or at least an indebted customer? He narrowed his eyes and studied the kid—even while he felt everyone else studying him.

"Is it true?" Grohms asked. "Are you her bodyguard?"

"I'm a bodyguard," Landon admitted. There was no point in denying what they could easily find out on their own.

"Why does Jocelyn need a bodyguard?" Dale asked.

"Didn't you hear about the shooting at her house last night?" the kid asked. And now the other men were studying him as intently as Landon was.

They were surprised that he knew, but they didn't look surprised about the shooting. They'd already known about it. How? Because one of them had been the shooter? Or was it now just common knowledge around the office?

"I don't envy you," Dale Grohms said.

Which surprised Landon because he'd thought the guy had a crush on Jocelyn. But of course, now he knew that Landon was just her bodyguard—not her boyfriend. Except after last night—or this morning, actually—Landon wasn't just her bodyguard.

He wasn't her boyfriend either. He wasn't sure what the hell he was but in trouble. Deep trouble…

"Why's that?" Landon asked.

"You have a very dangerous job," Grohms said.

"Jocelyn Gerber has a lot of enemies," Mike Forbes added.

A chill chased down Landon's back as he realized the other man spoke the truth. Jocelyn did have a lot of enemies. So keeping her safe was going to require all his concentration. He had to redraw that line and make damn sure he didn't cross it again.

Both their lives depended on him staying focused. He had to protect her. And he had to protect himself, as well.

Jocelyn stared down in confusion at the folder Landon slid onto her desk. "Where did this come from?"

He lifted his broad shoulders in a faint shrug. "Male paralegal. I didn't catch his name."

"I didn't ask him for this," Jocelyn said. She knew who her coworkers were; she didn't need a list of names with their addresses, marital statuses and criminal history. Fortunately, not many of them had a criminal history beyond some speeding tickets, and one had a driving-while-impaired charge on his record.

"You should have," Landon said. "You need to find out which of them is working for Luther."

She sighed. "I'm not sure it is one of them."

"You're not naive, Jocelyn," he said. "You know it has to be one of them. I would have noticed someone following us to your house. The shooter had to know where you live."

She shivered. "That doesn't mean they work with me. Someone in the police department could have found out."

He tensed, then begrudgingly nodded in agreement. "Maybe…"

"You said yourself it's possible that someone within the police department got rid of the evidence you and your unit brought me to bring to a grand jury," she reminded him.

"Not someone within my unit, though," he said defensively. "We were all determined to get Luther off the streets."

She hoped he was right. Or the chief had put the wrong franchise of the Payne Protection Agency in charge of protecting the people associated with Luther's trial. But another department had aroused her suspicions. Not like Landon aroused her, though.

Just looking at him chased away the chill of fear from her as passion rushed through her. He was so damn good-looking. And now she knew how magnificent his muscular body looked with no clothes.

How it felt.

How he'd made her feel.

She barely resisted the urge to wave the folder in front of her face to cool herself off. But she closed her eyes to shut out the temptation that he'd become.

"I think it could be a CSI," she admitted.

"Wendy Thompson?" he asked with a gasp.

She opened her eyes again. "Not Wendy. She didn't handle the evidence for those other cases—just this one." And that was why she'd been able to get a grand jury to indict—because the evidence hadn't mysteriously disappeared before she'd been able to present it to them.

He nodded. "That makes sense," he agreed. "But CSIs aren't the only ones with access to the evidence."

With the evidence locker in the police department, pretty much every officer had access. And when the evidence was sent to the district attorney's office…

"I know," she said. "But let's start with the CSIs. Let's talk to the chief." She could have just called Chief Lynch, but since she didn't have court today, she needed an excuse to get out of the office. The space was too small to share with Landon for too long.

His scent already filled her head. It was a combination of soap from the quick shower he'd taken mixed with male muskiness. She wanted to bury her face in his neck and breathe in it, breathe in *him*. And her body tingled with awareness and desire. She wanted him closer, wanted him touching her like she wanted to touch him.

No. They could not stay any longer in her small office. She jumped up from her desk. "Let's go."

"Don't you want to see if he's available first?" Landon asked.

She shook her head. "If he's not, we'll talk to Wendy Thompson and see if she has any suspicions. We should check on her anyway. With the witness missing, Luther will probably focus all his attention on taking out Wendy."

If anything happened to that evidence or the evidence tech, Jocelyn's case against Luther would be in serious trouble. Landon held the door for her, and when she passed him, her body reacted to his closeness—her pulse quickening, her skin tingling—and she knew she was already in serious trouble.

With him…

For years, there had been speculation that someone in the district attorney's office was working for Luther.

Some people even suspected it was Jocelyn. The real spy grinned at his reflection in the rearview mirror.

That was perfect. He would have to figure out how to frame her for it. But first he had to get rid of her—because he worried that she would figure it out first.

She was too damn smart.

And she worked too hard.

Or she had until this bodyguard had started protecting her. Of course, she'd been a little busy trying to stay alive to worry about work. That was why he couldn't stop trying to take her life—it kept her from tearing his apart.

And if she was dead, she could never discover the truth. He watched as they opened the door from the district attorney's offices and stepped into the parking garage. When he'd seen the bodyguard standing at her door, he'd figured they might be leaving, so he'd rushed to the parking garage and started the vehicle he'd rented a few days ago.

He hadn't wanted to risk anyone seeing his. He pulled his hood tighter around his face and adjusted his dark glasses. He didn't want to risk anyone seeing him either. But he had to take the risk of trying to kill her again.

The longer Jocelyn lived, the more likely she was to discover his connection to Luther Mills. He had to kill her and her bodyguard, too.

He couldn't wait until they got into the SUV. He'd tried to follow the bodyguard before, but he drove too damn fast. They would get away from him if they got into their vehicle.

Fortunately, he'd had his rental running beforehand. He'd already pulled out of his spot and gotten into position. So the minute they stepped away from the door to the building and headed across the parking area, he gunned his engine and bore down on them.

There was no way they could outrun him. No way they could escape him.

The man was definitely a bodyguard—with the quick reflexes and protective instincts. He shoved Jocelyn between two parked cars and jumped just as the rental's bumper neared him. Instead of striking the bodyguard or Jocelyn, the car struck those other cars. Metal crunched and screeched.

He pressed harder on the accelerator, cramming into that small space between those cars. Either they would crush Jocelyn and her bodyguard or his rental car would.

But the bodyguard surged up from the ground to which he'd fallen with Jocelyn. His arm was outstretched, the barrel of his gun pointed at the windshield, and he began to fire.

He ducked as the windshield shattered, but he kept his foot on the gas. He needed to take them out, needed for them to die. The shooting stopped, and he glanced up, peering through that broken windshield.

And finally his front bumper struck the concrete half wall of the parking structure. Either they were beneath his car or the ones he'd crumpled, or they'd gone over the wall.

He grinned. Either way, they were dead.

And he needed to get the hell out of there before he was caught. He shifted into Reverse and tried backing up. Those other crumpled cars caught on his, metal catching and twisting, rubber burning.

But it wasn't just the other vehicles he had to worry

about escaping. People had rushed up behind him, a security guard and a couple of burly men he'd noticed inside the building. More bodyguards?

They began to fire at his vehicle as they advanced on him. But finally his car jerked free of the wreckage. The back bumper struck one of the men, sending him flying back into another one—knocking them both to the ground.

He shifted into Drive now and accelerated, careening around corners as he headed all those stories down to the exit to the street. He sped up as he neared the garage exit and crashed through the gate at the end. It wasn't as if he could have used his parking pass. That would have been traced back to him.

He had to make sure that nothing could be traced because now he wouldn't just be facing conspiracy or aiding-and-abetting charges. He would be facing murder charges.

Jocelyn Gerber had to be dead. There was no way she or her bodyguard could have survived a fall from the fifth story of the concrete parking structure.

He waited for a flash of guilt or regret or something… but he felt nothing but triumph. Of course, if he'd had a conscience, he wouldn't have started working for Luther Mills in the first place.

Chapter 12

The parking structure had been designed in such a way that every other level had an area of uncovered parking. So when the car had kept coming at them despite Landon shooting at it, he'd had no choice. He'd grabbed Jocelyn up from the asphalt and he'd leaped over the half wall to the level below them.

It had just been a one-story jump down to the uncovered parking area. But the fall, and subsequent crash onto the roof of a vehicle, had knocked all the air from Landon's lungs. They burned as he struggled to breathe.

There was such a weight lying on them—on him. He moved his arms and reached up and found Jocelyn pressed tightly against him. He'd held her as he'd jumped, turning so that he took the brunt of the fall.

It was what Clint had done when he'd leaped out of the witness's apartment to avoid getting killed. But they'd fallen three stories into a dumpster. Landon had just struck the roof of an SUV. And Jocelyn was light. She hadn't hurt him.

But she wasn't moving.

He stroked his hand down her back and then up to her neck. He needed to check for a pulse. But before his fingers brushed her skin, she shivered and finally moved.

And he sucked in a breath as his ribs, which must have been bruised, ached in protest along with a twinge in his lower back.

"Are you okay?" she asked.

He should have been asking her that. But before he could, someone leaned over the half wall above them and called down, "Are you all right?"

He tried to reach for his holster, but it and his weapon were trapped beneath her body. He had no way to defend them—to protect her—if that person started firing.

But then he recognized the voice, and he focused on the face of the man leaning over the half wall. Unlike Cooper Payne's team, who were all former Marines who wore their hair in military brush cuts, this guy's hair was long and dark blond.

"You all right?" Garek Kozminski asked again. "An ambulance is on its way."

Maybe Jocelyn had recognized him, too, because she moved against him, struggling to sit up. Not wanting her to fall off the car, Landon caught and held her. He was finally able to draw in a deep breath again, so he sat up. Then he helped her down to the ground again.

Her legs nearly buckled beneath her. But he'd jumped

down from the car and caught her before she fell. "You're not okay," he said.

"I'm scared," she said. "But I'm not hurt. What about you?" Her gaze moved over his body, reminding him of how she'd looked at him and touched him the night before.

Heat rushed through his body. If he could feel attraction and desire, he wasn't in too much pain. He shook his head. "No. I'm fine." He glanced back up at Garek. "We don't need an ambulance."

"The security guard does," Garek replied as he glanced over his shoulder. "He got hit when the guy backed up."

"Did you get a look at him?" Landon asked.

Garek shook his head. "No. You?"

Landon cursed. "No. He had a hood drawn tight around his face and dark glasses."

"I'm surprised you saw that much with the tinted windows," Garek remarked.

Landon wouldn't have seen that much had he not broken the windshield. He must not have hit the guy, though, not if he'd been able to escape. "So he got away?" he asked for confirmation, a sick feeling roiling through his stomach.

Garek sighed and nodded. "Sorry…"

It wasn't his backup bodyguard's fault. It was Landon's. He should have made damn certain the man had not escaped. Hell, because of that disguise, he didn't even know if it had been a man trying to run them down.

He was no closer to finding out who was after Jocelyn than he'd been after the shooting. He only knew that the person was getting more and more bold, which meant he or she was getting more and more desperate.

That was not good. Desperate people were unpredictable. There was no way to know when they would try to take out Jocelyn again.

The only thing Landon knew for certain was that they would try again and would keep trying until they were either caught or succeeded in killing her.

Jocelyn could not deny that someone wanted her dead. She wanted to deny it. She wanted to go on believing all those threats she'd received were empty. But they weren't. Somebody was determined to make good on those threats.

Somebody was determined to end her life.

"Will the security guard be okay?" she asked Landon as the ambulance headed out of the parking structure with the middle-aged guard strapped to a stretcher in the back.

"Looks like it's just a broken leg," Landon said.

How did her bodyguard not have any broken bones? He'd taken the brunt of the fall when he'd propelled them off the half wall onto the level below and the roof of an SUV.

"Are *you* really okay?" she asked him.

"No," he admitted.

And she glanced at the ambulance, willing it back even as it raced out of the garage. "You should have said—"

"I'm pissed as hell," he said. "This idiot shouldn't keep escaping. We should be able to catch him. *I* should be able to catch him."

Whoever was after her wasn't one of Luther's young, careless crew members. It was somebody wiser and far more careful. Maybe it was someone within her department. She shivered as she considered it.

Some of them stood around now, watching her from the other side of the crime-scene tape Spencer Dubridge had had an officer string around the wreckage. They'd already told the detective what they knew—which had been damn little. And so much time had passed between the attempt on her and Landon's lives and the detective's arrival that their assailant could have ditched the vehicle and circled back to the garage to stand with her other curious coworkers. She knew they were just curious and not concerned about her. None of them was going to help her.

And neither she nor Landon could help the detective. They hadn't gotten a good look at the driver or at the car. They'd been too busy trying to stay alive. No. Landon had been too busy trying to keep her alive.

Once again, he'd willingly put his life at risk for hers. But he was just doing his job. She had to remember that, so she didn't get all sappy and fall for him.

Because for the first time in years, she felt sappy and overemotional. She blinked furiously against the tears stinging her eyes. And finally she dashed them away, hopefully before anyone had seen them. She didn't want to show any weaknesses to her coworkers or to the police officers present or especially to Landon.

He might suggest that she ask to be removed from the case. She probably wouldn't have to ask, though. She'd recognized the blond-haired bodyguard. At first she'd thought he was her boss's husband; then she'd realized he was her boss's brother-in-law. Either way, Amber was going to learn about this latest attempt on her life.

Detective Dubridge walked back from where he'd just peered over the half wall. Keeli Abbott stood near him, but not as close as Landon stood to her.

"Damn, Myers, I thought you and the others were taking the easy way out when you quit the vice unit to become bodyguards," he said. "Now I see how damn dangerous your job is." He glanced at Keeli now, and there was a furrow between his brows.

Landon shook his head. "It's dangerous for the same reason that vice was—Luther Mills."

"You think Luther was behind this?" Dubridge skeptically asked.

"Ultimately," Landon said.

And it was probably true—if someone from her office had tried to run them down—that person was working for Luther. That was why Jocelyn could not be taken off his case. She had to make sure that Luther was finally brought to justice.

She had to make sure that he couldn't hurt anyone else anymore.

Parker had just had a close call—too damn close. If not for Clint, he would have died. And he had too much to lose: his beautiful wife, his children…his agency. His friends.

He didn't want to lose any of them. So he'd made a call, warning them all that Luther was extra dangerous.

He might have put out a hit on all of them—not just the people associated with his trial, but on the people trying to protect them.

He might have put out a hit on the entire Payne Protection Agency. Unfortunately, few of them had seemed surprised by the news.

"What happened?" he asked Landon.

"Another attempt..."

"Are you all right?" he asked. "Is Jocelyn Gerber?"

"Yes and yes," Landon replied. But he didn't sound all right. He sounded angry as hell. But he'd survived and so had Jocelyn unharmed, so he'd done his job.

That wasn't enough for Landon, though. He was too much of a cop yet. He didn't just want to protect his principal. He wanted to catch the person after her. And he wanted to stop him permanently.

Parker had a feeling that wasn't just because of Landon's police background, though. This assignment had gotten personal for him.

Something was going on between him and Jocelyn Gerber, just like Parker suspected something was going on between Clint and Rosie Mendez.

Had he made a mistake when handing out assignments?

He'd known nobody would protect Rosie Mendez better than Clint would. Clint felt guilty over her brother's death and would do anything to make sure she was not harmed.

Nobody had felt guilty about Jocelyn Gerber. They'd all just been suspicious of her—no one more than Landon. So he'd assigned Landon to protect her because he'd known the former vice cop would find out the truth about her.

He hadn't realized that truth might have Landon falling for her. And it certainly sounded like he had—at least literally—when he'd fallen off the parking structure to save her.

Was he falling for her emotionally, as well?

"I'm sorry," Parker said. "I shouldn't have assigned you to protect her."

"What?" Landon asked, and he sounded befuddled.

Was he really okay?

"I know you didn't want this assignment," Parker reminded him. "So I'll take you off now. I'll have one of Logan's team protect her." That would be for the best—for all of them.

Parker couldn't risk losing one of his team. And he was already worried that Clint might not survive his assignment. He couldn't lose Landon, too.

Chapter 13

Landon silently cursed himself for putting Parker's call on speaker. Sitting in the passenger's seat next to him, she'd heard every word his boss had said. And she'd tensed more and more. It had been a while since he'd ended the call, but she had yet to say anything.

Making sure that the security guard was okay and giving Dubridge the report at the scene had taken so long that they'd decided to talk to the chief another day. Jocelyn had asked that he bring her home instead—to check on the cat and make sure she still had enough food and water in the laundry room.

Whoever Spencer Dubridge had recommended to repair the house must have had an opening because the windows had been replaced.

Jocelyn breathed a sigh of relief. "We can stay here now."

She obviously didn't want to go back to that hotel

with him. Did she regret what had happened between them? He wished he did, but he couldn't regret what had probably been the most powerful sexual experience of his life.

The way she'd fit him…the way she'd felt…and the pleasure she'd brought him.

He'd never known feelings like that before. But it didn't matter. He'd crossed a line with a client—a line that he never should have even gotten close to.

"Why didn't you let Parker remove you from this assignment?" she asked. "It's obviously what you want."

"It's true that I didn't want this assignment in the beginning," he said. "I wasn't a fan of yours."

"You thought I was working for Luther."

"I was wrong," he said. "About that, about you…" So very wrong. It might have been easier had he been right—then he wouldn't have succumbed to his attraction to her. He would have been able to resist her beauty, her sexiness.

But knowing her reasons for working so hard, for wanting justice so badly, had made her even more attractive to him—so attractive that she had become irresistible. He wanted her now.

He sighed. "Yeah, I should have had Parker reassign me."

"Dubridge would probably prefer you protecting him than Keeli Abbott."

"Keeli would prefer that more," he said. If anyone deserved to be reassigned, it was the blonde bodyguard. Her principal gave her nothing but disrespect and grief.

But Keeli was the strongest woman he knew; she could take it. Well, she was the strongest woman he'd known until he'd gotten to know Jocelyn Gerber. She seemed more upset about the conversation she'd overheard than having to jump off a parking structure earlier or getting shot at.

"Would she want to protect me?" Jocelyn asked. "Or, like everyone else, does she think I purposely failed to get those previous indictments against Luther?"

He flinched as he remembered previous conversations with Keeli about this particular assistant district attorney.

"So she's not a fan of mine either," Jocelyn murmured, and she hurried into the kitchen, as if trying to get away from him. But then she continued to the laundry room, opening the door to a mewling cat. Behind her, the water bowl and food dish were full. He remembered that, shortly after they'd left her house the night of the shooting, Jocelyn had called someone to check on her pet. Had it been a neighbor or that office intern?

Lady wound around her legs, purring rumbling from her furry body. Jocelyn bent over and wrapped her arms around the feline. "I'm staying here," she said. "The house is secure—especially with my alarm. And the glass I had them install is bulletproof. It's safer than the hotel."

She was right. It was.

"So you don't need to stay," she told him.

She really wanted to get rid of him. Because of what had happened between them? Or because of the conversation she'd overheard?

"I'm staying," he said. "I am your bodyguard." He crouched down, like she was, beside the cat, and he slid his fingers under Jocelyn's chin, tipping her face up so she had to meet his gaze. "And I am a fan now."

Her face flushed with color, and her eyes brightened. But then she blinked away the moisture in them. "Why?"

"Because you're tough," he said.

Her breath shuddered out. "I'm not sure about that..." she said. "Maybe I'm just hard to kill."

He hoped like hell that that was the case because he didn't want her to die.

"Or maybe you're just a really good bodyguard."

He chuckled. "I'd go with your being hard to kill." Because he hadn't been doing his job—at least, not as well as he usually did. And he was about to fail again and give in to the temptation to kiss her.

But then her phone rang, making the purse dangling over her shoulder vibrate. She pulled out the cell and accepted the call. But she didn't put it on speaker.

Landon had no idea who'd called her and why all the color suddenly drained from her face. "What's wrong?" he asked, fear gripping him because he could see fear on her face, as well. "What's happened?"

She shook her head, as if unable to speak. As if whatever she'd heard was too terrible to repeat. Finally she murmured, "The witness. It was about the witness..."

Had something happened to her? To them?

Now Landon wasn't sure he wanted to know what that call had been about—because he was worried that he might have just lost his best friend.

Even as upset as Jocelyn was, she was still aware of Landon, still attracted to him. She even felt bad that she'd worried him. But she didn't want to talk about that call she'd taken—not yet. She needed confirmation before she could believe it.

But she felt a sick churning in her stomach that it was true. So she didn't even notice the trip from River City to the Payne Protection Agency safe house near the shoreline of Lake Michigan. Landon didn't press her for information during the drive. He'd seemed more focused on the rearview mirror, and making sure they weren't followed, than on her—except for a few worried glances he'd cast across the console at her.

She'd wanted to reassure him. He was probably thinking the worst. And for him, this wasn't the worst. For her, though...

Landon made one last turn off the street, through the opening door of a garage on the main level of a townhouse condo. Once the door closed behind them, he opened his and hurried around to her side of the SUV. But she'd already opened her door before he could. She doubted she was in any danger in the garage.

No. The danger was upstairs, where Landon led her to meet with the witness. He released an audible breath, obviously relieved that his friend and Rosie Mendez appeared unharmed. But something was going on between them.

The minute Rosie saw Jocelyn, she turned toward Clint and implored him, "Please, can you give us a minute alone?"

Clint glanced over at Jocelyn, and his green eyes were narrowed with suspicion.

And that sick feeling roiled in her stomach. Apparently everybody had suspected that she worked for Luther. The thought made her physically ill.

Clint shook his head. "That's not possible."

"I'm not leaving either," Landon said.

Jocelyn grimaced. She would have preferred to speak privately with Rosie; she figured it might be her only way to get through to the frightened young woman. "Bodyguards don't understand that sometimes we need to be alone," she said with a pointed look at Landon, hoping he'd take the hint.

She probably should have told him about the call. But she'd been too focused on the argument she needed to present to Rosie to talk at all. She focused on the woman now, and Rosie shivered. She knew that Jocelyn knew. So she dropped all pretenses.

"What the hell were you thinking?" Jocelyn asked. But she directed the question at Clint Quarters. "Why would you bring her to the jail?" She didn't wait for his response, though, before she turned on Rosie. "And what the hell were you thinking? You might have jeopardized the whole case!"

"What?" Landon asked, his dark eyes wide with shock.

She should have clued him in after she'd taken the call. But she did so now. "She went to see Luther Mills." She pointed a shaking finger at Clint. "And he brought her!"

Landon turned to Clint, his brow furrowed with confusion. "What was the deal? Did you have her wear a wire?"

"Like Luther Mills would have said anything incriminating!" Jocelyn exclaimed. But then she turned back to Rosie and asked, "Did he?"

Rosie shook her head.

Jocelyn felt the case slipping away from her, felt Luther slipping away from justice once again. "His lawyer could have a field day with this—with you—when he cross-examines you on the witness stand."

"He won't," Rosie told her.

"The man is a shark," Jocelyn said. "Of course he will. He's going to tear you apart."

And Clint tensed, his hands curling into fists. Now he chose to act protectively? What the hell had he been thinking to let the witness anywhere near Luther Mills?

"No, he won't," Rosie said, "because I have no intention of testifying."

"What!" Clint beat Jocelyn to the exclamation.

And that was why Jocelyn hadn't spoken during the trip to the safe house; that was the fear she'd had. "That's why you shouldn't have brought her there. He intimidated her into changing her mind."

Landon, predictably, came to the defense of his best friend, turning on Jocelyn to ask, "You don't think all the attempts on her life were intimidation enough?"

Clint ignored his friend, though, and spoke only to Rosie, his voice soft. "I promised I would keep you safe."

"There's no need," she told him. "I'm safe now."

Jocelyn narrowed her eyes and studied the two of them, how intensely they were looking at each other. Had Rosie gone to see Luther for her sake or for Clint's?

Clint snorted. "You really believe that Luther Mills will keep his word to you? That he won't have you killed the minute you walk out of here with no protection?"

"Quarters is right," Jocelyn said. "There is no way

that Luther Mills will let you stay alive—not when you are the greatest threat to his freedom. You have to testify."

"You should be glad that I changed my mind," Rosie said.

Confusion furrowed Jocelyn's brow and she incredulously asked, "Why the hell would I be happy?"

"Because now you're safe, too," Rosie told her, as if she'd done her a favor. "He won't have any reason to threaten you or the others if there's not enough evidence to bring him to trial."

Horrified, Jocelyn could only gasp. "There's still enough evidence." And now the person who'd collected it was in even more danger than she'd previously been. She glanced at Landon. "The CSI tech—Wendy."

"Wendy Thompson," Landon said. "Hart Fisher is protecting her."

"She hasn't changed her mind about testifying, has she?" Had Luther gotten to her like he must have gotten to Rosie? Had she been nearly killed?

Jocelyn silently cursed the incident in the parking garage. If they hadn't been nearly run over, they would have talked to Wendy, and Jocelyn would know how badly her case against Luther was falling apart.

Landon shrugged.

"We need to talk to her," Jocelyn said, and she turned toward the stairs they'd come up from the garage. "We need to make sure Mills hasn't gotten to her like he has this witness." She suspected now that it was disgust churning in her stomach. She couldn't believe how many people would help a monster like Luther elude justice. She turned back toward Rosie Mendez and asked, "What did he give you? Money?

What did it take for you to sell out? To sell the justice your brother deserves?"

Rosie flinched. "You don't know my brother," she said. "Don't act like you know what he deserves or wanted."

She'd known other victims. She could have told Rosie about them—about her grandparents. But she was more worried about Wendy Thompson right now, so she turned on her heel and headed toward the stairs leading down to the garage.

Before following her down, Landon turned back toward his friend and murmured, "What the hell...?"

Jocelyn was glad he sounded as disgusted as she was. But when he joined her in the SUV, he defended his friend. "I don't think Clint knew that she'd changed her—"

"He shouldn't have brought her to the jail," Jocelyn said.

"I brought you there," Landon said.

"I am not the witness," she said. "And I didn't see Luther. She shouldn't have either. What the hell was he thinking? Is he working for him?"

Landon's hands tightened around the steering wheel until his knuckles turned white. "Absolutely not. Clint wants justice for Javier as much as you do."

"And apparently we both want that more than his own sister does."

"I think Rosie wants justice," Landon said. "I think she's just scared. She's nearly been killed so many times."

"So has Clint," Jocelyn murmured. So he probably wasn't working for Luther.

"That's his job," Landon said. "My job. That's what bodyguards do—risk our lives to protect our clients."

Jocelyn remembered the look that had passed between Clint and Rosie—an intimate look. They were more than bodyguard and client. Rosie hadn't seemed worried about her own safety before. And maybe she wasn't worried about herself now either.

Maybe she was worried about Clint instead.

Remembering the fall from that parking-garage half wall, remembering how hard Landon's body had struck the roof of that SUV... Jocelyn shuddered.

And she wished that Landon would have let his boss remove him from this assignment. She wished that he wasn't going to keep risking his life for hers. And she suspected that, just like Rosie Mendez, she was getting too attached to her bodyguard.

But unlike Clint Quarters, Landon wasn't in love with her. He was just doing his job. Jocelyn had to remind herself of that—so that she didn't fall for him like Rosie had clearly fallen for Clint.

Despite all the muscle he'd built up weight lifting in the jailhouse gym, Luther felt a hundred pounds lighter. He'd struck a deal with Rosie Mendez—a deal he had no intention of keeping. But that didn't matter.

She wasn't testifying against him either way. And now that he could focus on that annoying little evidence tech, he wouldn't have to worry about her much longer either.

He snickered, then pulled his cell phone from his pocket. He punched in the number that had dialed him last. The guy thought he'd taken out Jocelyn Gerber.

But he'd learned that those damn Payne Protection bodyguards were good at their jobs—too damn good.

"Hello?" the man tentatively answered.

"Hey," Luther said. "I am no longer concerned about that little problem you've been trying to take care of for me."

"You're not?" the man asked with obvious surprise.

Luther chuckled again. "No. I have no worries anymore. And I really want to see Jocelyn Gerber's gorgeous face when she loses. Again…"

Maybe he would offer to take her out for drinks afterward—to console her on yet another loss to him. After all the weeks he'd spent in jail with only ugly mugs around him, he'd enjoy looking at her.

Hell, he would enjoy doing a lot more than just looking.

"It's in my best interest to continue with the original plan," the man cryptically replied.

"Then you're the one with another loss on your record," Luther pointed out.

"I'd rather have the loss than a personal conviction."

Oh. He thought Jocelyn was onto him. And maybe she was. She was pretty smart.

He sighed. "Then do what you have to do…" But he felt a flash of disappointment as he clicked off the cell. It was too bad—really. She was so hot.

But soon she would be so dead.

Chapter 14

"I want you to fire the Payne Protection Agency!" Jocelyn Gerber demanded, her heels clicking against the tile floor as she paced the chief's office.

Woodrow's head pounded more with each click, but she seemed too wound up to slow down now. On the other side of the windows, Landon Myers watched her from the detectives' bullpen. He was probably getting dizzy from following her pace.

"I looked into your concerns that one of them could be working for Luther Mills," Woodrow told her. "And I can assure you that's not the case." Even though he trusted his stepson Parker's judgment, he'd wanted to make sure he hadn't made the mistake the ADA had claimed he had in hiring Parker's franchise of the Payne Protection Agency.

She stopped to cast him a speculative glance. Obviously she didn't believe he'd done a thorough investigation, for she just shrugged. "I'm less concerned about one of them working for Luther," she begrudgingly admitted, "than I am that none of them is working for me."

He glanced through those windows at Landon again. The man had not taken his attention from her for a second even though Spencer Dubridge was talking at him.

"I think you're wrong about that, Ms. Gerber," he said. "Myers is obviously taking his job very seriously. I've heard he's saved your life a few times now."

Her pale skin flushed, and she glanced down. "I'm not talking about Landon."

It was clear that she didn't want to. Woodrow narrowed his eyes and studied her. Did she want the Payne Protection Agency fired for another—more personal—reason? Was she falling for her bodyguard?

"I'm talking about Clint Quarters," she said.

He groaned. He'd been informed about the jailhouse visit and the witness changing her mind about testifying. "I understand."

"You know?"

He nodded.

"What are you going to do about it?"

He'd had an idea how to keep the young woman safe. But, like Jocelyn, Rosie Mendez wanted nothing to do with the Payne Protection Agency anymore. And Woodrow didn't trust any of his officers to keep her safe.

He wasn't sure who he could trust within his own damn department. And that was infuriating.

"Don't worry about the witness," he said. "She could still change her mind." If she wasn't already dead. "And you have all the evidence the CSI collected."

She drew in a deep breath before shakily releasing it. "I hope I do."

"Of course you do," he assured her.

"I thought I had evidence for prior cases, but when I tried to present it to a grand jury, it was gone."

"That wasn't the case this time," he reminded her. "Wendy Thompson provided you with the evidence then and will again for the trial."

"Wendy will," Jocelyn agreed. "But what about the CSIs in those other cases? Why didn't they produce the evidence I was told we had?"

He gasped. "I'll look into that."

"I need Wendy," Jocelyn said. "You need to make sure she stays safe."

"That's why I can't fire the Payne Protection Agency," he told her. "I need them."

She glanced through that glass at her bodyguard and her usually icy blue eyes seemed to thaw a bit. And he wondered if she'd had another reason for wanting him to fire the bodyguards. If maybe she'd begun to care about Landon Myers.

"I get why you're mad," Landon told Jocelyn. They'd returned to her office after her meeting with the chief.

She glanced up from her desk and studied him through narrowed eyes.

And he added, "I just don't get why you're mad at me."

She sighed, but it sounded ragged with frustration.

"I agree with you," he reminded her. "Clint shouldn't have brought Rosie Mendez anywhere near Luther Mills."

"Are you sure he's trustworthy?" Jocelyn asked.

"I live with the man," Landon said. "I'd know if he was on the take."

And now he understood why she was studying him so intently. He groaned. "You're not back to thinking I'm working for Luther, too, are you?"

She closed her eyes, as if she couldn't even bear to look at him anymore.

"What the hell is wrong with us?" Landon murmured. "Why can't we trust each other?"

Jocelyn opened her eyes and stared at him. But this time there was no suspicion, just confusion. "I don't know," she murmured. "Maybe we've both seen too much."

He moved away from the door to come around her desk and lean against the front of it. His thigh brushed across her arm, and they both tensed. "Maybe we're both worried about getting hurt."

"We have been hurt," she said. "You hurled us onto the roof of a car the level below us in the parking garage."

He stretched and flinched at the tense muscles in his lower back. "Yeah…but we both know that's not what I'm talking about…"

She jumped up from her chair then, as if trying to get away from him. But before she could move away, he caught her arm and held on to her.

"Let me go," she told him.

But he shook his head. He didn't want to let her go. He wanted to hold on to her. So he closed his arms around her and brought her tense body against his.

She felt so good. Smelled so good, too…like something cool and sharp. Just like she was—cool and sharp.

"Landon…" she murmured, and her gaze moved to his mouth. She stared it at as intently as she'd studied him moments ago. But there was no suspicion now— just a longing that he shared, that had his guts twisting into knots. He wanted her so damn badly.

"Let's go back to your house," he said.

She shook her head. "We can't."

"The workday's over," he said. "Pretty much everybody has left already…" So maybe he could take her here—on her desk. He needed her so intensely. He slid his hand down her back to her waist, then the curve of her hips, which were pressed against his.

Did she feel how she affected him?

She must have because her eyes dilated, the pupils swallowing all but a pale blue circle of her irises. "This is a bad idea," she said even as she leaned into him, arching her hips against his erection.

He groaned and nodded. "A very, very bad idea." But even as he said it, he lowered his mouth to hers.

While she smelled cool and sharp, she tasted so sweet. And she was hot, her body burning his everywhere they touched. He wanted to touch her all over, wanted nothing between them but their skin.

She pulled back, and he reached for the button of her suit jacket. But she caught his fingers in her hand. Panting for breath, she shook her head. "We can't…"

He glanced around and noticed a few shadows outside the office. Probably the backup bodyguards. But he needed to be certain. "Let's go back to your place, then," he said. "You've done all you can for the day."

But she shook her head again. "We really can't do this," she said, but she sounded conflicted and looked it, too, as her pulse pounded and she leaned against him yet. "We can't get distracted from what's important."

At the moment, he couldn't remember what was important. He couldn't think beyond the insistent throbbing in his groin. He wanted her so much.

"Like Clint and Rosie got distracted," she said. "They forgot how dangerous Luther is, how important it is to get him off the streets for good."

Landon released a shaky breath of resignation. "You're right…" He suspected the same thing with his friend and the eyewitness. They'd gotten personally involved. And those kinds of emotional attachments just caused problems.

In their business, it was better to stay single—easier to stay focused. But Jocelyn didn't step back, didn't move away from him.

He groaned again.

She rose up on tiptoe and pressed her mouth against his again. He kissed her back with all the passion burning inside him. But when he heard the door creak open behind him, with his back to it, he realized how damn right he'd been. How dangerous it was to get distracted.

How they might both wind up dead because he'd forgotten what mattered most was keeping Jocelyn safe.

Heat rushed to Jocelyn's face, and not just from passion. She was embarrassed to look up and find Dale Grohms standing in her doorway, though she could barely see him around Landon's broad shoulder. When that door had opened, he'd made certain that he stood entirely between her and whoever was coming into the office.

She wanted to take his protection personally, to believe that he really cared about her, but she knew he was just doing his job. Which was what she should have been doing.

"Sorry," her coworker said, although he sounded anything but. "Didn't mean to interrupt."

Jocelyn doubted that and opened her mouth to tell him as much.

But he continued, "Just figured you'd want to know about the latest attempt on the life of your witness."

She gasped. Rosie Mendez should have known better than to trust Luther Mills. If she'd told him during her jailhouse visit with him that she didn't intend to testify, he either hadn't believed her or had decided to take no chances that she might change her mind.

"Is she all right?" she and Landon asked together.

Grohms looked at Landon instead of her, and he grinned. "Figured you would have heard this before I did. You're the one who works for the Payne Protection Agency. Don't you guys talk to each other?"

Landon glared at him, and his hands clenched into fists. Jocelyn grabbed his arm and held him back in case he intended to leap over the desk and attack Dale. She kind of felt like throttling him herself, though.

"Is she all right?" Jocelyn asked.

He nodded. "Yeah, yeah. Her bodyguard saved her."

"Is he all right?" Landon asked, his deep voice gruff. It clearly galled him to have to ask Grohms.

Dale shrugged. "I don't know. The guy who tried killing her is dead, though. Some rookie cop who had originally been assigned to protect her before the chief learned about the threats. Guess the chief was smart for hiring the Payne Protection Agency." He turned to head back out the door.

"Wait!" She called him back. "How do you know all of this, Dale?"

"What?" he asked. "About the shooting at the cemetery? That's all over the news."

"About the Payne Protection Agency, too," she prodded. "How do you know the chief hired them?"

"Word gets around," Dale said. "We've all heard that someone within the police department is working for Luther. Guess we know who that is now. Only thing yet to learn is who within our office is working for Luther." He stared at her now, his brows arched as if he waited for her to confess.

And that sick feeling churned in her stomach again. All of Landon's coworkers seemed to suspect her. Now, apparently, so did all of her own.

Before she could say anything in her own defense, he shrugged, turned and walked back out of her office.

Landon cursed, then murmured, "I really hope he's the leak."

She smiled. "I wish, but I doubt it." She'd read the contents of the folder the DA had had the intern bring to her. Nothing incriminating had been found out about Dale Grohms. Mike Forbes was the one with the gambling debts. And the person with the driving-under-the-influence charge was a young ADA named Eddie Garza.

"And I doubt some rookie is the leak within the police department," Landon said. "It has to be someone higher up than that." His brow furrowed. "A detective..."

Did he suspect Spencer Dubridge?

"Or a CSI," she reminded him.

He drew his cell phone from his pocket and punched

in a number. Within seconds, Parker's voice emanated from the speaker. "You okay?" he anxiously asked Landon.

"We're fine," Landon replied. "How about Clint and Rosie?"

"You know about the attempt on Rosie Mendez at the cemetery?" Parker asked.

She must have been at her brother's grave site. Maybe Jocelyn had gotten through to her during their meeting at the safe house.

"Clint saved her," Parker said. "She's fine."

"And Clint?" Landon asked, his voice gruff with what was obviously fear for his friend.

"He's fine, too," Parker assured him.

"Where are they?" Jocelyn asked. She needed to talk to Rosie now—while the attempt was fresh in her mind, while she had to know that the only way to be safe from Luther was to put him away for life.

Parker paused for a long moment.

And Jocelyn groaned. "You don't know, do you?"

"No," Parker said.

"Damn it!" she cursed. How the hell was she supposed to try this case without the eyewitness?

"It's good I don't know where she is," Parker assured her. "The fewer people who know, the safer she'll be. But she will come back for the trial, though. She is determined to testify."

Jocelyn's breath escaped her lungs in a ragged sigh. "Oh, thank God."

"Don't be so happy," Parker cautioned her.

And she felt a flash of guilt. She shouldn't have been happy that the young woman must have been scared into testifying.

"Why not?" Landon asked the question.

"Mills will be even more dangerous now," Parker said. "Since he won't be able to get to the witness, he'll try extra hard to take out everyone else associated with his trial."

"Did you warn Hart and Tyce?" Landon asked.

"Yeah," Parker said. "But you two need to be careful, too. There is still a leak within the district attorney's office that we need to find ASAP."

Landon picked up that folder from her desk. "We're working on it," he assured his boss.

Working...

That was what they should have been doing. Not kissing.

Landon clicked off his cell and opened his mouth to say something. But Jocelyn pressed her fingers to his lips. "I know," she assured him.

What had happened between them could not happen again. Their lives depended on it. They needed to stay focused to stay alive.

Chapter 15

Being with her 24/7 and not touching her, not kissing her...

Now Landon knew what torture felt like. He wanted Jocelyn badly. But he wanted to keep her safe even more. There was no doubt that the danger had been heightened since Rosie and Clint had disappeared. More attempts had been made on the life of the evidence tech. Hart had saved Wendy from bombs and shooting attempts. Tyce had had his hands full with the judge's daughter, too.

Only Dubridge and Keeli knew what the hell was going on between the two of them. Landon didn't want to know. His only concern was keeping Jocelyn safe.

He wanted Jocelyn to disappear, too. But she insisted on working her other cases while following up on those leads on her coworkers. Mike Forbes currently occupied the chair in front of her desk while

Landon stood behind her desk, next to her chair, to protect her—and drive himself out of his mind with her closeness.

He didn't really expect anyone to try anything in her office. But with the way Jocelyn interrogated suspects, she might push them too far, might push them into snapping.

"Mike, I know about your gambling problem," she said.

The older man cursed her. "That's none of your damn business, Jocelyn!"

"Our boss made it my business," she said. "She gave me a folder of information she compiled on all of us."

"Why?" he asked, his blue eyes narrowed.

"Because she wants me to find out who the leak in our office is."

He snorted. "She's not going to find the real leak that way."

Jocelyn flinched. "It's not me."

He snorted again. "You're the one with the fancy house and car. Not me."

"No," she agreed. "You lost your house to your gambling debts."

"Do you think that would have happened if I was working for Luther?" he asked. "Don't you think he would have paid those off for me?" He jumped up from the chair.

And Landon stepped forward, making certain he didn't reach across Jocelyn's desk.

Mike glanced at him. "You were a cop," he said. "You must know she's the best suspect to be working for Mills."

"I thought she was," Landon admitted. "But she's not."

"I couldn't afford her place on the same damn salary she makes."

"Actually, Mike, you make more than I do," she informed him. "Seniority and all."

He glared at her. "If seniority mattered at all around here, I would have that case—not you!"

"Luther can't tempt me with money," she said. "My family has more than he does."

Instead of mollifying Mike, her words seemed to enrage her coworker. He stalked out of her office and slammed the door behind himself.

She flinched again and uttered a shaky sigh. "Well, this is fun."

"You should tell your boss you don't want to do this," Landon said.

"She's busy having a baby," Jocelyn reminded him. And she glanced down at her phone. Amber Talsma-Kozminski was at the hospital right now, and Jocelyn was obviously concerned about her.

"We can go see her," Landon suggested because he saw that concern.

She nodded. "We have one more meeting, though."

Her door rattled with a soft knock.

"Come in," she called out to a young man. "This is Eddie Garza," she murmured to Landon as the dark-haired man entered the office. He didn't look much older than the paralegal who'd brought her that folder. How was he already a lawyer? Already an ADA?

"You wanted to see me?" he asked. And he looked nervous. Way too nervous.

Of course, maybe he'd seen Mike Forbes leave. And

he didn't want to leave that same way—embarrassed and furious. This man was younger and bigger than Mike Forbes. So Landon stepped even closer to Jocelyn's chair. He had to keep her safe.

He had to keep his sanity, too, though, and standing this close, spending this much time with her, was sorely testing it.

"I'm sure you heard all the rumors going around the office," she began.

And the man glanced at Landon.

What were the rumors about him? That he was her bodyguard? Or that he was more than that? He wished he was more than that, but it was as if that one encounter had never happened, as if he'd just dreamed that he'd made love with her. It must have been a dream because surely nothing could have been as powerful as he'd imagined that was.

"Someone within our office is working for Luther Mills," she clarified.

The young man gasped. "You really believe that?"

"I don't want to," she said. "I hope that the rumor is wrong. But the DA wants me to look into it."

The young man tensed. "So you're looking into me?"

She nodded.

"You know about the under-the-influence charge?"

She nodded again.

His face flushed with embarrassment. "It wasn't alcohol or drugs—at least, not street drugs." He shuddered. "I would *never*." His voice shook like his body.

And Jocelyn tilted her head. "Why not?"

Eddie glanced at him again. "I had a brother who got hooked on them."

Had...

Jocelyn must have picked up on the past tense because she murmured, "I'm sorry."

He jerked his head in a nod. "That's why I would never work for Luther. I blame him and…"

"Who?" Jocelyn asked when he trailed off.

He glanced at Landon again, and he looked even more nervous than he'd been when he walked in. "Uh, I don't want to say."

"In front of me?" Landon asked. He'd never seen the kid before.

Jocelyn glanced up at him now. "Would you mind stepping outside for a moment?"

"Yes," Landon replied. "I'm not leaving you alone—"

"You'll be right outside the door," she said.

But it wasn't close enough—if Eddie Garza had a weapon. Hell, he was big enough that he wouldn't need a weapon. He could kill her with his bare hands.

"Please," she implored him.

Now he knew how Rosie had gotten Clint to take her to the jail. She'd asked. And Clint hadn't been able to say no even when he should have. Like Clint, Landon couldn't say no, so he walked toward the door.

But he stopped next to Garza's chair and warned him, "Don't try anything."

The guy nodded. Landon wasn't satisfied, but he stepped into the hall and pulled the door closed.

"When's my turn?" Dale Grohms asked with a grin, pointing toward Jocelyn's office.

"Your turn?"

"For the hot lights," he said with a chuckle. "For the interrogation."

"You sound almost eager," he said.

The guy shrugged. "I've got nothing to hide." And because that appeared to be the case, he wasn't on the list. But Landon was worried that something had been missed. He looked through the window in Jocelyn's door and shook his head. "Too bad Eddie can't say the same."

"What do you mean?" Landon asked.

Dale sighed. "I'm not sure why the boss hired that kid. He was in trouble—big trouble."

"The under-the-influence charge?" Landon asked. It couldn't have been too severe because he'd only been given community service.

Dale shook his head. "Guess it was on his juvie record. Must have been sealed."

Landon swallowed a curse. They hadn't thought to look for sealed records. "Sounds like we need to dig a little deeper," he agreed. But he was looking at Dale—not Garza.

Grohms just laughed as he walked away.

Jocelyn's door opened, and Garza stepped out. He didn't look at Landon as he passed him. And Jocelyn didn't look at him when he stepped back into her office.

"What?" he asked. "What did he say?"

She shook her head. "He explained that it was Adderall. Not his prescription, though. He was taking it, so he could stay up all night studying. He graduated high school and college early. Taking it at all, but especially driving under the influence of it, was dangerous and stupid, and he knows it."

So did he really have a juvie record?

Landon didn't know what to believe. But he suspected Jocelyn was holding something back. What?

She stood up and reached for her briefcase. "I would like to see Amber now."

He wasn't sure if that was because she wanted to make sure her boss was all right or if she wanted to talk to her about whatever she'd learned. Clearly she didn't want to talk to him about it.

Jocelyn couldn't tell Landon what Garza had told her. She didn't want to know if he'd already known and kept it from her. She didn't want to know if he'd betrayed her. But she had to tell someone.

But once she stepped into her boss's hospital room, she knew Amber was not the person she needed to talk to about that. Her boss looked exhausted. She was so pale with machines hooked to her.

"Are you okay?" she asked, concern gripping her.

"Yes," Amber replied, but her voice was faint with exhaustion.

Since hearing Amber had gone into labor, Jocelyn had been worried. Her boss had had so many difficulties with this pregnancy.

And now...

Jocelyn shuddered. Why would anyone put themselves through this? Through childbirth? She was glad that she'd decided long ago children and marriage were not for her. She didn't want any emotional complications—like Landon.

He stood so close to her that she could feel the heat of his body. He always stood so close to her that her heart pounded and her skin tingled. Sure, it was his job to protect. But she wondered if he was just trying to drive her out of her mind.

He was succeeding.

"Hey, there," a deep voice said as another man walked into the room. He carried something in a blanket. "Look who I found."

With his long dark blond hair and green eyes, the man looked like the one who'd been in the parking garage that day. But he wasn't. He chuckled when he saw Landon, though, and asked, "Any more falls?" So he must have heard about it from his brother. He settled onto the bed next to his wife.

She reached for the blanket with a trembling hand. "She's sleeping."

Milek Kozminski leaned down and kissed his wife's pale cheek. "You should be sleeping, too." He cast a pointed glance at Jocelyn.

"I'm sorry," she murmured. "I shouldn't have visited."

"No," he said. "She wouldn't have slept until she saw our little princess again anyways."

Amber smiled. "You know me so well."

Milek settled his head against hers. "Yes, I do."

And Jocelyn felt a twinge in her heart, one of longing for that kind of love. But of course, she didn't really want that.

Amber stared down at the bundle in the blanket, and the expression on her face caused another twinge in Jocelyn's heart. She'd never seen such a look.

"I want to hold her," Amber said. "But I'm so weak."

Milek shook his head. "No. No, you're not." But he helped as she held her baby, wrapping his arms around them both.

"We—we should go," Jocelyn stammered, feeling like a fool for having intruded on such a private moment. She backed toward the door and stumbled against Landon.

"Don't you want to hold her?" Amber asked.

This was another reason Jocelyn was glad that her old friendships had faded away. Everybody she'd grown up with was married with children now. That was probably why her parents kept putting so much pressure on her to do the same. They didn't understand and neither had her old friends. When she occasionally ran into them, they tried to hand off their babies or kids to her—like she was dying to hold a child.

She would really rather not. But this was her boss. And she didn't want to seem uninterested in what clearly mattered so much to her mentor. So she stepped forward.

"Sit down," Milek told her, pointing toward the chair next to the bed.

Jocelyn sat.

Milek laughed. "You don't have to look so terrified. She won't bite. She doesn't have any teeth yet."

"I—I don't want to drop her, though," she said, then forced a smile and added, "Congratulations on your daughter."

"Yeah, you can order the pink balloons for the office," Amber said. "But wait a few months. I don't intend to rush right back."

That was good—because she appeared to need a while to recuperate.

"Hold your arms like I have mine," Milek directed her.

When she imitated him, he settled the infant against her. The baby shifted, and Jocelyn tensed and closed her eyes. The child would probably start screaming now. But she emitted a tiny sigh and settled against Jocelyn.

And another twinge struck her heart. She was just happy for her boss, though, happy that Amber had figured out a way to have it all—the husband, the career, the kids.

Jocelyn didn't want to try to juggle as many things as her boss did.

"What are you naming her?" Landon asked the question. Once again, he was too close to Jocelyn, but he seemed more focused on the baby than he was on her. "Another Penny?"

"Another Penny?" Jocelyn repeated.

"Everybody likes to name their girl babies after Penny Payne," Milek explained.

"The chief's wife?" Jocelyn asked.

"You haven't met her," Landon said with certainty. "You would understand if you'd met her."

Jocelyn shrugged, and the baby shifted again, opened one eye and peered up at her. She braced herself, waiting for the scream. But the infant only stared at her. "She can't see yet, right?" she asked.

She didn't know much about babies. And she didn't really care to learn.

"She's not blind," Milek said. "But she can't see very far away yet. She can see you, though."

"Then why isn't she crying?" Jocelyn asked.

And the men laughed at her.

Amber smiled, though. "She recognizes her namesake."

"What?" She couldn't have heard correctly.

"Jocelyn Gerber, meet Jocelyn Talsma-Kozminski."

She stared at her boss. "I—I don't understand..."

They weren't friends. She only worked for her, but since they both worked hard, they had spent a lot of time together. Amber knew things about her, about her past, that few other people besides her parents and Landon knew.

"She's tough and determined," Amber said. "So she reminded me of you."

Jocelyn stared down at the baby now, but she couldn't see for the tears suddenly blurring her vision. "I—I don't know what to say…"

She couldn't remember the last time she'd been so overwhelmed. Then she glanced at Landon, and she remembered—with him, in his arms.

And she felt another twinge in her heart. But it was fear. After learning what she had from Garza, she was afraid that she'd made a mistake—that she shouldn't have begun to trust Landon Myers.

And she definitely shouldn't have started falling for him. But she was afraid that she had.

She was too close to learning the truth. He had to get rid of her. Now.

The hospital parking garage was set up like the one between the courthouse and the district attorney's office building. If he tried running them over, they could escape over one of those half walls. And since they'd parked only one level up, they wouldn't be hurt any worse than they'd been from their previous fall.

So he wasn't going to try to run them down. He was going to shoot them. He pulled his gun from the pocket of his trench coat. It was the same one he'd used to shoot up her house—the same one he'd taken from evidence a while ago. He'd saved Luther from an indictment then.

He would have saved him this time—if everyone hadn't been so damn careful about this case. His boss and Jocelyn and the evidence tech.

They'd made it impossible for him to get to the evidence. And Landon Myers was trying to make it impossible for him to get to Jocelyn now. He was always around, and now he had that backup team.

Or he thought he did.

They drank coffee. So he'd made sure to spike the pot at the office. While they'd followed Landon and Jocelyn to the hospital, they had since fallen asleep—their heads against the side windows of their Payne Protection Agency SUV. He snickered. But he wasn't sure how long he had before they awakened.

Landon and Jocelyn had to hurry.

What were they doing? What was Jocelyn telling their boss? Had she already begun to suspect him?

Nobody could, or he wouldn't be given the case once she died. And she would die this time along with her damn bodyguard.

Through the open window of his rental vehicle, he heard the click of her heels against the concrete. It could have been another woman wearing stilettos, but he doubted it. There was something distinctive about Jocelyn's walk—a sharpness that reflected her cold personality.

He stared through the new tinted windshield. Luther had referred him to a company that had replaced the glass—one that wouldn't talk to the Payne Protection bodyguards who'd asked if anyone had had to redo a shot-out windshield. They hadn't tracked him down yet.

And they wouldn't.

For soon they would be dead. He waited until they got closer—until Landon noticed his fellow bodyguards slumped in their vehicle. Then he raised his weapon and started firing at him and Jocelyn.

They dropped to the ground, but this time he was certain he hadn't missed. He saw the blood spattered across the concrete. He also saw the doors of the SUV open as the other bodyguards woke up.

And he tore out of the lot before they could catch him.

They would be too groggy to follow him. And too concerned about the wounded. Or the dead...

Chapter 16

Woodrow had already been on the way to the hospital when he got the call that there had been a shooting in the visitors' parking garage. His hand shook as he punched in the contact for his wife. He'd been on his way to meet her there, but a situation in the police lab had prevented him from leaving when he should have.

What if she'd been in the garage at the time? What if she was one of the wounded?

And there were wounded…

He'd seen the blood as he'd passed through the crime scene on his way to the hospital. With his cell pressed to his ear, he headed toward the ER. His stomach flipped when her voice answered, but he realized it was only her voice mail. She hadn't picked up. But his phone buzzed and he glanced down at the text flashing on the screen.

Where are you, darling? I am already cuddling this gorgeous new grandbaby.

He grinned with relief. The child technically wasn't their grandbaby, but that didn't matter to Penny. She'd long ago emotionally adopted the Kozminski children even though everyone had believed their father had killed her husband. Even if he had, Penny wouldn't have cared. She was so forgiving and loving.

She would forgive him for being late because she would understand why. If she'd known about the shooting, she would have been heading where he was, to the ER, to check on the wounded, especially if she knew what he did, that one of those wounded was a Payne Protection bodyguard.

She treated every bodyguard like they were her children. Of course, quite a few of them were. Panic struck Woodrow's heart, making it pound even faster than it had already been. It couldn't be one of his stepsons or stepdaughter, could it? Parker had had a narrow escape from death earlier in the week. And he'd brought in his brothers' teams for backup because of how damn dangerous Luther Mills had become, even more dangerous than they'd thought.

If he'd known how risky this assignment was, Woodrow might not have hired Parker for the job. But then, he hadn't had many options—not with being unable to trust his own damn officers. And now even the lab.

He hurried as he neared the front desk for the ER. He flashed his shield at the security guard who rushed up to meet him. "I'm the chief of police," he said.

It had been odd to say that in the beginning—after

so many years of being special agent in charge of a field office of the FBI. But now it felt right.

This was where he belonged. In River City with his wife and his ever-expanding family. And now one of those family members might have been injured, so he had no problem about cutting to the front of the line waiting in the ER. "The people who were wounded in the parking garage," he said. "Where are they?"

"Over here," the security guard said as he pushed open a door marked Employees Only. He led the way down a wide corridor. "A detective's already gone back to take the woman's statement."

So a woman had been attacked but survived. The man could have been referring to Jocelyn Gerber or to Nikki Payne-Ecklund. Nikki might have been working as backup for Landon. If anything had happened to Penny's daughter...

He shuddered and refused to consider it. For one, Nikki was damn tough and had already survived so many close calls that she had to be invincible. When the security guard pulled aside the curtain, he was relieved to see Jocelyn Gerber, with Nikki standing next to her.

They were both all right except for the blood oozing from cuts on Jocelyn's knees. She also had a scrape on her cheek.

"Are you all right?" he asked because she looked so very pale and fragile sitting on the gurney. He'd had his issues with Jocelyn Gerber, but now he felt a deep pull of sympathy and concern for her. While she could be brash and bossy, she was also a damn hard worker and a strong woman. Woodrow had so much respect and appreciation for strong women.

She nodded, and her black hair swung around her face, only slightly tangled from her ordeal. "Yes, but Landon's in surgery," she said, her voice shaking with concern.

"What happened?" He'd heard about the shooting—that it involved the assistant district attorney and her bodyguard—but he didn't know entirely what had happened.

"Landon and I were walking to the SUV when we noticed the backup bodyguards." Her voice caught. "They were slumped against the windows of their SUV. We thought they were dead."

Instinctively, Woodrow reached for Nikki, pulling her into a hug. "Are you all right? What happened?"

Nikki squeezed him before pulling back. Her face was flushed with embarrassment. "Lars and I must have been drugged," she said. "We fell asleep…only waking up when we heard the gunshots."

"Somebody was shooting at us," Jocelyn said.

"Did you see who?" Woodrow asked.

She shook her head. "Landon pushed me down so fast that I didn't even see where the shots were coming from."

Spencer Dubridge stepped behind the curtain with Keeli Abbott at his side. "Landon's out of surgery—"

"How is he?" Jocelyn asked, her blue eyes full of concern.

"The doctor said he'd be fine. The bullet just nicked an artery in his neck—that's why there was so much blood. But they've repaired it. Because he lost so much blood, though, he's not awake yet." Dubridge said the last with recrimination, as if he was angry that Landon was unconscious.

"Give him a minute or two to recover before you hassle him for his statement," Keeli remarked.

He glared at her before realizing everyone was staring at him with the same condemnation she was. "We need to find out who the hell this perp is," he said. "It's gotta be someone in the DA's office."

Nikki nodded. "He's right. It has to be. That's where Lars and I drank the coffee that must have been drugged."

Jocelyn looked even paler than she had moments ago. "You were right," she murmured to the chief.

"I'm sorry," he said. "It doesn't feel good to know you've been working with a traitor."

Now there was a sudden rush of color to her face. She looked around and asked the others, "Can you give me a few minutes alone with the chief?"

Nikki shook her head. "I promised Landon that I wouldn't leave your side," she said. "That's the only way he agreed to be treated."

"I know," Jocelyn said. "But this is private."

Woodrow swallowed a groan. Did she still suspect Landon was working for Luther—even after all the times he'd saved her life?

But he had things he needed to share with her, as well. "It's okay," he told the others. "I have some experience with law enforcement. I think I can protect her for a few minutes."

Dubridge chuckled. "Yeah, well, if you get into any trouble, let us know."

"So you're a smart-ass even to the chief," Keeli muttered as she followed him out of the area.

Nikki hesitated a moment longer. "Are you sure?"

Woodrow nodded. "Yes. Where's your husband? Is

he okay?" She was married to Lars Ecklund, the fellow bodyguard she'd mentioned who had also been drugged.

She nodded. "He's in the parking garage, looking for anything Detective Dubridge might have missed."

So nobody trusted his department anymore. But with a rookie cop nearly killing the eyewitness, Woodrow could hardly blame them—especially after what had happened today. Once Nikki left, he turned back to Jocelyn and told her, "You were right."

She tensed. "You know?"

He nodded. "About the CSI, yeah. You were right that it had to be one of them getting rid of evidence."

She gasped. "Not Wendy Thompson."

"No. Terrance Gibbs."

"I thought he was retired," she said.

"Just a short time ago," he said. "But he came back recently to *help* out." He hadn't been trying to help the River City PD, though. He'd been trying to help Luther Mills to get rid of the evidence against him.

Her brow puckered as if she was searching her memory. Then she nodded. "I think he collected some of the evidence that went missing…"

"Well, he won't be a problem anymore," Woodrow assured her. The former CSI had died while he'd been trying to kill Wendy.

"That's good," she said. "Because we have another one."

And this was what she'd wanted privacy to tell him. Dread settled heavily into the pit of his stomach. "What is it?"

"I told you I had concerns about Parker Payne's team of bodyguards…"

He released his groan this time. "How can you—after how many times Landon's risked his life for you?"

"I don't know if he even knows this," she said. "That's why I wanted to tell you first. But then the judge has to hear it, too. He needs to be warned."

"Warned about what?"

"Luther Mills's brother works for the Payne Protection Agency."

Just as Woodrow hadn't been the chief for very long, he hadn't been a resident of River City for long either. He didn't know the history everyone else seemed to know. "I wasn't aware that he had a brother."

"Neither was I," she admitted. "I just learned today."

"Who is it?"

"Tyce Jackson. The man protecting the judge's daughter."

Woodrow sucked in a breath, shocked. He shook his head. "Are you sure that's true? Where did you learn that?"

"From someone within my office," she said.

"Can you trust that person?"

She shook her head. "I can't trust anyone." She looked speculatively at him, as if she was wondering if she could even trust him.

"Then you don't know that's true," he pointed out.

"I doubt this person—another assistant district attorney—would have told me something that could be easily disproved," she said. "It would only make him look guiltier."

Maybe that was all the man had been trying to do—cast guilt onto someone else. But she was right. Woodrow needed to look into it—to hopefully disprove it. Like the other bodyguards, Tyce Jackson had risked his life several times to save the judge's daughter, so Woodrow couldn't believe he was any threat to her.

"I'll find out," he promised, and he pulled back the curtain. He didn't see Nikki or the others. But he doubted Jocelyn, with her scraped knees, was going anywhere. And as she'd said, she didn't trust anyone right now.

So he wasn't worried about her. He was worried about the judge's daughter and just how far reaching Luther Mills's influence was.

Jocelyn had had her doubts about his hiring Parker's team. He hoped she was wrong, though. Or he had put everybody in greater danger—just as she'd feared.

Pain shot through Landon's neck, blood spurting from the wound. Instinctively, he reached for Jocelyn, pushing her to the ground. But had he been too late? Had she been shot, too?

He reached out, but something tugged on his arm. And he jerked awake. Then he flinched and squinted against the bright lights. "Jocelyn!"

"She's fine," a deep voice assured him. And he turned to find Spencer Dubridge sitting next to his bed. That was not who he'd wanted to see.

As if he'd guessed as much, Dubridge chuckled. "She's talking to the chief in the ER. That's why she's not here."

"In the ER," Landon said. "So she is hurt!"

Spencer shook his head. "Just a little bruised and scraped from you shoving her down."

He flinched again with regret that he'd hurt her.

"You saved her life," Dubridge said. "Did you see who it was? Who was shooting at you?"

He shook his head. "It looked like the car—same make and model—that tried hitting us the other day. But the tinted windshield had been replaced."

Dubridge cursed. "I checked all the glass replacement companies in the area."

Landon shrugged. There were a lot of places that didn't like giving information to cops, even if served with a warrant. He cared less about finding the car than finding the driver. He had a feeling the guy was smart enough to make sure the car couldn't be traced to him anyway.

"What're Jocelyn and the chief talking about?" he asked. And why hadn't she come to see him yet?

"She didn't want us to know," Keeli said, speaking up from where she stood at the door—as if protecting both the detective and him.

Dubridge nodded. "Yeah, she wanted to talk to him in private."

Landon tensed. He didn't like the sound of that. Was she trying again to get the chief to fire the Payne Protection Agency?

Ever since she'd spoken to Garza alone, she'd been acting strangely. He needed to see her—needed to make sure she was all right. He gripped the railings on his bed and sat up.

"What are you doing?" Keeli asked as she stepped toward his bed.

He pushed down one of the railings and tried to swing his legs over the side. But his body felt so damn heavy that he could barely move them.

"You have to take it easy," Keeli said. "You lost a lot of blood."

He lifted his fingers to his neck and felt the bandage covering the wound. "It was nothing…"

"If you hadn't kept your hand on it…" Keeli shuddered. "You were lucky."

He had a feeling that luck was about to change as a strange chill chased down his spine. "You need to check on Jocelyn," he said.

"I need to take your statement," Dubridge told him.

"I gave you my statement," he said, frustration tightening the muscles of his already aching stomach. "I saw nothing more than I did the last time. I don't know who the hell is after Jocelyn."

"Someone in her office," Dubridge said. "That's where Nikki thinks she and Lars were drugged. They were lucky they made it to the parking garage without crashing."

"Lars was driving, and he's a big guy," Keeli said. "So the sleeping aid didn't work as quickly on him as it did on Nikki."

"Another reason petite women should not be bodyguards," Spencer murmured.

Ignoring their bickering, Landon managed to get to his feet. The room tilted for a moment, and spots danced before his eyes. But he powered through—because, like Lars, he was a big guy. Yet it wasn't just his strength driving him. It was his concern for Jocelyn.

And once he got dressed, with Dubridge's help, and made it down to the ER, he found his concern was warranted. She was gone.

Jocelyn knew she shouldn't have slipped out of the ER without telling anyone. That she shouldn't have gone off alone. But she thought she might be safer alone than with anyone else right now. She did not know whom to trust.

Sure, Landon kept saving her life, but had he known the whole time who was putting her in danger? Was he aware that one of his team members—one of his friends—was Luther Mills's brother? And he hadn't told her?

She wanted to trust him. Most of all, she wanted to make sure he was all right. But Dubridge had assured her that he would be. Still, she felt a sickening lurch in her stomach as she stepped out of the cab onto the sidewalk outside the front entry of the district attorney's office building.

While she wanted to trust Landon, she could not bring herself to trust the others. She didn't know what they knew about Tyce Jackson's relationship to Luther—if they were keeping him apprised of everyone else's whereabouts. So she hadn't told them hers.

It was bad enough that Tyce was protecting the judge's daughter. So she'd warned him.

Judge Holmes had been shocked, the way she had been.

She had to make sure she had no more surprises. She needed to find out who in her office could be working with Luther. She could no longer deny that someone was, not after the backup bodyguards were drugged.

Dubridge had probably already sent a crime-scene tech to retrieve the coffeepot. Since she worked in an office of caffeine junkies, she suspected everybody's prints would be on it. And the break room didn't have a security camera that might have caught the culprit in the act. They didn't have enough cause to *legally* search everybody's office.

She swiped her ID badge through the reader outside, and the exterior doors opened for her. She hurried through the lobby to the elevators. Despite it being way after hours, the elevator worked. The cleaning staff was in the building.

Jocelyn searched until she found one of the unmanned carts and lifted the ring of keys from it. Even if whatever she found wouldn't be admissible, she intended to search everybody's offices; she needed to know who was working for Luther.

But the first office she unlocked was her own. She intended to put her briefcase inside while she searched the others, so she left the door open behind her. But when she opened the bottom drawer of her filing cabinet to slide her briefcase inside it, she found a couple of things.

Things that she had not put there.

An orange prescription bottle with the label torn off, as well as a cell phone. So someone else had already lifted the office keys from the cleaning person's cart. And they'd used those keys to plant evidence in Jocelyn's office.

But it made no sense. Why would she drug the bodyguards who were protecting her? She'd nearly been killed—too many times. And she clearly wasn't the one firing those shots or running herself down.

She stared down at the bottle. She needed a plastic bag or something to put it in so that it could be checked for prints. Whereas the coffeepot would have a lot, she doubted the bottle would have any. The same with the cell phone. She would bet it had been wiped down and was an untraceable burner phone—a phone that no doubt had a record of calls to Luther Mills or to his lawyer.

Whoever had put the prescription bottle and phone in her filing cabinet was desperate not to be caught. Maybe that was why the things had been placed in her office, just to get them out of the one in which they had really belonged. Hopefully, even with the label torn off, there was a way to trace the pills—some pharmacy serial number or something.

She leaned over to peer closer at the bottle without touching it when she felt a sudden presence. Before she could straighten up and turn around, something slipped over her head and wound tightly around her throat.

She gasped for breath as she clawed at it, trying to scream for help.

No. She shouldn't have gone off without her bodyguards because now there was no one to save her from her attacker.

Chapter 17

Landon had been torn between heading to Jocelyn's house or to her office. He'd chosen the building for the district attorney because he figured she had left the hospital determined to find out who in her office was working for Luther Mills.

He'd had to wait for a security guard to let him into the building, though. The guard confirmed that her key card had opened the doors just a short time ago. So he wasn't far behind her.

But even a few minutes was too long for her to be alone—with someone very determined to kill her. Her attacker would take any opportunity she gave him, and by going off alone, she'd given him a big one.

Landon rushed over to the elevator and stabbed the button for her floor. If he was feeling stronger, he would have used the stairs. But it would take too long for him to make it up the five flights.

Finally the elevator dinged, and the doors slid open. He jumped into the car and pressed the button for five. And he willed it to hurry as a sudden urgency gripped him. She would have been safer had she gone home to her cat and her high-tech security system.

Here the distracted security guard was her only protection. And there was no way he could hear her screaming from the lobby. The elevator lurched to a stop, the movement adding to the dizziness Landon was already fighting from all his blood loss. He pressed his fingers to his head and tried to clear it.

Maybe he should have waited for Keeli and Dubridge. But he'd rushed off without them as backup—without any backup. He regretted that now as he worried that he might not be strong enough to save Jocelyn if she needed saving.

And he was afraid that she did the moment he looked through the window in her office door and noticed two dark shadows. One leaned over the other. He shoved open the door and rushed into the room.

The taller shadow charged him, knocking Landon over as he ran into the hallway. The other shadow dropped to the floor. The lamp on Jocelyn's desk cast a glow onto her pale face. She lay across the open bottom drawer of her filing cabinet. Her skin was so ashen but for the angry red mark across her throat.

Whoever had been inside the office with her had been strangling her.

"Jocelyn!" Landon shouted her name.

But her long black lashes lay against her cheeks. Her lids didn't so much as flicker. She had to be unconscious.

He refused to consider the alternative. That he'd been too late.

That he'd lost her.

"Jocelyn…" He murmured her name as he crouched over her. Then, with shaking fingers, he reached out and checked her damaged throat for a pulse. Panic pressed on him when he felt nothing but the coolness of her silky skin.

His chest ached, and his lungs burned. "Jocelyn!"

He leaned down and pressed his lips to hers, breathing through her lips as he began compressions. He was trained in CPR and regularly recertified, and he was never more grateful than now for that training.

He couldn't lose her.

She had to come back to him.

Jocelyn choked and sputtered, her throat and lungs burning as she struggled to breathe. She reached up to tear that rope or whatever it had been away from her neck—but it was gone. Her hand bumped against a shoulder, though, and she opened her eyes to see a dark shadow leaning over her. She tried to scream, but she could make no sound but a rasp.

"Shhh…" a deep voice murmured, his voice sounding nearly as raspy as hers. "You're safe. It's me. It's me."

Landon! She sat up and threw her arms around him, clinging to him. She'd known she shouldn't have left the hospital without checking on him. But she hadn't wanted to put him in danger, too. She grasped his arms and pulled back. "We…" Her voice cracked, and she struggled to clear it. "We need to get out of here."

"He's gone," Landon said. "Whoever it was took

off when I came in." He reached for the phone on her desk. "I need to call down to Security—see if they saw him leaving."

"Did...did you see who it was?" she asked.

He shook his head. "He ran out fast—so fast that he has to be long gone. I couldn't get a good look at him, but he was big enough to knock me over."

She saw the blood seeping through the bandage on his neck and touched it. "Did he reopen your wound?"

Using his free hand, he covered her fingers with his. "No. I'm fine. We need an ambulance, though. We need to get you to the hospital."

She grabbed the phone from his hand. "No. I'm fine."

"You weren't breathing when I found you," he said, and his voice was raspy again with emotion. "You need to be treated."

"I'm breathing fine now." And while her throat hurt, she could speak even though it sounded hoarse. "I'm fine."

"You could have died," he said. "You shouldn't have left the ER without protection."

She shook her head. "I shouldn't have left without checking on you." He'd saved her life over and over again, putting himself in danger every time. And she hadn't even seen him after he'd been shot.

"Why did you?" he asked, and his eyes darkened with pain.

A twinge of regret struck her heart. She felt bad about hurting him. "I didn't know what to do."

"Or you didn't care..."

She gripped his arms again. "No. I do care." And maybe that was why she hadn't wanted to see him—

because when he'd been shot, she'd cared too much. Seeing that blood—*his blood*—spurt from the wound in his neck had nearly paralyzed her, she'd been so afraid. For him...

If he hadn't shoved her to the ground, she would have been shot, too. He'd saved her then, even when he'd nearly been mortally wounded. And not fully recovered from that wound, he'd saved her again.

She slid her hands up his arms to his shoulders. "I care."

He chuckled. "But you don't want to."

"No," she agreed. "I don't."

"Because you don't trust me," he said. "Even now..."

She closed her eyes and sighed. "I—I..."

"You're keeping something from me," he said. "Something you told the chief in private."

Dubridge must have told him that or maybe Keeli had. Because if he'd talked to the chief, he would probably know what she'd told him. She doubted Chief Lynch was going to keep it secret, so it was going to come out soon anyway.

She opened her eyes and studied Landon's face, needing to see his reaction when she told him.

"Luther Mills has a brother," she said.

He shrugged. "He probably has a few half siblings. His parents were never married."

"He has one who works for the Payne Protection Agency, and before that, he worked for the vice unit."

Landon's brow furrowed with confusion. "What are you saying? That one of my friends is Luther's brother?"

"Tyce Jackson."

He laughed, but then the laughter stopped, and the

grin slid away from his face as he must have realized it was a strong possibility. "It doesn't matter if they are."

"Of course it does," she said.

He shook his head and flinched as his neck moved. "No. Tyce was even more determined to bring down Luther than the rest of us in vice ever were—even Clint. And Clint blames Luther for the death of his cousin."

She sighed. So Clint Quarters had had a personal reason for wanting justice—an even more personal reason than hers.

Landon continued, "If Tyce and Luther are related, it's by blood only. They weren't raised together, and they are nothing alike."

Even while she admired his fierce loyalty, she wondered if he was just fooling himself. "Isn't the saying that blood is thicker than water?" Then she grimaced as she remembered how the bullet had sprayed Landon's blood around the parking garage. It had seemed like water then.

How was he alive?

How had he saved her life once again?

"I'm sorry," she said. "I shouldn't have told you."

"You should have told me sooner," he said. "Before you told the chief."

"And that's why I didn't tell you," she said. "Because I knew you'd try to protect him." Like his fierce loyalty, being protective was second nature to Landon. He had made the right choice to leave the River City Police Department to become a bodyguard.

She only hoped that his new career choice didn't get him killed—that protecting her didn't get him killed.

"I'm not protecting him," he said. "I'm defending him. As a lawyer, you should realize the difference.

And you should know that everybody's innocent until proven guilty."

"Everybody?" she asked. "Even Luther Mills?"

"Luther's never been innocent," he said. "If the rumors are true, he was just a kid when he killed for the first time."

"I heard that rumor, too," she said. "I heard the person he killed was his father. Maybe Tyce Jackson's father, too."

"So if anything, Tyce might want revenge against Luther," Landon said, "not to aid and abet him."

She sighed. "Maybe you should have been a lawyer. You're mounting a strong defense for your friend."

"Tyce is my friend," he said. "But he's my friend because he's a good man. I know he's not working for Luther. Not when he worked vice and not now. He's working against him. Just like you are. Just like I am. That's why we need to find who the hell's working for him in your office. We need to find out who the hell just tried to kill you."

She wasn't about to argue with him about that. "You're right," she said. "Let's talk to the security guard."

Landon helped her up from the floor. Maybe she'd stood too quickly, for she swayed on her heels and nearly fell. But he caught her, sliding his arms around her to pull her close to his chest.

His heart pounded so hard that she could feel its frantic beat. "Are you all right?" she asked him.

He shook his head.

"You left the hospital too soon." Because of her. Because he'd been worried about her.

"We need to go back," she said. He'd just had surgery to repair the gunshot wound. She doubted doctors had released him yet.

"Yes," he agreed. "We need to go back for you to be treated."

And of course he would be more worried about her than he was about himself. Just as he supported his friend who'd obviously lied to him. And just as he protected her—with no concern for his own life or health.

She felt that panic again that she'd felt when he'd gotten struck in the garage. That feeling that she was falling…but it wasn't over a half wall to the pavement below. She was in far more than physical danger.

She was in danger of falling in love with her bodyguard.

He was shaking. He couldn't stop shaking. He'd come so close to getting caught.

How the hell was that damn bodyguard even alive?

He'd seen the blood spurting out of him. He should have died. But like some avenging angel, he'd rushed to her rescue. He hoped Myers had been too late, though—too late to save her.

She'd stopped fighting him. She'd stopped breathing. She had to have died.

But if Landon Myers had come back from the dead, she might have, as well. So he waited on the street outside the building—deep in the shadows where hopefully no one would see him. He tilted his head, listening for the sound of an ambulance or a police car.

If the bodyguard had been real and not a ghost, wouldn't he have called for help by now? Wouldn't he have tried to save her? And even if he hadn't, the police should have been called…

What the hell was going on?

Then, after several long minutes of waiting, he saw them—standing in the lobby. Both of them. They were alive.

Why the hell couldn't he kill these people no matter how damn many times he'd tried?

He reached for his gun—desperate enough to risk shooting at them again. They might have seen him—might have recognized him. He had to kill them.

But before he could pull out the gun, his phone began to vibrate. Not his real phone but the disposal cell that only one person used to contact him.

Luther Mills.

Damn it. He couldn't talk now. He could barely think for the fear coursing through him. What if they'd seen him?

He'd pulled that hood up around his face again. He wore gloves. They shouldn't have...

But it wasn't a chance he was willing to take. Neither was missing Luther's call, though.

He stepped deeper in the shadows, into an alley between two buildings across the street from the district attorney's offices. "Yes?" he asked in a low whisper.

"It's time," Luther told him.

He'd already been trying, but he didn't want to admit that to Luther—not after the man had told him to back off from Jocelyn Gerber. Did every man she meet fall for the black-haired bitch?

He shook his head. "So you want me to do it now?" He reached for his gun again. Maybe he'd give Luther the satisfaction of hearing the shots ring out...

"Not that," Luther said. "We have bigger concerns."

His stomach lurched with dread. Someone must have figured it out.

Luther continued, "A couple of *things* have gone missing, but not the way I wanted them to. I'm pretty damn certain that they're going to turn up at the worst possible time."

Like his trial.

He knew that the eyewitness had already disappeared to some safe house nobody had been able to find. But now Luther was making it sound like the evidence tech had disappeared, as well. With the evidence?

"So we need that little insurance policy we talked about," Luther said.

"What does that have to do with me?" he asked.

"I need someone I can count on to carry this out," Luther said.

He didn't feel any pride that Luther thought he could count on him. In fact, he just felt sicker, like the walls were closing in on him. Or maybe the bars.

He did not want to wind up in a cell next to Luther Mills. But if he didn't help him, Luther had enough on him to make damn sure he went down with the drug dealer.

He sighed. "What do you want me to do?"

"Pick up that little insurance policy for me," Luther said. "Make sure it's known we have it."

Even though Luther couldn't see it—or maybe because he couldn't—he shook his head. "That's too risky."

"It's necessary," Luther said. "Our insurance policy will be of no use if nobody knows we have it."

But Luther wouldn't have it. He would. It was his freedom he was risking now. Luther had already lost his.

But he was willing to pay dearly to get it back. And he needed money. Badly.

Especially now. The longer Jocelyn Gerber lived, the closer she would get to discovering that he was the one helping Luther. Then he would need that money to escape before he was the one she was prosecuting next.

"Okay…" He murmured his agreement.

And Luther chuckled. "As if you had a choice."

He had one—but it involved giving up his freedom. Jocelyn Gerber didn't offer immunity in exchange for evidence. That was why she couldn't get any of Luther's crew to turn against him.

No. The only way he would get immunity was to kill her and get away before anyone figured out what he'd done.

Chapter 18

Landon swiped the key card through the hotel room door and pushed it open. He pressed his back against it to hold it until Jocelyn walked past him. Then he closed and locked it.

"We're safe here," he assured her as he flipped on the lights. "I made sure nobody followed us. Not even the backup…"

They hadn't caught up with him, though. He suspected they'd gone to her house instead to look for her there. Or maybe they were busy protecting the judge's daughter since Tyce had probably been removed from that assignment.

He didn't give a damn who the hell his friend was related to; he knew Tyce Jackson was a good man, one who could be trusted with anyone's life. But Jocelyn didn't trust Tyce or anyone else at the Payne Protection

Agency right now but him. That was why he'd agreed to her request that nobody know where they were.

"Thank you," she murmured, her voice still raspy.

The line around her neck was still a deep red and even more swollen than when he'd found her not breathing. He shook his head. "Don't thank me," he said. "I should have brought you to the hospital instead of a hotel."

Her lips curved into a smile. "You're the one they would have kept. I'm sure you left against doctor's orders."

He hadn't even bothered to wait to receive doctor's orders, much less follow them. "I'm fine," he insisted.

"So am I," she said.

"I don't know how long you were gone…" His voice cracked as he thought of that moment when he'd felt no pulse.

He touched her neck now, just above the swelling. And he felt her pulse leap beneath his fingertips. He uttered a sigh of relief.

"So you haven't just saved my life," she said as she stepped closer to him. "You brought me back to life." She rose on her tiptoes and pressed her lips to his. "Thank you," she murmured against his mouth.

That kiss jolted him to his core, sending a rush of desire and some other—even stronger—emotion coursing through him. The gunshot wound to his neck and the subsequent blood loss had made him feel so weak—even lifeless. But she…

He lifted his head and murmured, "Now you're the one who's brought me back to life."

Tears rushed to her eyes, making the blue glisten

with moisture. She blinked furiously, but a few drops spilled over and trailed down her cheeks.

He lifted his hands to her face and wiped the tears away with his thumbs. "What's wrong?" he asked. "Why are you crying?" She had every right to cry, but she'd been so brave—so strong.

"I don't want to cost you your life," she said. "I don't want you to die because of me."

He leaned his forehead against hers and sighed. "It won't be because of you. It'll be because of Luther and whoever's working for Luther."

"You really don't believe Tyce Jackson could be...?" she asked.

A slight grin tugged at his lips. "You just can't stop yourself."

"What?" she asked.

"From cross-examining a suspect," he said.

"You're not a suspect," she replied.

He arched a brow. "Really?" he asked. "When you found out one of my best friends could be Luther Mills's brother, you didn't wonder about my allegiance? You didn't worry that I had been recruited to work for Luther, too?"

Her silky skin finally flushed with color. "I was shocked," she admitted. "I didn't know what to think or feel at that point."

He flinched. But he wasn't surprised that she'd doubted him. And he really couldn't blame her. He struggled with trust, too. As a cop, he'd seen too damn much—had been lied to too damn many times—to easily trust anyone.

"I'm sorry," she said again. "I shouldn't have doubted you."

He sighed. "I want you to trust me," he said. "I want you to trust the other bodyguards, so you don't run off by yourself again." He forced himself to step back—to move away from her. "But I can understand why you can't. Hell, maybe you're right to trust no one."

Because he had failed her. His attraction to her had caused him to lose focus. He'd saved her life, but she never should have had the close calls that she had. That was his fault.

He had to fight this attraction—he had to stay focused—for both their sakes.

For both their lives...

His rejection stung. But Jocelyn could understand why he was upset with her. She'd nearly gotten him and herself killed too many times.

Because she couldn't trust...

He'd done nothing to make her doubt him. It was clear he'd had no idea that his friend might be related to Luther Mills. Her pride and her heart stinging with that rejection, she'd retreated to the bathroom. She'd needed to shower and clean up. But she had nothing but the robe over the back of the door to wear. They hadn't gone back to her house. She had no bag—no essentials. Not even any makeup or a comb.

Her face looked so pale and washed out. The dark circles beneath her eyes were the only color on her skin, except for the angry red mark around her throat.

What had the man used? A tie? A rope? She peered closer into the mirror and saw no fibers. It must have been a tie. But it had been too dark for her to see it, to identify who might have been wearing it earlier that day.

The door rattled beneath the tapping of a big fist. "Are you okay in there?" he called out.

No. She wasn't. Like at the hospital, she was hesitant to see him again—because she was so damn worried about how much he was beginning to mean to her.

Too much.

And all she was to him was an assignment, one he was worried that he was going to fail. But her getting hurt, nearly killed, was her fault. She should not have gone off alone like she had.

"Jocelyn?" he called out again, his deep voice sharp with concern. "Are you all right?"

She forced herself to open the door. The steam from her shower rolled out like fog, encasing them in a dreamy, warm cocoon. "I'm fine…" she said.

"I ordered some tea and food from room service," he told her. "You must be sore and starved."

Her stomach pitched at the thought of eating. She didn't want food. She wanted him.

She needed him.

But he'd stepped back from her earlier.

Dare she risk another rejection?

She reached for the sash of the robe and tugged it loose. And the soft terry cloth parted, revealing her naked body.

A low groan tore from his throat. "Jocelyn, you're killing me…"

She tensed, worried that she might. She wouldn't be the one pulling the trigger, but it would still be her fault if something happened to him. "I'm sorry…" And she reached for the sash.

But he tugged it from her fingers. Then he tugged the robe from her body, leaving her completely naked but for the flush spreading over her skin. And that angry red mark around her throat.

She lifted her fingers to her neck to cover it. But he wasn't staring at her wound. He was staring into her eyes—deeply, as if he was looking into her soul rather than at her body.

His breath shuddered out in a ragged sigh. "You are so damn beautiful…"

She shivered. But she wasn't cold; her skin flushed as heat raced through her. He stepped closer to her, leaned down and brushed his mouth across hers. Slowly—just their lips meeting and clinging and moving.

He might have meant the kiss to be tender, gentle, but Jocelyn was too hungry, too overwhelmed with passion. She linked her arms around his neck and held his head to hers. Then she kissed him deeply, passionately.

He groaned and lifted and carried her to the bed. After he laid her down, he stared down at her again, with so much heat and hunger in his gaze. He stripped off his clothes until he was as naked as she was—physically.

Then she saw the hunger and need in his dark gaze, and she knew he was just as naked as she was—as vulnerable. He needed her as badly as she needed him.

But yet he took his time with her, moving his hands and lips slowly, seductively, over every inch of her skin. She touched him, too, sliding her fingertips and her lips over muscles that rippled beneath her touch.

"You're the beautiful one," she told him. She'd never seen a man as perfectly built as he was.

His body slid over hers, skin sliding over skin. She

shivered and clutched at him. She wanted him—so badly.

Then he was there, making love to her with his mouth, making her cry out as she came. But it still wasn't enough. She felt an ache inside her that only he could fill.

He moved off the bed just long enough to sheathe his erection in a condom. Then he returned, but he flipped on his back and pulled her on top of him. She straddled his hips, then guided his erection inside, and finally that emptiness was filled.

She moved and rocked and rose up and down, driving them both out of their minds. He gripped her hips to hold her steady for a moment.

"You're driving me crazy," he said, his eyes bright with passion.

She was burning up—physically and emotionally— as tension wound tightly inside her. She needed a release. So she ground her hips against him, fighting toward that release.

He slid his hands from her hips up her sides until he cupped her breasts. He stroked his thumbs across her tight nipples and she felt the pull from them to her core.

And finally the release hit her, a powerful orgasm moving through her. Her toes curled as she cried out his name.

His hands moved to her hips again, but this time he didn't hold her still; he propelled her to move faster. And she came again, nearly sobbing as pleasure overwhelmed her.

Then his big body tensed beneath her. He groaned and shouted her name.

She collapsed onto his chest. But he didn't let her

rest. Instead, he picked her up and carried her into the bathroom with him.

"What are you doing?"

"Taking a shower," he said as he turned on the faucet.

"I already had one," she reminded him.

"Not with me." And he pulled her under the spray with him. They made love there, too—in the shower, water pouring over them.

Her legs wrapped around his waist, he held her against the tile wall as he thrust into her. She touched the damp bandage on his neck. "Landon, you shouldn't have gotten this wet."

He shrugged, and muscles rippled in his arms and chest. "I'm fine."

He was better than fine. He was perfect.

And Jocelyn was scared…that she was falling in love with her bodyguard.

Parker cursed as Landon's cell phone once again went immediately to voice mail. What the hell had happened to him? Was he all right?

He'd left the hospital against doctor's orders Friday night, and he'd lost his backup bodyguards. Of course Parker had had to pull them for another assignment.

He cursed as he thought about how abysmally they'd failed. He hoped that Landon hadn't, too. He hoped that he and Jocelyn Gerber were all right.

When the voice mail beeped, he said, "Call me back ASAP. Ms. Gerber is going to want to know what Luther's done now. It's going to affect her case."

She'd gone missing, too. Of course, it had only been for the weekend. But this assistant district attorney was known for working weekends. Hell, for working every waking moment.

Was she all right? He'd tried her cell, too, and had left her a similar message. She must have finally played hers because his cell began to vibrate in his hand.

He moved farther into the foyer of Judge Holmes's house. He didn't want to disturb the judge or the others who were crowded in his den.

"What's going to affect my case?" Jocelyn Gerber asked without preamble.

"First off," Parker said, "are you all right?" She had sounded all right when he'd picked up, but now she hesitated. So long that he asked, "Is Landon all right?"

He shouldn't have left the hospital.

"He's fine," she said. "We're fine."

But she didn't sound fine; she sounded unsettled, on edge. But maybe his messages had caused that. Jocelyn Gerber's first concern had always been her case.

"What's going on?" she asked again.

"Bella Holmes has been kidnapped."

She cursed. "I told the judge to take Tyce Jackson off her protection duty. He's Luther's bro—"

"I know," Parker interrupted. "And the judge did remove him, which is probably how she was taken. Tyce would have made damn sure nothing happened to her." He suspected the bodyguard had fallen for the beautiful heiress.

"We have to get her back," Jocelyn said. "Or the judge will need to be recused. And I don't trust anyone else."

"You think Luther could have a judge on his payroll?"

"If he has police officers, evidence techs and someone in the district attorney's office, why wouldn't he have a judge?" Jocelyn asked.

And Parker groaned. If that was the case, then Luther would want Judge Holmes to recuse himself so someone else could preside over his trial. That meant he had no reason to keep Bella Holmes alive.

"We've got to find her," Parker said.

"Yes, we do," Jocelyn agreed. "We'll come to the judge's house."

"He doesn't want you here," Parker said. He hadn't even wanted him to call her. But Parker had been worried about her and Landon anyway. And he'd thought she had a right to know.

"Of course," she said. "He doesn't want any hint of impropriety."

Impropriety was the least of the judge's concerns at the moment. He was probably upset that he'd removed Tyce as his daughter's bodyguard because of what Jocelyn had told him. And it didn't matter to whom Tyce was related. He loved Bella Holmes.

"We have to get her back," Parker murmured aloud.

"I'll talk to Luther," Jocelyn said.

And a deep voice murmured in the background of the call—probably in protest.

Landon wouldn't want Jocelyn anywhere near Luther Mills. Not when he was threatening her, too. And legally Landon couldn't sit in on that meeting to protect her.

Jocelyn Gerber would be alone with the ruthless killer and his corrupt lawyer. No wonder Parker could hear Landon protesting in the background. But was he just worried about protecting her?

Or had he fallen for the beautiful ADA?

Chapter 19

For two days there had been no attempts on her life. Nobody shooting at them or trying to run them down. The only danger had been that Landon was falling harder and harder for the beautiful assistant district attorney.

But Parker's call had reminded him why a relationship between them would never work. Jocelyn cared only about her career—even more than she cared about her life.

"It's too dangerous," he told her even as he drove the Payne Protection Agency SUV toward the jail. "You should not meet with him."

"I won't be alone with him," she said. "His lawyer will be there, and a guard will be right outside the door."

"His lawyer is a sleazebag," Landon said. He didn't

know who was representing Luther, but that anyone who did was as immoral as he was. "You can't trust him."

"The guards—"

"Can't be trusted either," he reminded her. "Especially now. They have to know that they're being investigated. They may blame you for that."

"The chief and I are working together on that investigation," she admitted. "But they don't have anything to worry about—"

"Unless they're working for him," he said. And that concerned him. Luther had gotten to too many people. He'd bought or manipulated them into doing what he wanted. And what he wanted was for Jocelyn Gerber to die, probably so that his mole in the DA's office could take over his case. "You can't do this," Landon said even as he pulled up to take a ticket from the parking meter for the jail visiting lot. "It's not safe."

"I'm a hell of a lot safer than the judge's daughter is right now," Jocelyn said. "I don't even want to think about what might be happening to her…" She shuddered, so it was apparent that she was thinking about it.

Landon sucked in a breath. From his years of working vice, he knew, too.

"We have to do what we can to find her," Jocelyn persisted.

He nodded and pulled the SUV into a parking spot.

She flipped down the visor and looked into the mirror to adjust the scarf she'd looped around her neck. After spending two days in that hotel room barely wearing anything, they'd had to stop at her house to pick up clothes and to make sure the neighbor had been taking care of the cat like she'd promised. Jocelyn had grabbed a couple of scarves to hide the angry bruise around her neck.

"Are you sure you're up for this?" Landon asked her.

She nodded. "I have to be."

"Jocelyn—"

"I am," she assured him. "I feel fine. I just don't like how it looks. And I don't want Luther to see it."

"And know how close he came to succeeding in having you killed?"

"We're not sure that he was behind the attack."

He sighed. "You'd still rather believe it was someone else."

"I don't know what to believe," she said. And she turned toward him, her blue eyes soft with regret. "I was wrong about your friend. Parker made it clear that if Tyce hadn't been removed as Bella's bodyguard, she probably wouldn't have been abducted."

"He can't know that," Landon said. Jocelyn had nearly died several times with him protecting her. "Tyce might have been killed trying to protect her."

"I think that's what he meant," Jocelyn said. "That Tyce would have died before letting anyone take her."

"So you saved Tyce's life," he assured her. "And we'll save Bella's." If she was still alive…

He wasn't sure exactly what Luther wanted with her. Did he really think he'd manipulate the judge into ruling in his favor and that Jocelyn would let that happen? He had to know she'd make the judge recuse himself.

And maybe that was what he wanted. He could have a judge in his pocket just like he had an ADA and who the hell knew how many cops.

"Okay," he said. And he opened his door and walked around the hood, careful to check the parking lot for any sign of that car with the tinted windows. But he'd made certain nobody had followed him here.

The shooter could have been waiting for them, though, because Jocelyn had had to call that sleazy lawyer to set up this meeting. It wouldn't have been legal if she hadn't.

He walked around and opened her door. Jocelyn swung her legs out. And an image flashed through his mind of those long, toned legs wrapped around his waist, wound over his shoulders, bent over...

Desire rushed over him, heating his blood. They'd made love so many times, but he still ached for her.

Jocelyn drew in a deep breath, as if bracing herself, before she stepped out onto the asphalt.

Landon knew she didn't like visiting the jail any more than he liked her visiting it. But it was part of her job, and Jocelyn didn't shy away from any part of her job—no matter how tough or how dangerous.

A guard at her side, Jocelyn walked up to the door of the little conference room where she would meet with Luther and his lawyer. Her heels clicked against the concrete floor, sounding like small-caliber gunshots echoing off the concrete walls and ceiling, too. Instinctively, she felt the urge to duck and take cover.

"His lawyer is already inside," the guard told her as he reached for the door. "But we're bringing Luther down from his cell right now."

Luther. Not the inmate. Not even Mills...

Landon was right. She couldn't trust the guards—at least, not one who was on a first-name basis with a dangerous murderer. She glanced behind the burly guard, wishing she would see Landon. But the guards searching him must not have been done yet. She'd been searched and had headed back alone.

She'd hated to leave him—especially after the two days they'd had together. Two days that had seemed like a dream. They couldn't have been real; she couldn't have experienced as much pleasure as he'd given her.

But she had.

The guard opened the door and held it for her. "Ms. Gerber, have you changed your mind?"

She shook her head and stepped inside. The lawyer sat already at the table in the conference room. Even though it was late at night, he looked perfectly coiffed, his black hair slicked back. His suit was perfect, too.

Jocelyn lifted her fingers to her throat, checking that the scarf hadn't slipped. She wore it for protection, to hide the bruises, but now she realized it could be used as a weapon like her attacker must have used his tie. Maybe she shouldn't have worn it.

But it was too late now. The door on the other side of the room opened and Luther Mills stepped in, a grin curving his lips when he saw her.

"It's like my dream come to life," Luther murmured as he took the seat across from her. "The things you and I were just doing, Jocelyn…" His dark-eyed gaze slipped from her face down over her body, and he wriggled his brows at her.

She resisted the urge to shudder with revulsion. That was what he wanted—to affect her, to scare her. So she stared down her nose at him. "I am not here to discuss your dreams, Mr. Mills."

"That's a damn shame," he said. "I think you might like what I was doing to you."

Her disgust churned in her stomach, but she only

glared at him, acting as unmoved as possible. Luther Mills was a predator looking for the weakest victim, so she could show no weakness to him.

"Mr. Mills," his lawyer intervened, sweat beginning to bead on his high forehead. "Ms. Gerber called this meeting with concerns that you're behind the abduction of Judge Holmes's daughter." And it was clear that he shared her concerns but wanted no part of this one of Luther's crimes.

Luther widened his eyes with obviously feigned innocence. "The judge has a daughter?" he asked. "I didn't even know that."

Jocelyn glared at him again. "Everyone knows how much the judge's daughter means to him."

"More than justice?" Luther scoffed. "I find that hard to believe."

Luther had apparently never loved anyone more than himself or his money. He didn't understand how far a person might go to protect someone they loved.

She thought of Landon, of that bullet striking his neck. She could have lost him so easily. But then, he really wasn't hers to lose—despite their idyllic weekend. He was still just her bodyguard.

And the reason she needed a bodyguard was because of this man. Sure, other people had threatened her, but it was too much of a coincidence for them to act on those threats now—when Luther was trying to take out everyone associated with his trial. Even the judge's innocent daughter.

"Your plan is not going to work," she told Luther.

He leaned forward, so that his face neared hers.

She forced herself not to pull back as he studied her very intently and unsettlingly.

"What do you think my plan is?" he asked her.

"You're going to use his daughter to make the judge rule in your favor," Jocelyn said.

"You think he would do something like that? That he would compromise the system like that?" He sounded as if he really wanted her to answer.

And that worried her. She had to be honest, though. "No. Your plan won't work," she answered him. "Judge Holmes will recuse himself, and another judge will get assigned to your trial."

He grinned, probably unable to not gloat over what he considered another victory over justice.

She gasped as she realized that was what his plan really was. "That's what you want. Another judge—one who works for you."

"Everybody thinks you work for me, Jocelyn," Luther taunted her.

Heat rushed to her face. It was so damn embarrassing that everyone thought that. She shook her head in denial.

But he continued, "Because you've conveniently lost every case against me."

"Nothing about that was convenient," she said.

"Hurt your career a bit, huh?" He snickered. "We both know you wouldn't be trying this case if your boss wasn't on maternity leave."

"In all those other cases against you, I didn't have Judge Holmes."

"Of course, I don't know what you're talking about, but you won't have him now either. If something happens to his daughter…"

"It won't," she said, and she was forced to bluff. She hoped like hell that her bluff proved to be the truth.

She could not lose Judge Holmes. "Tyce Jackson has found her."

He leaned closer and narrowed his eyes, studying her even more intently. "Really?" Luther asked. "He found her?"

She nodded.

"Alive?" he asked with surprise.

Jocelyn heard the surprise in his voice, and her heart slammed against her ribs. That poor girl.

It sounded as if Luther was certain she was dead. And there was only one way he would be certain—because he'd ordered her killed.

She gasped.

He wasn't entirely certain, though, because he kept staring at her. "You were lying, right, Ms. Gerber?" he prodded her. "Tyce didn't find her, did he?"

He sounded worried about the man she now knew was his brother. He didn't claim him as much, though, so he probably hadn't ordered anyone to spare his life. Did he think Tyce had been killed trying to rescue her?

It was a distinct possibility. And she felt sick as she thought of Landon losing his friend, of a man losing his life. She hoped like hell if Tyce had found her that he and the judge's daughter had made it out alive.

She stood up and headed toward the door. Just as Landon had warned her, this had been a waste of time. For her...

She had a horrible feeling that Luther had gotten more information out of her than she had him. She had no proof that he'd ordered the judge's daughter abducted or worse.

She had nothing to use against him to coerce him to turn over the girl. She could only hope that Tyce Jackson was as good at his job as Landon was at his, and that he would save Bella just like Landon had saved her.

Over and over again…

Luther whistled as the ADA turned and walked out into the hall. He hadn't been lying about dreaming about her. It would almost be fun to face her in court. And it definitely sounded as if that was where they were heading. He hadn't been able to get the charges thrown out before the trial.

So he had to win the trial.

And he needed Judge Holmes to either be on his side or off the bench for that to happen.

"What the hell did you do?" his lawyer asked him. But then he held up a hand, with a lot of rings on it, and shook his head. "No. Don't tell me. I don't want to know."

Luther sighed. "Deniable culpability…whatever the hell you go on about."

"I don't want to talk about this," the man said as he began to rise from the chair.

"You're not going anywhere," Luther told him. And he held out his hand now—for the lawyer's phone. He'd hidden his untraceable cell in his jail cell—just in case Jocelyn had ordered him searched when he came into the room. He wouldn't have put it past her.

She was so damn smart.

And careful…

That had to be the only reason she was still alive, that and her damn bodyguard, Landon Myers. Landon had always been a pain in the ass with that protective streak of his. No wonder he made such a good body-guard.

Was Luther's half brother as good a bodyguard?

Had Tyce found Bella Holmes?

Luther punched in some numbers on his lawyer's cell phone and pressed it to his ear. "Tell me you still have her."

The lawyer closed his eyes and pressed his hand over them. If he was trying to be one of those little caricature monkeys, he should have covered his ears, so he would hear no evil. Closing his eyes just meant he couldn't see it.

"I'm not with her," the ADA on Luther's payroll replied.

"Why the hell not?"

But Luther knew—he was afraid to get caught.

"She's not going to get away. Your crew members are protecting her."

Not enough of them, just some young, dumb kids. Luther needed to send in more mature and more dangerous backup. But thanks to the damn Payne Protection Agency, he kept losing crew members.

Like Tyce. He'd once been a member of his crew. But he'd just been undercover, trying to get evidence to bring down Luther. If he died trying to save the judge's daughter, then so be it.

He probably wasn't the only half sibling Luther had anyway. "You didn't notice anyone watching the place?" he asked.

"No. You think someone found her?" the guy asked, his voice rising with a hint of panic.

Tyce could. He knew the area. He knew a lot of Luther's crew. He felt a flash of panic, too. "I better get more guys out there just in case."

Just in case little Ms. Gerber hadn't been bluffing.

Before he could disconnect to make another call, the ADA said, "I shouldn't have been involved in this. I've met the judge's daughter. She might have recognized my voice."

"Then I guess you should have made sure she was dead before you left the warehouse," Luther said.

And his lawyer groaned.

"But then, I don't think you have the stomach for killing," Luther told the guy. "Or Ms. Gerber wouldn't have just paid me a visit."

"She was there? At the jail?"

"Yup. Alive and well."

The ADA snorted. "Not that well. She's been missing since I strangled her the other night."

That was why she'd worn that scarf around her neck. "Tried," Luther said. "You didn't succeed. Just like I said, you don't have the stomach for it."

"You told me to back off," the ADA reminded him. "So I was just going to slip some evidence into her filing cabinet."

"Evidence? Against me?"

"Against her," the man replied. "The drop phone I used to talk to you."

"Are you framing her or me?" Luther asked. Maybe he needed to take out this ADA instead of Jocelyn Gerber.

"It wouldn't hold up in court, but it makes her look guilty," the man replied. "I saw her coming in as I was about to leave."

"So you decided to strangle her even though I told you to back off."

"I'd put her bodyguard in the hospital, so she was

finally alone," the man explained. "I had to take advantage of the opportunity."

"Landon Myers is in the hospital?"

"Was—but just for a little while. He got out in time to save her again."

That was what those damn bodyguards did—swooped to the rescue. He had to get more of his crew over to the warehouse to make sure nobody got the judge's daughter out alive. But before he clicked off, he told the guy, "You better not fail next time you try to kill her."

"When's that?"

"Now." The guy had been able to get close to her because no one had suspected him yet. But if the judge's daughter lived and was able to identify him, he would never get close to Jocelyn Gerber again. And if the guy died trying to kill his coworker, like the rookie cop had died trying to kill Rosie, it was just one more loose end Luther wouldn't have to clean up.

Chapter 20

Landon closed his eyes and tried to shut out the sound of water running in the bathroom. As soon as they had returned to her house from the jail, Jocelyn had headed to the shower—needing to wash off her visit with Luther Mills.

Landon wanted to join her in the shower, but guilt was already weighing heavily on him. While his assignment was to protect Jocelyn, he was also part of a team—a team he hadn't been supporting as much as he should have been. He was worried about his friends.

Fortunately, Clint and Hart were safe now—since the people they were protecting had agreed to go into safe houses far from Luther's reach. But since they were safe, Keeli and Tyce were in even more danger. Especially Tyce.

He had to be trying to find the judge's daughter.

Landon didn't want to bother him, but he had to know if he was all right.

Even though he expected the call to go straight to voice mail, he punched Tyce's contact on his cell screen. When a male voice answered, he nearly dropped it—especially when he realized it wasn't Tyce who'd picked up the call.

"Parker?"

"Yeah…" His boss uttered a ragged-sounding sigh that rattled the phone.

"What's wrong?" Landon anxiously asked. "Why are you answering Tyce's phone?"

"He was shot. He's in surgery."

Landon's stomach flipped as it filled with dread. "What happened?"

"He rescued the judge's daughter."

"Is she all right?" Landon asked. Or had Bella Holmes been shot, too?

"She's fine," Parker said. "Tyce found her and saved her—all on his own. But he got shot in the process. I'm not sure if it happened before or after we arrived as backup. We got there just as Luther's backup arrived. It was…" His voice cracked. "It got crazy…"

"Is anyone else hurt?" Landon asked.

"I don't think any of Luther's crew survived."

"What about the Payne Protection bodyguards?" Landon asked. "Are they all okay?"

"Everyone is except for Tyce."

"How bad is it?" he asked, fear making his voice gruff.

"He carried her out of the warehouse, got her to safety, made sure she was treated before he collapsed," Parker said.

But that was because Tyce was a beast. He was big and strong and determined.

"How bad is he hurt?" Landon asked again.

"I don't know," Parker said. "He's been in surgery for a while."

Which meant that there was considerable damage. "Damn it…" he said.

"It was weird how Luther's crew showed up," Parker said. "It was as if they'd been tipped off that Tyce had found her. What the hell did Ms. Gerber say to him at the jail? That was where you brought her, right?"

"Yeah…" he conceded. "But I wasn't in on the meeting."

"So you don't know what she told him."

"She wouldn't have said Tyce found her," Landon said. "Until now, I didn't know Tyce had any idea where to find her." But he should have known that he would figure it out. Tyce had been undercover for a long time as part of Luther's crew. So he might have had some idea where she was being held.

Parker sighed. "I don't know."

"What?" Landon asked.

"I don't know if we should trust Jocelyn," he replied. "You might have been right about her this whole time."

"No, I wasn't," Landon said. "And you know it. All the attempts on her life prove she's not working for Luther."

"But you're the one who's gotten hurt all those times," Parker said. "Not her…"

"That's not…" And he remembered he hadn't told Parker about the attempt in her office—when she'd nearly been strangled. So he did it now.

Parker cursed him.

"That's why we disappeared for a while," Landon said.

"Because you didn't trust anyone?" Parker asked. "Because you believed her about Tyce being in collusion with Luther? I don't know what happened in her office, but I think you were smart not to trust her. And I don't think you should now, not after what happened to Tyce."

Landon knew his boss was upset, so he wasn't going to argue with him—even though he wanted to hotly defend Jocelyn. "Let me know when Tyce is out of surgery," he said.

"Don't bring her near the hospital," Parker warned him. "Nobody wants her around here."

That wasn't true. Landon wanted her. Badly...

Understanding that Parker was rightfully worried about Tyce, Landon just disconnected the call. He was sliding his cell into his pocket when he heard the ding of another cell phone receiving a text. It wasn't his, or he would have felt it.

And he could have sworn Jocelyn had brought her cell upstairs with her when she'd gone to take her shower. The sound dinged again, and he realized it came from the briefcase she'd left on the coffee table. Curious as to why she would have two phones, he walked over to it. She must have shoved something in it as they'd come inside because the briefcase wasn't fully closed. Usually it was shut and locked.

He took the opportunity to flip it open, and his stomach pitched when he looked inside. Lying on top of a pile of folders was the phone and a prescription bottle with the label torn off. What the hell had been in the bottle?

The sleeping pills that had drugged their backup

bodyguards? Why would she have drugged them, though?

He stared down at the phone. The text highlighted on the screen said, Thanks for the heads-up that Tyce had found our insurance policy.

He sucked in a breath, feeling like he'd been sucker punched. He'd wanted to go into that room with her and Luther to protect her. But he'd needed to be inside to protect his friend and himself.

Because not only his stomach hurt; his heart ached, too, feeling as if it was breaking.

He'd been such a fool to change his mind about her. An even bigger fool for trusting her. And the biggest fool for beginning to fall for her.

Jocelyn had been hoping that Landon would join her in the shower. Once she'd washed off the revulsion she'd felt from her visit with Luther Mills and his sleazy lawyer, she'd still felt chilled. Scared that Luther might just get away with murder again.

And she'd needed Landon's arms around her, holding her, comforting her, keeping her safe.

She'd needed the heat of their passion to chase away all her fears and concerns again, like it had this weekend. But the weekend hadn't lasted forever, no matter how much she'd wished it had. And because she'd wished they could go back—to the weekend and that safe hotel suite—she'd gone downstairs, in only her towel, to find him.

She found him leaning over her briefcase, and she gasped in shock. "You're still snooping through my stuff?" she asked. And despite the towel wrapped around her, she felt completely naked and vulnerable and incredibly hurt. "You can't still think I'm working for Luther?"

"I can't?" he asked, as he turned toward her. His handsome face was flushed with anger, his jaw rigid with it. "When he sends you a text thanking you for the tip about Tyce knowing where Bella Holmes was being held?"

"What?" she asked. "My phone's upstairs." Out of habit, she'd brought it with her into the bathroom. She never knew when her boss might call her. She'd also wanted it close in case someone called her about the situation with the judge's daughter.

"Not that phone," he said. "This phone." And he pointed to the cell phone lying atop the folders in her briefcase. "The one you use to communicate with Luther Mills."

She shook her head. "That's not my phone."

"The bottle isn't yours either?" he asked.

"No," she said, and now anger gripped her, that he could actually suspect even for a moment that those things were hers. "I found the phone and bottle in my filing cabinet in the office..." Her voice cracked with that anger now as it overwhelmed her. "...right before someone tried to strangle me to death."

Before they'd left her office, she'd shoved them into her briefcase with the intent of turning them over to the chief when she felt safe, when she'd been confident that she could trust anyone besides Landon.

Clearly now he didn't trust her. He closed his eyes as if he couldn't bear the sight of her.

"Do you honestly think I did that to myself?" she asked. "After everything you know about me now, how can you think I would ever work for Luther Mills?"

He sighed and opened his eyes, which were full of regret. "I'm sorry. I just talked to Parker—"

"Have they found the judge's daughter?" she asked. He nodded.

"Is she okay?"

"She is," he confirmed, but there was fear yet in his voice.

And she knew. "Tyce isn't…"

"He was shot rescuing her," Landon said. "Parker said it was as if someone tipped off Luther and he sent in reinforcements." He held up the cell phone. "Then Luther sent this text to this phone."

She looked at the screen now, reading the thank-you message. She shuddered in revulsion and felt as if she needed to shower again. "That's not my phone," she repeated. "And, unfortunately, there's probably no way to prove that message came from Luther."

But why had he sent it? Did he know she had it now? Was he just messing with her?

Tears stung her eyes, and she blinked furiously to fight them from falling. "But it is my fault," she murmured as guilt pressed on her lungs. "I was trying to scare him into giving up information that might lead to where Bella was being held, so I bluffed that Tyce had already found her." She shook her head at her stupidity. "I should have known that Luther was too smart to fall for it."

"You weren't bluffing," Landon said. "Tyce had figured out where she was being held."

"Is he going to be okay?" she asked, her heart pounding hard with dread and fast with fear.

Landon's broad shoulders lifted in a weak shrug. "He's in surgery."

That didn't sound good.

"But Tyce is tough. He got her out and got her to the hospital to be checked out before anybody even realized he'd been shot."

What kind of people were the Payne Protection bodyguards? Shot in the neck, blood gushing from his wound, Landon had still managed to save her.

She pointed toward the pill bottle. "That must have been what was used to drug the backup bodyguards," she said. "Why would I do that? Why would I help Luther Mills? You know I don't need money. All I need is justice."

And him—she needed him. But he couldn't trust her. So they had no future. Hell, even if he could trust her, they had no future. She had to focus on her job, on making sure criminals like Luther Mills were brought to justice.

Landon stepped closer and cupped her bare shoulders in his big hands. "I'm sorry," he said. "I shouldn't have doubted you."

"I understand why you did," she admitted. "I can't believe Luther sent that text."

"Who else—"

"No," she said. "I know it's him." Even if they would never be able to prove it. "But I don't know why he would have."

"To mess with you," Landon said. "To make you feel guilty, to knock you off your game—because he knows he's going to court now."

She sucked in a breath as she realized he was right. She would soon have to face Luther Mills again—in court. And she could not lose or he would be free and even more dangerous than he was behind bars.

"That's not all he's going to do, though," Landon said. "He's going to step up his efforts to try to take you out, so that whoever is working for him in the DA's office can take over his case."

She shivered, very cold despite his touch on her bare skin. But she was not about to back down—from Luther Mills or from Landon.

She wanted him. But she was afraid that wasn't all. She needed him. Hell, she might even love him. She lifted her arms to link them behind his neck, and she pulled his head down to hers.

"Jocelyn…" he murmured, his brown eyes even darker with desire and something else. Fear. For her or for him?

It was clear he wanted to say more—about Luther, about the case, about her prosecuting the case—but she didn't want to hear it. She didn't want to think about it.

She only wanted to feel that passion only he had ever made her feel. She rose up on tiptoe and pressed her mouth to his, kissing him deeply.

A groan emanated from his throat as he kissed her back with the same intensity and hunger she felt for him. He pulled away and murmured her name again. But then he lifted and carried her toward the stairs. He rushed up to her bedroom, where he set her on her feet again.

The towel had loosened and dropped from her body, leaving her naked before him. But she wasn't just physically naked. She felt emotionally stripped, too.

Hurt that he'd doubted her. Vulnerable that she'd cared so much that he had.

Did she already love him?

She was more afraid that she might than she was even afraid of Luther Mills. She didn't want to be in love.

But Landon was her hero in so many ways. She reached for the buttons on his shirt, needing him as bare as she was, needing to feel his heart beating against hers. As she attacked the buttons, he slipped off his holster and placed it on the table next to the bed. Then he shrugged off the shirt and unbuttoned his jeans, dropping them and his boxers to the floor.

He obviously wanted her as badly as she wanted him. His erection jutted toward her. But when she reached for him, he pulled back. Then he leaned down and fumbled in his pocket for a condom.

Before he could roll it on, she reached out and closed her fingers around him. Then she leaned over and made love to him with her mouth.

He groaned and tangled his fingers in her hair, gently pulling her back. "I need to be inside you," he said, his voice gruff with desire. "I need to be part of you."

That was how it felt when they made love—like they were no longer separate, like they became one being. She lay back on the bed and held her arms out for him.

His hand shook as he rolled on the condom. Then he joined her on the bed. She parted her legs and he knelt between them, easing gently inside her. She arched up and wrapped her limbs around him, holding him tight as she took him deeper.

A low moan tore from her throat as the first orgasm moved through her. The tension had been wound so tightly inside her, that was all it took. But he built the tension again with slow, deep strokes, as he lowered his head and kissed her.

First he brushed his lips over hers. Then he moved

them down her throat. She gasped as his tongue stroked across her bruised skin.

"I'm sorry..." he said.

The strangling wasn't his fault, and he knew that. She was the one who'd gone out with no protection. So she suspected he was apologizing for earlier—for those brief moments he'd doubted her.

Warmth flooded her, but it wasn't just desire this time. She felt so much more for Landon, things she'd never wanted to feel for anyone or anything but her job.

He slid his arm under her back and lifted her up as he eased back on his haunches. She straddled his thighs, then locked her legs around his waist. In this position, her body was aligned with his, so that her breasts were nearly on the level with his face.

He took advantage of that fact, and he closed his lips around a taut nipple. He gently tugged on it, and she moaned, the tension winding so tightly inside her again.

He thrust up, sliding even deeper inside her. Desperate for release, she moved and rocked against him as she clutched at his broad shoulders. Then she lowered her head and nipped at his shoulder.

He chuckled, then groaned as she swiped her tongue across it. Then she shifted her lips to his throat and then his mouth, kissing him deeply. They moved as one, their rhythm completely in sync, and that was how they found their pleasure, crying out as it overwhelmed them.

Shaken and spent from the powerful orgasm, Jocelyn felt boneless and limply sank into the mattress when he released her. Within seconds, after cleaning up, he was back with her, pulling her into his arms.

His chest rose and fell with pants for breath and the powerful beat of his heart.

Hers beat with the same intensity. Even though she'd found release, she'd also found more fear—because she knew without a doubt that she loved him.

He had his emergency bag packed, complete with a forged passport and a substantial amount of cash. He would get more—so much more money—if he stayed and made sure that Luther Mills got away with murder again. But if he stayed, he risked getting caught and losing his freedom.

And despite the money he'd made working for Luther, he didn't have enough to get away with his crimes like Luther did. And once it was known what he'd done, he would have no allies—only enemies.

A phone vibrated on the table near his bed. Two of them sat on it, the one on which Luther called him and his real cell phone. He stared at them, wondering which it was.

Luther calling…wondering if he'd killed Jocelyn Gerber yet. Or Jocelyn calling…wondering why the hell he wasn't at the office yet.

He stepped away from the suitcase he was packing on the bed and stared down at the phone. Judge Holmes…

Was it a trick? Was the man calling to put him on speaker for his daughter to identify his voice? He'd been careful to disguise it when he'd spoken to the judge during her abduction. He'd even used a special device to digitally alter the sound of his voice. But because he hadn't thought Bella Holmes would make it out of captivity alive, he hadn't bothered disguising it around her.

Of course, he'd met her only a couple of times in the judge's chambers. And being the social butterfly she was, she met new people all the time. He doubted that she would be able to place him.

So he punched in the accept button.

"This is Judge Holmes." The older man needlessly identified himself. "I am trying to get a hold of ADA Gerber. Do you have any idea where she might be?"

Before he answered, he coughed and sputtered, so that the judge would think he had a cold. "No, Your Honor. I'm sorry. I don't know where she could be."

"She's not at the office."

"I'm not at the office either," he replied. "I've been battling a flu bug for a couple of weeks now." An illness would explain his disappearances and absences over the past couple of weeks—if anyone had noticed.

"I'm sorry to hear that," the judge replied. "I thought you might be Ms. Gerber's second chair for Luther Mills's trial."

He should have been first. "I think Jocelyn has determined she can handle the prosecution on her own. And isn't that trial a couple of weeks off yet?"

"An opening came up in the docket, and we're able to start sooner than expected," he replied, "as long as the lawyers have no objections."

Luther would have objections and more demands on *him*. Jocelyn had to die now before the trial could start. Of course the judge was eager to begin the trial, because he wouldn't be able to bring his daughter home from wherever he'd hidden her until it was all over.

"I will be heading into the office soon, Your Honor," he said. "If I see Jocelyn, I will tell her to contact you."

"Thank you." The judge clicked off the cell.

He tossed his phone down and uttered a low growl of frustration. He had no choice now. He could not fail again. This time—when he tried—he had to make damn certain he killed Jocelyn Gerber.

Chapter 21

Jocelyn trembled against him, a cry slipping through her lips. Landon had already been lying awake, unable to sleep, because he was so damn worried about her. She must have been worried, too, because even in her sleep, she could not rest. He tightened his arm around her and rubbed her bare back with his other hand.

"Shhh," he murmured. "It's all right. I have you."

She jerked awake and stared up at him, her blue eyes wide with fear. She reached out a shaking hand and touched his face. "You're okay…"

So her nightmare hadn't been about something happening to her, but to him.

He shook his head. "I'm not okay," he said.

"No." Her fingers skimmed over the healing wound on his neck. "You're going to have a scar."

A scar was the least of his concerns. He was more worried about having a broken heart. And he would if anything happened to her. "I'm not okay," he said, "because I'm worried about you. I want you to give up the case."

She tensed and stared up at him, the fear turning to confusion then anger in her blue eyes. "What? How can you ask me to do that?"

"Because it's too dangerous."

She shook her head. "What's too dangerous would be letting Luther Mills back on the streets. He can't keep getting away with his crimes. He needs to go to prison."

"You don't have to be the one to send him there," Landon pointed out. "Someone else can do it."

"You're the one who's been adamant that someone within the DA's office is working for him. If I give up the case, that person might get it, and then Luther would once again escape justice." She shook her head. "I can't risk that. I can't be the one who lets him go free."

"If you try this, you might be," he goaded her. "You don't know that he'll get convicted even with you prosecuting him."

Her already pale skin grew paler, and her breath escaped in a shaky sigh. "You still don't think I'm good at my job."

"I don't trust Luther Mills," he said. "And neither should you."

"Of course I don't!"

"You don't know what he might pull next," Landon said. "It's too dangerous for you to take him on."

"It's too late," she said. "I already have."

And she had the marks for her trouble—the scrape on her shoulder, the dark bruise around her neck. She could have already been killed. He didn't like her chances for surviving the trial.

"And I'm not backing down," she said.

Fear filled Landon's heart—fear for her and for himself. But he had to say it. He cared too much not to lay it all out there, not to lay himself bare.

"Not even for me?" he asked.

Her brow furrowed. "I can't believe you would ask me to do this… You've wanted to get Luther Mills probably as long as I have."

"I still do," he said. "But I don't want to lose you in the process. I care too much, Jocelyn." He loved her, but before he could open his mouth to say those words, she put her fingers over his lips.

"Don't…"

Before he could say or do anything else, she tugged free of his arms and rushed out of the bed into the adjacent bathroom. Then he heard it, too, the ringing of her cell phone.

She'd rather take a call than hear his declaration of love. Was that because she didn't feel the same way?

"That was a quick trip back," Luther remarked as he walked into the small conference room to meet with his lawyer. He watched the other door, but it didn't open. "Just you and me?" he asked as he took a seat at the table.

His lawyer nodded, but not a slicked-back hair on his head moved.

Luther rubbed his hands together, feeling that fortunes were at last turning back in his favor. That ADA must have finally successfully gotten rid of Jocelyn Gerber.

"What's up?" he asked.

"Your trial," the lawyer replied.

He nodded. "Yeah, in a couple weeks," he said.

The lawyer shook his head now. "No. A couple of days. Judge Holmes cleared his docket and got it moved up."

Was that the judge's way of getting back at him for messing with his daughter? Not that he could prove Luther had anything to do with that.

Nobody could. The only person alive who could testify to his involvement was too smart to risk it. Not only would it implicate himself, but it would end his life.

Luther's heart began to race, and not with the good kind of excitement. "No. That's too soon. We haven't found the witness or gotten rid of the evidence yet."

The lawyer shrugged.

"Why the hell did you let that happen?" Luther demanded to know. "I pay you the big bucks to help me." But he'd done damn little of that so far.

"I had no argument to use against the judge moving up the date," the lawyer replied. "I thought you'd be eager to get out of here."

"To go to court?" Luther asked. He shook his head. "I want to get out of here for good." Not just to be brought back at the end of each day of the trial.

Another plan was already taking shape in his mind, though. He wasn't giving up yet. And if Jocelyn Gerber was to suddenly turn up dead, the trial would have to be postponed while another assistant district attorney was brought up to speed on the case. That would give him a little more time to perfect his new plan, so it wouldn't fail as badly as his previous one—to take out everyone associated with his trial—had failed.

That would have been ideal, would have gotten the charges against him dropped. But since that wouldn't work, he would have to adapt.

The lawyer looked at him uneasily. He probably knew that Luther was coming up with something. But he didn't ask what it was, because of that plausible deniability thing he kept talking about. He was going to have to forget about that, though, and finally earn all the money Luther was paying him.

Because this new plan could not fail. Luther was not going to prison for the rest of his life. Hell, once he got out of jail, he intended to never return. Luther Mills was not going down for the crimes he'd already committed or for the ones he was about to commit.

Jocelyn loved Landon so damn much. That was why she'd stopped him from saying whatever he'd been about to say. If he'd been about to declare his feelings for her, she hadn't wanted to hear them. If he felt the same way about her...

Then she might not be able to follow through with what she needed to do. She needed to prosecute Luther Mills. And she would be doing that sooner than expected per the call she'd just taken from Judge Holmes.

She couldn't give that her full attention if she knew that Landon was in danger because of her. And if he continued to be her bodyguard during the trial, he would be in danger.

She wouldn't be able to get him removed from the assignment, though. After she'd been so wrong about Tyce Jackson, she doubted that Parker Payne would listen to her. Like the rest of his team, he didn't even like her. Those people were Landon's friends. Even if she survived the trial, she knew that she and Landon could never have a relationship.

The people who mattered most to him couldn't stand her. They would never support their being together. So it wasn't as if she had the hope of a future with Landon anyway. But she wanted him to have a future.

So she had to get him to quit his job. She had to make him mad enough to no longer want to protect her. She wasn't sure what that might take since being protective was such a part of his nature.

She reached for the bathroom door and drew in a deep breath, bracing herself for what she had to do. She'd pulled on the robe she'd left hanging on the back of the door and had tied it tightly around herself, as if it might hold her together when she felt like falling apart.

She didn't want to lose Landon. But it was better to lose him as a lover than for him to lose his life. Just as she'd struggled after her grandparents' murders, she would struggle after Landon's—struggle with living in a world without him. He might hate her, but she wouldn't care as long as he was safe.

She pulled open the door and stepped out.

"Who was that?" Landon asked. He'd pulled on his jeans but left them unbuttoned and riding low on his lean hips. He was so damn good-looking it wasn't fair—not to Jocelyn's furiously pounding heart.

She wanted him again. But she loved him too much to keep putting him in danger. She replied, "Judge Holmes."

"Is Tyce okay?" he asked.

She nodded. "Yes. He and Bella are going out of

the country, so nobody can get to her during the trial. The judge has also managed to move up the trial date."

Landon gasped. "Why would he do that?"

She suspected that it was for the same reason she was happy that he had. "So all this will be over soon."

"It's too dangerous," Landon said, as he had just a short time ago.

She agreed, but instead, she shook her head. "It's smart. We need to get Luther convicted and sentenced to a high-security prison with guards who will hopefully do him no special favors."

She hadn't figured out yet which ones were helping him, but she and the chief would. Woodrow Lynch was as determined to stop Luther as she was.

"You don't need to have any part in this," Landon said. "You can let someone else do this."

"The only person I would trust to try Luther besides me is off on maternity leave," she reminded him. "I have to do this."

He drew in a deep breath. "Okay, then I'll do everything in my power to keep you safe."

That was her greatest fear. She shook her head. "I don't think that's a good idea," she said.

His brow furrowed. "What?"

"Your protecting me," she said.

"Why not?"

She gestured at the bed with the sheets tangled from their lovemaking. "We crossed a line, Landon."

"We did more than that," he said, and he moved closer, his arms outstretched for her.

But she stepped back. He could not touch her. If he did, she might not stick with her plan. "No." She shook her head. "We didn't."

"What are you saying?"

"That being with you was a good distraction from worrying about the case," she said. "But that's all it was. And now I can't afford any distractions."

He snorted. "Just a distraction…"

Maybe he knew her better than she'd realized now. Maybe he already knew how she felt about him, that she loved him.

She turned away from him, so he wouldn't see the longing on her face. And hopefully he would think she was dismissing him and what they'd shared. She opened her closet door and peered inside, but she couldn't see any of the clothes hanging from the rods because tears were blurring her vision.

She kept her voice clear and sharp, though, when she replied, "Yes. You must know you and I have no future together." And they wouldn't, if he died. But she forced herself to sound haughty and snobbish and added, "My parents would never approve of my involvement with a *bodyguard*."

She silently apologized for misrepresenting the people who'd raised her. They were not snobs. They didn't care what anyone did for a living as long as they were a good person. And they didn't come any better than Landon.

Her parents would love him…just like she loved him.

He sucked in a breath, though. "I didn't realize I wasn't good enough for you."

He was too good; that was why she had to let him go. She forced herself to turn back to him and look down her nose at him. "Come on, Landon. You see where I live." She gestured at the massive master bedroom. "You see how hard I work. I have big aspirations."

For law and order—nothing else.

"I don't have room in my life for someone like you," she continued coldly.

A muscle twitched in his cheek just above his rigidly clenched jaw. "No," he agreed. "You don't."

That was what she'd wanted—to make him angry, to hurt him, so that he would give up his assignment. But she felt a twinge of pain for causing him pain.

She loved him so much…that she hated hurting him. But it was better than getting him killed.

"Good," she said. "Then you agree that I need to have another bodyguard for the duration of the trial."

He nodded. "We agree," he said. "You don't need me." He walked out of the bedroom with a finality that had panic flashing through her.

Would she see him again? Was he leaving now? Without even really saying goodbye…

But then, she'd already said it all—cruelly. And she knew that he would probably never forgive her.

Chapter 22

She was never going to forgive him. But she'd left Landon no choice. He needed to save her life, and since she didn't want him as her bodyguard, that left him only one option: to make sure she was not able to prosecute Luther Mills.

If she wasn't threatening his freedom, then Luther would have no reason to want her dead. She would be safe.

Safe but furious.

Did it matter, though? If he believed what she'd just told him, then he had no chance of a future with her anyway. But he wasn't entirely sure that he believed what she'd told him…or if she'd only been trying to make him mad enough to quit his assignment.

Something she almost confirmed when she descended the stairs and remarked, "I'm surprised you're still here."

She'd expected him to run off in anger. Maybe she'd been counting on it.

"I wouldn't leave you unprotected," he said. He was too well aware of what had happened the last time she'd taken off alone. Even though she'd looped a scarf around her neck, he could still see a bit of the bruise from her nearly being strangled to death.

How had she not learned how vulnerable she was from that experience?

She moved her hand to the bright-patterned scarf, pulling it up enough that it covered the bruise. "Is Parker sending over someone else?" she asked, and she sounded impatient, as if she couldn't wait for him to be gone.

Before he could answer, the doorbell rang. And she breathed a sigh of relief, probably thinking his replacement had arrived. She would not be happy when she saw whom he'd called and figured out why.

But he would do anything to protect her, even if she hated him for the rest of their lives over what he'd done.

"It's Dubridge," a deep voice called through the door as Landon walked toward it.

"Are you and Keeli switching assignments?" Jocelyn asked almost hopefully.

Keeli was a damn good bodyguard, but Landon didn't trust her to protect Jocelyn any more than he trusted himself right now. Luther was entirely too dangerous. The only way the bodyguards had been able to protect their principals from harm had been to take them away where Luther would not be able to find them.

But Jocelyn refused to leave River City. She refused

to give up the case. So Luther would know right where to find her: the courthouse.

Or her office as she prepared for the trial. He had no doubt that was where she was heading now. But she wouldn't get there. He unlocked and opened the door, stepping back to let Dubridge and Keeli walk past him.

They both looked at him as they passed. Dubridge appeared skeptical. Keeli looked triumphant and sympathetic at the same time. She reached out and squeezed Landon's hand as she passed him. And both Jocelyn and Dubridge noticed and narrowed their eyes as if jealous.

Which was funny since Jocelyn had said she cared only about her career and all Dubridge had done was give Keeli grief since she'd been assigned the job of his bodyguard.

"You have to be wrong," Detective Dubridge told Landon.

"No, he's right," Jocelyn said. "I want a different bodyguard. It's for the best."

"Why?" Keeli asked. "Because he figured out what you've been up to?"

Jocelyn's brow furrowed with confusion. "What?"

Landon quickly glanced away from her, though. He couldn't look at her when he did this. So he focused on the detective. "The evidence is in the briefcase," he said. Fortunately, she hadn't had time to close it yet, so the phone and pill bottle were easily visible.

"You called him about that?" Jocelyn asked. "I was going to bring it to him."

Landon shook his head. "No. You weren't." But he was talking to Dubridge instead of her. "If I hadn't heard the text Luther sent her, I wouldn't have found it."

Keeli sucked in a breath. "Luther sent her a text?"

Landon nodded. "Thanking her for tipping him off about Tyce finding the judge's daughter."

Dubridge cursed.

But Keeli cursed louder and lunged toward Jocelyn. Landon stepped between them. He was trying to protect Jocelyn—not put her in more physical danger.

"How could you!" Keeli shouted. "He could have died."

"I didn't purposely tip him off," Jocelyn defended herself.

But it was too late. Dubridge was inspecting the phone and the pill bottle. "She drugged the backup bodyguards," he murmured. "But why...?"

"To get rid of Landon," Keeli replied. "Just like she tried getting rid of Tyce. She's trying to get us all killed—it's part of her and Luther's plan."

Jocelyn gasped in outrage. "I am not working with Luther Mills."

But Dubridge just shook his head and pulled his handcuffs off the clip on his belt. "I have to bring you in, Jocelyn."

"This is ridiculous," she insisted. "I can explain the phone and the pill bottle. Someone planted them in my filing cabinet in my office."

"A locked office," Landon said, and he shook his head as if he didn't believe her. "And she only claimed that after I found the items in her briefcase."

"You don't believe her?" Dubridge asked, and he focused his dark gaze on Landon now.

He didn't want to lie. But he had to—to keep her safe and alive. He shook his head. "No. I don't."

A cry slipped through her lips, as if he'd slapped

her. And maybe he had—emotionally instead of physically. "I can't believe you're doing this," she said. "I don't understand."

"I couldn't let you get away with it," he said.

She cursed him. "How could you! You know I hate Luther as much as you do. That I want to bring him to justice!"

Dubridge linked her arms behind her back and snapped the cuffs around her wrists.

And both she and Landon flinched. He didn't want her hurt. He hadn't thought Dubridge would actually lead her away in handcuffs. But that was the kind of cop he was: by the book. The kind of cop Landon had been.

Shame flashed through him that he'd caused her arrest when he knew the truth. But finding those items in her briefcase looked bad for her.

"What are you doing?" she asked. "You're going to screw up the whole case against Luther. You're going to delay the trial and get another ADA assigned to it." Then the color drained from her face, leaving her eyes wide and bright. "You're the one working for him. You must be. You're trying to get me taken off the case."

He wasn't working for Luther. He was working for her—to keep her safe. But just like he'd had his doubts about her when he'd first found those things in her briefcase, she clearly still had doubts about him.

No matter how much he cared about her—even loved her—he realized she was right. They could never have a relationship, and not just because she claimed he wasn't good enough for her, but because they couldn't completely trust each other.

And now, after what he'd done, he realized he'd destroyed that trust even more as well as what—if any—chance he'd had for a future with her.

But at least she would have a future—if she was taken off the case. Luther Mills would have no reason to kill her now.

Now Landon was the one in danger, though, because as Detective Dubridge led her away in handcuffs, Jocelyn looked as though she wanted to kill Landon.

She's a lawyer, Landon had warned Dubridge before he closed the door and locked Jocelyn into the back of his department-issued sedan. *She's good at presenting arguments, so don't let her get to you.*

She'd glared at him then—like she glared at him now as he sat in on the meeting she'd convinced Dubridge to call with the chief and the district attorney and Parker Payne. Fortunately for her, the detective had listened.

"You let her get to you," Landon remarked to Dubridge.

The detective shook his head. "I think you're the one she got to."

No. Landon had gotten to her, had gotten her to trust him. Then he'd betrayed her. He could have destroyed her had she not convinced the detective to take off the cuffs and hold off on booking her until he spoke to the others.

With the cuffs off, she was able to pull down her scarf. "If I'm working for Luther, why would he have tried so many times to have me killed?" she asked. She pointed to the bruise on her throat. "This happened just as I found that stuff—" she gestured toward where the bottle and phone sat on the chief's desk "—in my filing cabinet. Someone had planted it there, and then they nearly killed me."

If not for Landon, she would have died. How could he save her one moment and then betray her the next? Her heart ached with pain so intense she wanted to double over and wrap her arms around herself. But she would not let him affect her. So she lifted her chin with pride and met the gaze of everyone in the room but him.

She couldn't look at him, not without her heart breaking over his betrayal.

Amber Talsma-Kozminski rose slowly from her chair and walked over to Jocelyn. She pulled her into a hug. "I'm so glad you're all right."

"Why didn't you tell anyone about that attack?" the chief asked. But he was addressing Landon—not her.

She answered, though. "I didn't know who to trust then. I'd just found out that Tyce Jackson is Luther's brother."

"You were wrong about him," Keeli remarked.

"He is Luther's brother," Parker said.

"But I was wrong that Tyce was working with him," Jocelyn admitted. "And you're all wrong if you think I'm working with him." She glanced at Landon then. But he was looking away from her. And she knew that, while he'd initially had doubts about her when he'd found that phone in her briefcase, he didn't still believe she was working with Luther Mills.

So why had he tried to convince the detective that she was?

Amber squeezed her shoulders and assured her, "I don't think that. You're trying this case because you're the one I trust the most. I know nothing and nobody will prevent you from doing your best."

Nothing and nobody would. Not Luther Mills and not Landon Myers.

"Thank you," Jocelyn said, "for believing in me."

Amber turned toward the chief. "I do believe in her," she said. "And I will not bring any charges against her."

"She didn't report her assault. She held on to evidence," Detective Dubridge interjected.

The chief looked at him and then at Keeli. "Have both of you reported everything that's been happening?"

Keeli's face flushed a bright red. And Dubridge looked down.

What the hell had been going on with them?

The chief turned back to Jocelyn. He was beginning to show his age with a few more lines in his face and dark circles beneath his eyes. "I know you're not the leak in your office," he assured Jocelyn. "I know you're the best ADA to prosecute Luther Mills."

She released the breath she hadn't realized she'd been holding. She hadn't wanted to admit to herself how scared she'd been that someone might think her guilty of conspiring with a monster like Luther Mills.

But she knew now that she had been sleeping with the enemy. Landon had proved to be her enemy.

"Then I better get back to work," she told him, "so I can do my job." She turned toward the door and faced Landon. She saw no regret or remorse on his face. He wasn't sorry for having made her look guilty to the others.

And all that love she'd thought she'd felt for him turned to loathing. "I hate you," she whispered as she passed him on her way to the door. But before she could escape that room, the chief called her back.

"Please, stay a few more moments," he implored her.

Did he actually believe her? Or did he only want to interrogate her alone? Because he dismissed everybody else—politely—one by one until only he, she and Parker Payne remained in the chief's office.

She braced herself for an inquisition. But what she got instead had her furiously blinking back tears.

Parker knew an apology was not enough. So he wasn't surprised that Jocelyn Gerber didn't accept it. She just turned away from him, as if unable to look at him. He understood. He had to force himself to look at the chief as he apologized to him, as well.

"I'm sorry," he said. "I thought my team could be professional."

"I hired you and your team because I knew it was personal," the chief replied. "And that because it was personal, you'd all do your best."

Guilt weighed heavily on Parker's shoulders, though, compounded when he noticed Jocelyn's shoulders shaking slightly. She hadn't turned away out of disgust; she'd turned away to hide her tears.

This strong, independent woman had been reduced to tears, and he felt horrible over that. "I'm sorry," he murmured again—to her.

"Everybody is alive," the chief pointed out. "That's the important thing."

"Keeping them alive is the important thing," Parker said. "I'll protect you myself, Ms. Gerber." Because he knew she would never let Landon close to her again.

He'd been close enough to hear what she'd whispered to her bodyguard.

She shook her head. Then she turned around, and her eyes were dry and cold. Maybe he'd only imagined that she'd been crying. "No. You and your team think I'm conspiring with Luther. Nobody's going to protect me."

"I can give you an officer for protection," the chief offered.

She shook her head again. "One that could be working for Luther, too?"

The chief flinched.

"No, thanks," she said. "I think I'll be safer on my own than trusting anyone else ever again." She turned for the door again.

But Parker called out, "You know why he did it, right?"

She gripped the knob so tightly that her fingers turned white. "I don't care."

"It was because he cares," Parker said. "He wants you off the case, so Luther stops trying to kill you."

"If he cared," she said, and her voice cracked slightly, "he would know that I have to do this. I have to make sure Luther is finally brought to justice."

"He cares more about you than about justice for Luther," Parker said. "And that's a hell of a lot."

Jocelyn didn't argue with him, just pulled open the door and walked off—alone and unprotected. And Parker flinched. Landon's efforts to protect her had put her in even more danger.

Chapter 23

She hated him. He could still hear her whisper ringing in his ears even hours later. She hated him.

Landon had lost her. And not just her trust.

He'd lost her respect and whatever feelings she might have had for him. He'd been such a fool. He knew that, but Parker had called him into his office at the Payne Protection Agency, probably to make damn certain he knew how badly he'd screwed up and maybe even to fire him.

Landon didn't care about his job, though. All he cared about was making sure she was safe. "Who do you have on her?" he asked the moment he stepped into Parker's office.

His boss's black hair was tousled like he'd been running his hands through it. A muscle twitched in his cheek just above his rigidly clenched jaw. He was furious with Landon.

"I'm not going to apologize," he warned Parker.

"You deliberately misled Dubridge," Parker said.

"To protect her," Landon said.

"You could have done that without trying to destroy her career," Parker said.

And Landon flinched. He knew how much her career meant to her. He had no intention of ruining that for her. He'd only wanted to cast enough doubt on her to get her removed from the Mills case. "She can't try Luther or she's going to die."

Parker sighed and ran his hand through his hair again. "She might now," he admitted. "Because she refuses to have anyone protect her."

Landon gasped.

"She doesn't trust anyone anymore—thanks to you."

A stabbing pain struck Landon's heart, and he sucked in a breath. "She can't be alone. She nearly died the last time she was."

If he hadn't found her when he had, she would have died for certain. How long had she already been alone? Since that meeting in the chief's office?

He glanced at his watch. It was after hours in her office now—with only that one security guard in the lobby paying no attention to what went on in the offices floors above him. His heart began to pound fast and furiously now.

He'd screwed up. He'd already known that before Parker had pointed it out to him. He just hadn't realized how badly he'd screwed up. He only hoped it hadn't cost Jocelyn her life already.

The words on the notebook blurred before Jocelyn's eyes. She'd been working on her opening statement for weeks. Hell, ever since she'd learned she was the one who was going to be prosecuting Luther Mills. But now she couldn't see or remember the clever words she'd written. She could see only Landon's handsome face.

How had he made love with her so passionately to betray her so coldly such a short time later?

Was it because he cared, as his boss claimed? He'd wanted her off the case—just like Luther Mills. Or why had Luther tried so many times to have her killed?

She touched her throat. The skin was still tender where it was bruised. That was why she'd pulled off the scarf. Even having the thin silk rub against it bothered her, but maybe she was overly sensitive because of what had happened. She closed her eyes. It wasn't as if she could read the notebook anyway. And she thought back to that night.

She'd been so shocked over what she'd found in her filing cabinet—over what Landon had used against her—that she hadn't heard her door open. But then she hadn't shut it because she'd intended to search the other offices. She hadn't had a chance to do that before something had looped around her neck. It had been silk—like the scarf—but narrower and thicker. It had to have been a tie.

A silk tie…

Mike Forbes didn't wear ties unless he was headed to court, and then he clipped on bow ties. Unfortunately, he'd taught Eddie Garza the same bad habit of clipping on a tie for court. And like Forbes, Eddie preferred bow ties.

The only man who always wore a tie—and a very expensive silk one—was…

She opened her eyes on a gasp and found him standing in her doorway. Dale Grohms.

The guy was tall, like Landon, but not nearly as broad. He had more of a runner's build. His features were more refined, too, but he wasn't nearly as good-looking as he thought he was. He leaned against the jamb as he fumbled with his already loosened tie.

Her heart slammed against her ribs. And she reached down for her purse and the Taser she kept inside it. But the purse wasn't there. She'd shut it in the bottom drawer of her filing cabinet—along with her briefcase.

She glanced at it, remembering what had happened nights ago when she'd put the briefcase in there, what she'd found and how she had nearly died. Now she knew who had tried to kill her, but she couldn't let him see that knowledge or that fear.

"Hi, Dale. You're working late, too?" she asked.

"You sound surprised," he remarked, and that little grin that always played around his mouth slipped away.

She'd never given Dale much thought beyond thinking he was a pompous ass. That was why she'd figured he always looked so smug, but now she knew the truth. He felt smug because he'd been fooling everyone.

Including her.

"I knew Eddie and Mike were still around," she lied, "but I thought you'd left."

"I saw Eddie and Mike leave a while ago," he said, and the smug grin was back.

"Just for dinner," she said. "They're coming back."

"Not once they get drinking," Dale said. He glanced around. "So it looks like it's just us. Unless your bodyguards are hanging around somewhere."

She nodded and managed a short laugh. "Of course they are. They never let me out of their sight."

"Seems like they did some nights ago."

Now she knew beyond a doubt. He was the one who'd tried to strangle her earlier. That meant he was probably also the one who'd shot at her and Landon and who'd tried running them down in the parking garage.

So he had a gun as well as the tie he pulled free of his collar. She had to get to her Taser.

"But Landon showed up," she said, forcing a smile. "He always shows up."

Dale shrugged, as if he didn't care. Or maybe he knew about what had happened today, how angry she was with Landon.

She'd told him she hated him. She'd thought she never wanted to see him again. But now she longed to see him, and not just so he could save her life again. If she died, she didn't want Dale's face to be the last one she saw.

She wanted to see Landon's. She wanted Landon...

But she couldn't count on him anymore. She could count only on herself. She uncrossed her legs from beneath her desk and planted her feet on the floor. She would have to act quickly if she had any hope of getting to the filing cabinet and her Taser. But when she jumped up, Dale moved quickly, stepping in front of her filing cabinet.

He grinned as he leaned back against it. "Have your purse and briefcase locked up in here again, huh?"

She reached for the phone on her desk, but he made a tsking noise. And she knew what he was going to say even before he said it.

"By the time Security gets up here, you'll already

be dead, Jocelyn. And then whoever rushes to your rescue is going to die, too."

"Why?" she asked. And she wasn't just trying to stall him now. She really wanted to know. "Why would you do this?"

"Kill you or work for Luther Mills?" he asked, as if both were a matter of fact.

He was convinced that this time she would die. So he didn't care that she saw him, that she knew…

She shivered. But the Taser wasn't the only weapon she had. A letter opener sat atop her desk. Its blade wasn't sharp enough to do much damage, but maybe it would buy her some time.

Some time for what, though?

For Security to check on her? Or for Landon to do that? If he really cared, like Parker claimed he did, why had he left her unprotected?

Dale felt a rush of power at the look of fear and revulsion on her beautiful face. She didn't look so haughty and superior now.

He grinned. "Why would I kill you, Jocelyn?" He repeated the first part of her question and acted as if he was truly pondering it. "Because you're a pain in the ass of everybody in this office."

She shivered again.

"It's true," he insisted. "We all hate you. You're such a sanctimonious bitch."

"I've never had a problem with you," she said.

"Or a compliment," he reminded her. "Or any interest at all. Hell, you didn't even interrogate me like you did the others to see if they worked for Luther."

"You weren't on the DA's list."

He chuckled. So he'd fooled her, too.

"You have family money, so it's not hard for you to live on an assistant district attorney's salary," she said. "You're not on drugs or addicted to gambling." She shook her head. "So why?"

"I've got to be poor or on drugs to want to kill you?" he teased with a smirk. This was fun.

So much more fun than shooting at her or trying to run her down...

Or strangling her from behind.

This was fun to play with her beforehand, to stoke her fear before he would watch her die. And this time she would die for certain.

"To work for Luther," she persisted. "I don't understand why you would help him."

He felt a sudden chill, as if a door or window had opened somewhere. But the windows weren't able to open. And the only door was to the stairwell. So the chill was all in his head even as it raced over his skin.

He shouldn't talk about Luther. He knew that. But it wasn't as if she was going to live anyway.

Still, he hesitated.

"Why, Dale?" she persisted.

He shrugged. "Your family money and mine are a little bit different," he said. "You have a lot more."

And what he'd passed off as coming from his grandmother had mostly come from Luther Mills. He'd just put it in his grandmother's trust first.

Jocelyn nodded as if she'd been privy to his thoughts. No doubt she had figured it out; she'd obviously investigated him even though he hadn't been on their boss's list.

That was why she needed to die—even more so than

Luther ordering it. She had to die because she was a pain in the ass.

"I do have a lot more money," she said. "And if that's all you want, I can give it to you."

He moved away from the filing cabinet to lean over her desk. "I wanted something else from you, Jocelyn," he admitted. "But you turned me down."

"We work together," she reminded him.

"You worked with the bodyguard, too," he said. "But that didn't stop you."

Her face flushed, confirming what had only been suspicions. She had been romantically involved with Landon Myers. So where was he? That chill intensified, and he realized it was nerves now. Where the hell was Landon Myers?

Dale hadn't shot him again. Or tried to run him down...

Where was he?

He glanced toward the open door and into the hall. But nothing moved—not even the shadows.

"That was a mistake," she said, drawing his attention back to her.

Had she moved? She appeared to be sitting on the edge of her chair now. Did she intend to try to fight him?

As tall as she was, she was thin and delicately boned, too. And he was strong. Far stronger than she knew.

"And this is a mistake, Dale," she said. "You haven't killed anyone yet. So you can survive this. You can make a deal."

He snorted. "I know about your deals, Jocelyn. They always include jail time. And I'm not going to jail."

She shook her head. "No, no, of course not. You'll be a hero, Dale. You'll be the one who brings down Luther Mills."

He shook his head and sighed. "You're pathetic, Jocelyn. And condescending and superior as hell. Do you really think I'm going to fall for your bullshit?"

Her blue eyes widened with feigned innocence.

"I know you too well," he said. And maybe that was why he should have been prepared when she lunged at him.

But the letter opener struck him, stabbing the corner of his eye. He blinked at the sting of pain and blood that trailed from the wound. Then he grabbed her wrist, squeezing hard until the letter opener dropped to her desk.

"You bitch!" he said. And he swung his other hand at her beautiful face, striking her hard.

Then he reached for her throat. He wasn't even going to use his tie this time. No. This time he wanted to squeeze the life from her body with his own damn hands.

But she wasn't done fighting. She clawed at his hands and tried kicking out—struggling so much that she knocked her chair over and fell to the ground.

He leaped over the desk and jumped on top of her. Her breath whooshed out as his weight hit her lungs and stomach. He grinned as he stared down at her.

She was so scared.

So beautiful…

Maybe he'd take a little more time before he killed her. Maybe he would take what she'd denied him…but had freely given to her damn bodyguard.

Chapter 24

Fear pounded in Landon's heart as he rushed up the stairwell. He'd had to argue his way past the security guard in the lobby, who'd informed him that Jocelyn wasn't alone on the district attorney's floor. Dale Grohms hadn't left yet either, which had surprised the guard, who'd remarked how much the male ADA was in and out of the office.

Landon's heart had sunk then as he'd realized Grohms had to be the one working for Luther, the one who'd tried to kill her. But would he try again when the security guard knew he was present yet in the building? On the very same floor with Jocelyn?

Not wanting to alert Grohms to his presence, Landon had taken the elevator up only as far as the floor below the district attorney's. Then he'd switched to the stairwell, running up the last flight of steps. As he pushed open the door at the top of the stairs, he'd heard her scream.

And his already madly pounding heart had slammed against his ribs. He'd never heard her like that, despite all the dangerous situations they'd found themselves in. He'd never heard her sound so terrified.

He drew his weapon and ran toward her office. Grohms must have been the one trying to kill them, so he had a gun, too. One he drew and fired as Landon neared the doorway. A bullet whizzed past Landon's head and broke the window on the door across from Jocelyn's.

He heard another cry, but it didn't sound like Jocelyn's, and something clattered to the floor. Barrel raised, Landon darted into the room. Dale didn't fire at him, but he charged, knocking him aside as he headed toward the hall.

Instead of running after him, he checked on Jocelyn to make sure she was breathing. "Are you okay?" he asked.

She nodded, but her cheek was already swelling from a blow. And her hair was tangled around her face. She clutched a letter opener in her hand, blood dripping from the blade onto her desk.

Instead of him saving her, she had probably saved Landon, for Dale's gun lay on the floor. She must have stabbed him to make him drop it. He wanted to reach for her, to pull her into his arms—not to comfort her, but to comfort himself. He had to make sure she was really all right.

She gestured with her letter opener at the doorway. "Get him, please." Then she stumbled back and, trembling, dropped onto the edge of her desk.

"Jocelyn…"

"We need him to testify against Luther," she said.

And he nodded. If they got Dale to turn, there might not even have to be a trial. Luther might realize he needed to plead guilty.

Landon rushed off in the direction Dale had run, toward the elevators. But he hadn't waited for one of them. The door to the stairwell clicked as it closed, drawing Landon's attention there. He shoved it open to the echoing of footsteps striking against the steps.

He ran down those stairs, trying to catch up with Dale. The man was bleeding from the wound Jocelyn had inflicted. A couple of times Landon slipped on droplets of blood and nearly fell. "Dale, stop!" he yelled after the man. "You need help."

And he would probably need more if Landon caught him. He wanted to kill him for what he'd put Jocelyn through—for all the times he'd tried to kill her.

But despite his injury, Dale didn't stop running. Another door clicked as it swung open. Landon caught up to him just as Dale darted out into the parking garage. "Stop!" he yelled again.

And Dale suddenly stopped, his body going stiff before he dropped to the ground. Gunshots reverberated off the concrete walls.

Landon cursed as he raised his weapon. Someone else was out there, in the shadows of the garage. "Come out!" he yelled. "Show yourself!"

But the only thing he heard was the sound of footsteps running away. He dropped to his knees next to Dale's bullet-hole-ridden body.

"Hang in there," he said as he pressed his hand over the wound in the other man's chest. Blood pumped from it as his heart pumped its last. Landon reached for his cell with his other hand and punched in 911.

But he knew help would not arrive in time to save Dale Grohms. He heard more footsteps coming from the building and turned with his gun.

Jocelyn ran toward him. "What happened? Did you shoot him?"

He shook his head. "Somebody was waiting out here," he said.

But he wasn't sure if that person had been waiting for Dale or for him and Jocelyn in case Dale had been unsuccessful. He kept his gun clutched in one hand now, the barrel swinging toward the shadows.

"They shot him and ran off," he said. And he peered around, trying to see how far they'd run.

She dropped to her knees beside them. "Tell me, Dale. Tell me that it was Luther. Tell me you have proof that it was," she urged him.

But the man stared up at her with a blank gaze. He was beyond help—for Jocelyn or for himself.

He was already gone.

The chief did not like this. They'd caught the leak in the district attorney's office. Hell, they'd caught two, since the security guard was apparently the one who'd shot ADA Grohms. He claimed it was because he'd thought Grohms was armed. But the man had dropped his weapon in Jocelyn's office—when he'd tried to kill her.

After Landon had headed up to the DA's floor, the guard was seen on the security footage placing a call on his cell phone. To Luther Mills?

At least Luther had given him the order to kill

Grohms instead of Landon and Ms. Gerber. Or maybe he had wanted them dead, but the guard had worried about being blamed for their murders. Now that Detective Dubridge had busted him, with the help of the man's own security footage, the guard was trying to act the hero—even though he couldn't explain why he'd run away from Landon.

The chief sighed with frustration as he paced his office at the River City PD. A knock rattled his door moments before it opened to the beautiful face of his bride.

Penny walked across the office and right into his arms, as if knowing how much he'd needed her warmth and love. He held her tightly against his madly pounding heart.

She leaned back and stared up at him, her brown eyes wide with worry. "Are you okay?"

He nodded. "Just worried."

"About?" she prodded him, tilting her head to the side and tousling her auburn curls. She was so incredibly lovely and loving.

"Everything," he said. He was worried about everything. "We almost lost Ms. Gerber tonight."

"Oh, no, is she all right?"

He nodded. "Thanks to Landon Myers. He saved her." But had that been enough to earn her forgiveness? Would she let him remain as her bodyguard?

She had to know that she needed one. Even with Dale Grohms dead, she was still in danger. Hell, they all were.

With the trial being moved up on him, Luther Mills had to be getting desperate. There was no way he could escape justice this time—not with the eyewitness and the evidence against him.

And Jocelyn Gerber prosecuting the case.

Penny ran her fingertips along his cheek. "There's something else bothering you."

Woodrow groaned. "I think I've got one of those feelings you get."

Penny Payne-Lynch was infamous for her premonitions of danger. "You feel like something bad is going to happen."

"I don't just feel it." Although the sensation seemed all consuming. "I *know* it…"

His sweet wife didn't try to assure him nothing bad would happen—probably because she had never lied to him. She just hugged him closer, offering him comfort.

Jocelyn couldn't stop shaking, and not just over how close she had come to dying. Dale had been determined to kill her and had probably intended to assault her first. He'd reached for the buttons on her blouse just as Landon had pushed open the door to the stairwell. Then her coworker had pulled the gun she hadn't even realized he'd had tucked into the waistband of his dress pants. And he had fired that gun at Landon.

She'd grabbed the letter opener from the desk and swung it into his biceps. She hadn't wanted him dead; she'd just wanted him to drop the gun—which he had. But then he'd run off to his death.

"Do you really think the security guard was acting on Luther's orders?" she asked Landon, who was checking all the doors and windows in her house despite having activated the high-tech alarm. If he was trying to make her feel safe, he wasn't succeeding. She felt more vulnerable now than she ever had.

But that had nothing to do with Luther Mills and everything to do with him.

He turned away from the windows and walked over to the couch where she sat, petting a purring Lady. He nodded. "Yes, I do."

She shivered, and the movement made Lady jump up off the couch and head toward the kitchen.

"Unfortunately, I think a lot of other people could be working for him, too," Landon said. "We don't know who to trust."

She groaned and closed her eyes and murmured, "I can't trust you." Not after what he'd done, after he had tried to have her arrested.

But then when she'd needed him, he'd been there for her. He had saved her life. Again.

"I'm sorry, Jocelyn," he said. "I'm so sorry."

She felt him settle onto the couch next to her. He didn't touch her, but she still felt the heat of his closeness. As always, his nearness made her pulse quicken, her skin tingle, but he also gave her a feeling of comfort she hadn't felt since she'd realized Dale Grohms was the one trying to kill her.

"I was an idiot," Landon berated himself. "An idiot in love."

She opened her eyes now and stared at him. His handsome face was twisted with a grimace.

"That's why I did it," he said. "I couldn't stand the thought of you being in danger any longer. I wanted to make sure you would be safe."

She loved him, too—so much—but she had no hope for a future with him. "You've seen all those other threats," she reminded him. "You know that I'm always in danger."

He flinched.

"And you need to know and accept that I'm not going to stop doing what I love because of those threats or even because of the attempts on my life."

He drew in a deep breath and said, "Then I guess it's good you're going to have a bodyguard around all the time."

"I am?" she asked.

He nodded. "Even after this trial is over, I don't want to leave you. Ever…" He reached out then and covered her hand with his. "Please, Jocelyn, forgive me for being an idiot. Don't make me leave."

Her heart ached, then swelled and filled with warmth. But while she loved him, trusting him was going to be harder for her. "You're not going to keep pressuring me to give up this case or my job?"

He shook his head. "I promise. I know that your job means everything to you."

But she shook her head now. It didn't mean everything. Not anymore. He did.

He continued, "And it's a part of you, makes you who you are—and that's the woman I love. If you lost that part of you, that job, that quest for justice, I wouldn't love you like I do."

She pulled her hand from beneath his, and he lowered his head, as if defeated. "Landon…" She reached up and cupped his face in her hands, tipping it up again. He was so handsome, but he looked so miserable, too. "I love you, too."

He released a shaky sigh. "I thought I wasn't good enough for you."

She shook her head in denial and regret of the cruel things she'd said to him. "I didn't mean that. I was just trying to get you to quit—to protect you." Which was really no different from what he'd done. She'd hurt him in order to try to protect him. Smiling at the irony, she said, "We're both idiots."

"Yes, we are," he agreed. "We're idiots in love."

She smiled bigger, her heart overflowing with love for him. "I do love you…so much…"

He leaned closer and brushed his mouth over hers. The kiss was so tender that tears sprang to her eyes. His love was in that kiss and in the look he gave her, his eyes so warm and adoring.

She linked her arms around his neck and clung to him as he lifted her from the couch. Then he carried her up the stairs to the bedroom. They undressed each other, tearing at buttons and zippers in their haste to be naked, to have nothing separating skin from skin— soul from soul.

Once her bra and panties dropped to the floor, Landon staggered back a step as if she'd struck him. But she wanted him closer, not farther away, and she held out her arms for him.

He shook his head. "I just want to look at how gorgeous you are…" But his gaze met hers and held. Then finally he stepped forward and pressed his muscular body against hers.

His erection swelled between them, prodding at her. She needed him inside her, needed him joined with her again. But he was focused on her, on kissing her lips, then her neck and her shoulders.

Her legs began to tremble, threatening to fold beneath her. So she fell back on the bed. And he followed her down. But he held his body off hers, as he moved his mouth over every inch of her skin.

She squirmed and writhed from his attention, needing release from the pressure he built so tightly inside her. His lips closed around a taut nipple, and she arched off the bed, crying out at the pleasure.

She clutched at his shoulders, his back, trying to pull him down with her. But he moved down her body instead, making love to her with his mouth.

The tension broke, making her cry out again with pleasure. But it wasn't enough. She wanted more. She wanted him.

But he rose from the bed before she could pull him down onto her. He was only gone a second, though, to roll on a condom, before he joined her again literally, easing inside her. She wrapped herself around him, clinging to him, as they found the rhythm that was theirs alone. They moved together, perfectly, in their own dance.

The tension wound through her again, building and building, until it let go, and she screamed Landon's name. And her love. "I love you! I love you!"

He tensed and then yelled as he found his release, too. For a moment, he rested his forehead against hers. Staring deeply into her eyes, he said, "I love you."

Then he pulled away, disappearing for just a few moments to clean up, before coming back into bed. He slid his arm around her as he untangled the covers and pulled them up, over them both.

But she wasn't shivering and trembling anymore. She felt safe and warm…with him.

He stroked his hand down her back, but his fingers trembled slightly. Was he worried about the trial?

"Are you okay?" she asked him.

"Yes…"

But she heard the concern in his voice. She settled her head against his shoulder and murmured, "We need to trust each other. I need to trust that you'll stay safe protecting me and you need to trust that you'll be able to protect me."

He tensed for a moment, but then his body relaxed beneath hers. "We will," he said. "We have. We've survived everything Luther has thrown at us."

Jocelyn knew, though, that Luther wasn't done trying. He wasn't going to give up. He had probably already begun to formulate another plan to get away with murder while committing more.

Landon knew it, too, because his arm tightened protectively around her. But he just squeezed her in assurance as he said, "Together—with our love—we are too strong for even Luther Mills to hurt."

He was right.

Together they were much too strong for Luther to hurt. But she had no doubt that he would try.

Epilogue

The trial...

Court had gone even better than Landon had expected. But then Jocelyn—when she had all the evidence and an unshakable eyewitness—was damn good at her job. If she'd had the evidence and witnesses she'd needed for any of Luther's many previous crimes, Javier Mendez would not have died.

Nor would have so many members of Luther's crew that he'd sent after the Payne Protection Agency and the people they had been hired to protect.

Landon still felt horrible over all those times he'd doubted her and had thought she might have purposely failed to get indictments against the drug dealer. Jocelyn Gerber was too honorable for anyone to bribe and too zealous about justice for anyone to threaten and manipulate.

Even Luther Mills.

He kept trying, though, with the way he stared at her in court. Every time Luther looked across from the defendant's table to Jocelyn's, Landon clenched his hands into fists. He wanted to take the guy down just for the way he looked at her. As if he was undressing her...

But then he'd glance back at where Landon sat in the gallery behind the prosecutor's table, and he would chuckle. And Landon realized he was purposely goading them. Hell, he'd been purposely goading them all. He was smug—too damn smug—like he had no worries about going to jail.

Why?

The judge was ruling against every cheap trick and ploy Luther's sleazy lawyer tried, while every bit of evidence and testimony Jocelyn presented was accepted. Her case wasn't just circumstantial—it was insurmountable for Luther's defense. He was going to prison.

He had to know it.

So why did he look so damn smug? What the hell did he have planned now? Because Landon had no doubt, Luther had something up his sleeve, something dangerous and wicked and certain to result in more deaths.

Landon peered around the courtroom. After testifying, the witnesses and their bodyguards had left it, going back into protective custody until after the sentencing. The judge's daughter and Tyce were still out of the country somewhere well away from the reach of Luther Mills.

The only people who sat near Landon were Parker Payne, a few bodyguards from his brothers' branches of the security agency and the chief of police. The side behind Luther had surprisingly filled up, though.

With so many crew members dead or in jail and denied bail, how did the drug dealer still have so many supporters? And they were supporters, not just spectators. It was obvious from the way they grinned at Luther, who turned back to look at them, and from the way they glared at the judge.

And that uneasy feeling churned harder in Landon's guts. Something was going on. And he saw the moment that Luther put his plan in motion—the moment he and the judge's bailiff exchanged a significant glance.

All Landon had time to do was leap toward the prosecutor's table and Jocelyn as he shouted, "Get down!"

Then the shooting began.

Jocelyn fell to the floor of the courtroom, not because of the bullet that whizzed past her head but because of the muscular body that knocked her down. Landon moved quickly, turning the table on its side to use the solid and thick wood top as a shield as the gunshots continued to ring out.

Jocelyn had already been ducking when he'd called out—because she'd noticed the same look between Luther and the bailiff that Landon must have. The judge probably had, too, because he'd dropped down behind the bench. Hopefully before he'd been hit.

Landon had been allowed his weapon in court, so he returned fire. The other bodyguards and the chief hopefully had been allowed theirs, as well.

Shots rang out all around them…until finally either everyone had run out of ammunition like Landon, who'd replaced his clip twice—or they were dead. The sudden silence was nearly as deafening as all the gunfire had been, or maybe her ears were damaged from the noise and close shots.

"Are you okay?" she whispered. Or at least she thought she was whispering; her words reverberated inside her skull, though, as if she'd shouted.

"Yes," Landon whispered back, his mouth close to her ear as he continued to crouch protectively over her—just as he'd promised he would. They had kept their vow to each other that they would survive the trial.

So far they had anyway. But the trial really wasn't over yet.

"Is it safe?" she wondered aloud.

"Luther is gone," Landon replied as he peered over the edge of the thick table.

She gasped. "He's dead?"

"No. He's gone," Landon regretfully replied. "He made it out of the courtroom with a shield of shooters surrounding him."

And she heard it now, the shots ringing out elsewhere in the courthouse. Hopefully he would not get out of the building, though.

"How about everybody else?" she anxiously asked. "Are they all right?"

Landon moved to stand up, but she pulled him back down, worried that it wasn't safe yet. "Wait, wait!" she advised him. Some of Luther's shooters could have stayed behind; maybe they weren't out of ammunition yet.

He leaned forward and kissed her. "It's okay," he assured her. "All of Luther's crew are either with him or dead." He stood up then and helped her to her feet.

And she saw that the bailiff was dead. He must have been working for Luther. He had to be the one who'd smuggled all those guns into the courtroom for Luther and his crew in the gallery. The guns must have been taped beneath the seats and the defendant's table.

"Judge Holmes!" she called out.

The gray-haired judge rose shakily from behind the bench and gazed around his courtroom. He shuddered at the destruction and carnage.

And Jocelyn looked around, seeing what he saw. The holes in the walls and furniture and the blood everywhere.

She cried out, then pressed a hand over her mouth to hold back a louder scream. So many of those young men who'd been sitting on Luther's side of the courtroom were dead. Even his lawyer lay cowering on the ground, his briefcase held over his head as if he was afraid that someone might blow it off his shoulders.

She was afraid to look at the other side, at where Landon had been sitting with his boss and some of the Payne Protection Agency bodyguards.

Landon shouted, "Is everyone okay?"

Parker and those other bodyguards were checking on Luther's fallen crew members and collecting their weapons. The only one sitting behind the prosecutor's side of the courtroom was the chief. He was slumped on the bench seat, his hand pressed to his shoulder. He had been hit.

"Chief Lynch!" Jocelyn rushed over to him.

Parker rushed to the chief's side, too, but the bodyguard's stepfather waved them off. "Go after him! Don't let him get away!"

All the bodyguards hastened to follow his orders, rushing out of the courtroom. Except for Landon...

He stayed beside her with his gun in one hand and his cell in the other. He dialed 911.

"Help's on the way," she assured the chief of police.

"I'm fine," he told her even as he flinched. "The bullet went right through my shoulder."

From the amount of blood oozing from the wound, she suspected it had done some damage on its way out, though. She pulled her scarf from her neck and wadded it up against his wound.

The chief's face was pale, but his grasp was strong when he covered her hand with his, which was bloodied from his wound. "Luther..." he murmured urgently at her. "They've got to get Luther..."

Unlike the chief, who was injured, and all those other people who lay dead on the floor, she doubted the drug dealer even had a scratch on him. But he could not be as invincible as he thought he was.

"He just got out of the room," she told the chief. "He won't get out of the courthouse." There were guards at all of the exits, and the bodyguards had gone after him.

He would not get away.

But Jocelyn and Landon exchanged an uneasy glance. Even if Luther did manage to escape, though, the two of them would be fine. They, strengthened from the love they shared, would keep each other safe—just as they had during the shoot-out, and like they would for the rest of their lives together.

Forever...

* * * * *

HARLEQUIN

*Uplifting or passionate,
heartfelt or thrilling—
Harlequin has your
happily-ever-after.*

With a wide range of romance series that each
offer new books every month, you are sure to
find the satisfying escape you deserve.

Look for all Harlequin series new releases on the *last Tuesday* of each month in stores and online!

Harlequin.com

"Rayna." Raising her chin, he kissed her, cutting off her words. "I'm glad you didn't. I don't know what it is, this thing between us, but it's strong. More than physical, I think. Or at least that's how it seems to me," he amended. For all he knew, she could feel completely different.

"Same here," she told him, pulling him close for another lingering kiss. "Logistically, I should totally stay away. But I couldn't stop thinking about you. I know how badly I hurt you and I'd do anything to make up for it."

Horrified, he recoiled, looking askance at her.

"Is that what this is? Your way of making reparations?"

She frowned. "Is that really what you think? After the wild passion we manage to generate between us? Seriously, Parker. I'm not here as some sort of repayment of a debt. I came because I wanted you. Needed you. As you can see."

This made him relax. Somewhat. He hated being vulnerable, yet that was how he felt around her. His emotions raw, open and exposed.

"Don't ever doubt me again," he ordered, tightening his arms around her. "Because I honestly don't know if I would survive it."

She nodded. "Me, neither. I know better than to jump to hasty conclusions. You deserve better." She bit her lip and looked down.

"I do." At her startled look, he laughed. "Seriously, though. If I'd been in your shoes, I might have taken that same leap of rapid logic."

Unsmiling, she shook her head. "You're not the sheriff. I am. That's not the kind of mistake I should be making, whether with you or with some stranger I don't even know. As a law enforcement professional, I've been taught to look at evidence. Instead, I let emotion overrule my training. I assure you it won't happen again."

"It better not." He kissed her. Neither of them spoke for a while after that.

Don't miss
Texas Sheriff's Deadly Mission *by Karen Whiddon,*
available August 2021 wherever
Harlequin Romantic Suspense
books and ebooks are sold.

Harlequin.com

Get 4 FREE REWARDS!

We'll send you 2 FREE Books plus 2 FREE Mystery Gifts.

Harlequin Romantic Suspense books are heart-racing page-turners with unexpected plot twists and irresistible chemistry that will keep you guessing to the very end.

FREE Value Over $20
